the world is
decorated
with
Stars

Denice
Kronau

The World Is Decorated with Stars

Published by Wheatmark®
1760 East River Road, Suite 145, Tucson, Arizona 85718 U.S.A.
www.wheatmark.com

ISBN: 978-1-62787-165-5 (paperback)
ISBN: 978-1-62787-166-2 (ebook)
LCCN: 2014911689

For Michael

Tho' far I go, and far from you reside,
No distance can congenial souls divide;
And may I hope for sure some joy 'twill, be,
That you far distant sometimes think of me.

—Phebe Folger Coleman,
untitled poem to her family, 1809

1

Abigail

March 1843, Nantucket

Abigail Gardner Starbuck quickly climbed the steep ladder to the roof, hauling a pail of sand. She could smell the accumulating smoke coming from the chimney fire. Opening the small door at the top of the ladder, she pushed the bucket of sand onto the floor of the roof walk, gathered her skirt in her left hand to keep from tripping, and climbed up on it. Standing on her tiptoes, she lifted the pail of sand over her head and dumped it down the chimney. Within a few seconds, she was rewarded with a billow of black smoke, followed by clear air.

"Mother, I think the fire's out," shouted thirteen-year-old Sarah from the street in front of the house. "Can I go back in now?"

Abigail peered over the railing of the roof walk and looked at her daughter standing in the middle of Union Street. Sarah was small for her age, but from three stories high, she looked absolutely tiny; and Abigail could see that she was shivering in the cold March air.

"Yes, go back in. I'll be down in a minute."

She stood at the railing on the roof walk and looked out to the harbor. It was a sunny, clear, cold day with very little wind. The water in the harbor was a vivid dark blue reflecting the blue of the cloudless sky. Gentle waves rolled toward shore, and she could see three whaling ships docked on Long Wharf. As she looked at the ships in the harbor, she wondered when Matthew would be back. Her husband, Matthew Starbuck, was captain of the whaling ship *Young Hero* and had been gone for three years and five months. She had gotten sporadic letters from him as his path crossed other captains' during his travels. Sea captains and their crews would visit each other's ships, called a "gam," when they met at different whaling grounds around the world. Traditionally, the officers would meet on one ship and the crew on the other. They would exchange news, letters, and goods as they spent a couple of days at anchor before sailing off again. She got his last letter, dated June 1842, four months ago in December 1842. He wrote that he was in Callao, Peru, with a partially full ship's hold of 500 barrels of whale oil, well short of his 1,500-barrel quota. With such a poor result, she estimated that the earliest he would sail into Nantucket's port would be July 1843. She missed her husband. The children missed their father. She knew that they were self-sufficient, by necessity, but she hated that he was gone for so long. She worried that he wouldn't recognize his own children when he came home; they had grown so much.

Collecting the pail, she carefully descended the steep steps from the roof walk, pulling the rope to close the trap door behind her and securing it with a cleat hitch to the railing of the steps.

"Right over left, left over right, makes a knot both tidy and tight," she murmured as she tied the knot.

Nantucket's winds could be both unpredictable and

fierce; she didn't want the trap door to blow open in inclement weather, which was typical for March. As she reached the bottom of the stairs, she briefly looked around the attic. Sunlight streamed through the small windows at the east end of the room, illuminating a few neatly stacked boxes. BABY CLOTHES and BABY TOYS were written on the boxes closest to her. Every time she saw them, she felt a twinge of guilt, thinking that she should give them to someone who could use them. *It feels selfish to leave them sitting here in the attic*, she thought. *But I'd be so sad if we don't have any more children.*

Abigail had always pictured herself having at least five children, but with Matthew away so much, she wasn't sure anymore. She would be devastated if she couldn't have any more children. She wasn't ready to give the things away. She was optimistic by nature, so she cheered herself up with the thought that, at thirty-four, she still had time. Many women on Nantucket had children well into their forties. Her mother, Phebe, always told her that if it was God's will, she would have more children. Abigail, being extremely practical, was less inclined to believe children were entirely up to God. *You needed a husband who was home more than a couple of weeks every few years*, she thought. She paused for a moment, remembering the last time she needed these items: when her eight-year-old son, Thomas, was just four years old. She still found it hard to believe that the last time Matthew saw their son, he had just turned five and, to her, was still her baby. Now eight, and big for his age, he already was doing chores that Matthew would normally be responsible for: chopping wood—which, truth be told, scared her every time he picked up his little ax—, hauling water, and feeding the chickens. Both children were a tremendous help around the house, which she was grateful for every day. She shook her head, bringing herself back to the present, and descended the two flights of stairs to the ground floor and kitchen, bucket in hand. She replaced the bucket by the back door after refilling it with sand; while they hadn't had a chimney fire in a very long time, she wanted to be prepared, just in case there was another flare-up that morning.

"We got lucky this time, Mother," said Sarah who looked up from the dough she was forming into loaves of bread. She had left it covered with a dishcloth on the kitchen table when she ran out of the house until Abigail had doused the chimney fire. "We only needed one bucket of sand to put out the fire."

"Yes, this time it was easy."

Abigail smiled as she watched her small daughter heroically push and pull at the big lump of dough in front of her. Being small for her age didn't stop her from trying to keep up with the larger children and her mother.

"I'll check the temperature of the oven. Is the bread ready to bake?"

Their house had one of the few beehive ovens on the island. It was a large brick dome-shaped oven, just behind the fireplace in the cellar. She loved it as it baked bread, pies, and cakes perfectly.

"Yes, in ten more minutes. I'm making four loaves, three to get us through the week and one to give to the Alms House."

No wonder the waist of my dress is getting loose, thought Abigail as she went down into the cellar. *All I do is run up and down stairs all day.*

At five feet eight, she was tall like her father; and while she was never overweight, no one would ever say she was thin until recently, when her mother remarked that her dresses were hanging loose on her. Her best features were her dark brown eyes with their long dark lashes and her shiny chestnut-brown hair, which fell in soft waves to her waist when she undid her bun at night. While her mother was considered a beauty in her day, Abigail knew that she was just attractive in an ordinary way, which was fine by her.

She could feel the heat from the oven as she reached the bottom step. She stepped into the cellar and put her hand close to the iron oven door, which was on the back wall of the fireplace. The construction of the beehive oven and fire-place was unique, and it took a skilled mason to build it. It looked like a normal fireplace, except for the small square iron door two-thirds of the way up from the floor in its back wall. When she opened this door, she saw a good-sized chamber with a flat bottom and a concave roof—all made out of brick. In building the oven, the mason built another struc-ture backing up to the fireplace in the main room and sharing the same flue. This structure, also made of brick, was shaped like half a ball, sitting on top of a tiny firebox. From the back, it looked like a beehive, which was how it got its name. She walked behind the oven and continued her inspection. She saw that the coals in the firebox were glowing red and just starting to turn gray and, luckily, had not been affected by the bucket of sand. The fire and the bread dough were perfectly timed: the coals would provide sufficient heat for the time required to bake the bread.

As young as she was, Sarah was very competent in many aspects of running the house, especially baking. Her grand-mother had taught her how to bake and how to do nearly everything else necessary to run a household. She had a knack for timing the readiness of the oven with the readi-ness of the bread dough—something Abigail rarely got right. Phebe always despaired at her daughter's lack of com-petence in running a house.

From a very young age, Abigail had been more interested

in her father William's work than in the activities needed to run a household. Like many other girls on Nantucket, she loved learning ever since she was a little girl and was especially interested in math—anything to do with numbers fascinated her. She loved solving problems and could get lost for hours in complicated math proofs. She and three of her friends started a math club when they were twelve, which met at her house every Wednesday afternoon after school. William would often help them with their math problems, encouraging Abigail and being the envy of all her friends, whose fathers were not so interested in algebra and calculus. He often took her to his office and warehouse near Straight Wharf when most girls her age were staying home and learning the household arts. It was no wonder that she was merely adequate at running a household; she'd much rather work on the company's ledgers than bake a loaf of bread.

ABIGAIL HEARD SARAH coming down the stairs to the cellar. "Do you need help with the bread?"

"No, I have them."

Sarah stepped into the room. Abigail grabbed a cloth to protect her hand and opened the hot oven door, holding it for Sarah as she slid in the four loaf pans. She closed it quickly, knowing that every degree of heat was precious.

"What would you like to do for the next hour? It's cold out, but we could walk down to the wharf and see if there's any news of your father."

"If there were news, someone would have come to the house and told us already. We only live five minutes' walk from the wharf." Sarah was definitely Abigail's logical child.

Abigail sighed. While she loved her daughter beyond all reason and would never criticize her, sometimes she wished that Sarah could be a bit less serious and more like a carefree little girl. She looked at her daughter's lovely heart-shaped face with its big chocolate-brown eyes and saw in their depths a quiet maturity unusual in a young girl. Her daughter's gentle spirit reminded her of Wonoma. She was a Wampanoag Indian woman who, as legend had it, was a skilled healer who brought peace to the warring tribes of the island before the English arrived in the 1650s—Abigail could easily picture Sarah in a similar role.

"Fair point." Abigail smiled, taking Sarah's small hand into hers and giving it a squeeze. "Let's go down to the wharf and hear if there is any news about *other* people's fathers. We can stop by your grandmother's on the way back to pick up the thread she has for your sampler."

They set out for Old North Wharf wearing their warmest hats and cloaks. There were a lot of people on the street, hurrying toward the wharf, which could only mean that a ship was arriving. As they turned the corner from Union Street onto Main Street, Abigail caught the arm of her next-door neighbor, Elizabeth Coffin, who was headed to the wharf at a hasty clip. Elizabeth's husband, Michael, was the captain of the *Omega* and had been gone even longer than Matthew.

"Elizabeth, what's happening?"

Abigail stepped alongside of her closest friend, quickening her pace to keep up with her. Sarah had to nearly run to keep up.

"Abigail, good morning! Didn't you hear?"

"No, Sarah and I have been home all morning, and Thomas, who is always the first in our house to announce the arrival of a ship, is off playing with his friends in the schoolyard."

"I think the *Omega* is sailing into port! A farmer rode in from Madaket saying he spotted her offshore, but he wasn't certain it was she. Wouldn't you know it? The wind is blowing southeast. He's so close, yet—"

"I know. It's always frustrating when the wind doesn't cooperate in bringing the ship the last yards to the wharf. Let's hope it changes direction quickly!"

Abigail linked her arm through Elizabeth's. The two women walked faster as they headed down Main Street to the wharf.

"I'll meet you at Grandmother's," said Sarah. "I see Betsy up ahead, and I want to talk to her."

"Don't forget that you have to finish two letters on your sampler before sunset today. You know how hard it is to do fine needlework by candlelight."

Sarah belonged to a needlework club hosted by her grandmother, and because of this, she liked to set a good example for the other girls in the club by completing her embroidery assignments on time.

As Sarah skipped ahead to catch up with Betsy, Abigail said, "I'm always torn. On one hand, I wish that she wasn't so serious and would play and have fun like other girls her age, but on the other—I know that she could be married in four or five years, and she has so much yet to learn."

"If I remember correctly, we weren't perfectly prepared when we got married." They both walked a little faster toward the wharf. "And besides, when Sarah gets married, both you and Phebe will be here to help and guide her."

"I guess you're right." Abigail sighed. "I'll hold off worrying about Sarah until I learn that she's marrying someone from America and not the Nation of Nantucket."

Elizabeth smiled at her friend's reference to the Nation of Nantucket. While Nantucket was always part of the United States from its inception, it was reluctant to take sides at the time of the Revolution, petitioning both England and the

Continental Congress to stay neutral to protect its whaling industry.

"I'm pretty sure that we live in America too. You're being very old-fashioned when you refer to the mainland as 'America.'" Elizabeth's gentle teasing made Abigail laugh and dispelled her worries about Sarah for the moment.

SINCE THEY WERE little girls, Elizabeth could always cajole Abigail out of her worries. She was three years older than Abigail. They first met at the school on Fair Street. Both girls came from families who believed that daughters should receive the same education as the sons. Abigail was a serious little girl, like Sarah, and Elizabeth took her under her wing from the first day of school, sensing that she could use a friend. It was Elizabeth's friendship and encouragement that coaxed Abigail into being more outgoing. If you asked either of them when their friendship had started, neither could answer; they had been best friends their entire lives.

Abigail could feel the shift in the wind as they reached the wharf and joined their neighbors who had gathered there. There were several ships docked at the wharf, and she could hear their riggings slapping against the masts in the stiff wind. The odor from the harbor was usually pretty bad, but the cold weather and favorable wind direction made it tolerable as they waited for the *Omega* to reach the wharf.

A ship sailing into port was big news, not only for the family of the ship's crew, but also for everyone in town. Like Abigail, other families were hopeful that the ship would bring news of their loved ones at sea and the outside world. While there was almost a carnival atmosphere as they waited for *Omega* to come into port, there was also an undercurrent of worry. A lot could happen to the crew in two or three years at sea—illness or death, attacks from pirates, and on rare occasions, attacks from other countries' navies who were known to press sailors into service with little chance of escape. People still talked about Captain Robert Calder, from Liberty Street, who had been captured at sea by the British during the War of 1812 and imprisoned in England's Dartmoor prison. He miraculously managed to escape in 1820 and reached Nantucket in 1822. His family had long thought he was lost at sea and were astounded when he walked through the front door, alive and well. Unfortunately, this was not true for many of the sailors from Nantucket who had met the same fate.

With the change in wind direction, the *Omega* reached the dock in just a short time. As the *Omega* approached Old North Wharf, Elizabeth could see her husband, Michael, standing on the bow shouting commands to his first mate as they pulled down the sails, slowing the ship's progress. The *Omega* was one of Nantucket's finest whaling ships; it was 363 tons and had six whaleboats. The sailors on the ship's deck threw the lines to the men standing on the wharf who caught them and secured them to the pilings. They watched as the gangplank was extended from the ship to the dock. Abigail knew that Elizabeth would have loved to charge up the gangplank to embrace her husband, but like all captains' wives, she knew that she had to wait until he had finished his docking activities before he could disembark.

"Unfortunately, I need to run to my mother's. I would love to wait to hear if there's any news of Matthew, but I don't have time to wait. Could you send Samuel over?"

Samuel was Elizabeth and Michael's oldest child and, at twelve years of age, had sailed with Michael on this voyage: his first time at sea. He was excited to go to sea when he was only twelve—most boys went to sea at fourteen after spending two years at a cooper's, learning to make barrels.

Once on ship, boys started as rowers and graduated, in order, to steerers and harpooners. The best of them went on to become officers and, eventually, to captain their own whaling ships.

"Of course. I'll see you tomorrow." Elizabeth knew that, like all sea captains' wives, Abigail would take comfort from hearing about Michael's voyage, especially if he had met Matthew while at sea.

Abigail walked west toward Main Street; if she hurried, she had just enough time for a quick cup of tea at her mother's before going home to take the bread out of the oven. Her mother, Phebe Gardner, still lived at 16 India Street in the house Abigail grew up in.

She called out to her mother as she opened the front door to the large, clapboard-faced house. Unlike her house, which had shake shingles on all four exterior walls, the front of Phebe's house was covered in white-painted clapboard in a style known as Federal. The spare, clean lines gave an impression of elegance, which was further enhanced by the semicircular blind fan over the front door. She loved her family's home as much as she loved her own. She removed her cloak and hat, leaving them on the bench by the front door, and walked to the back of the house.

Phebe was in the kitchen with Sarah and Betsy, who were at the table, eating thick slices of bread with butter and drinking hot chocolate. She was stirring something in the cast-iron pot that hung in the fireplace.

"Smells delicious," said Abigail. "What are you making?"

"Potato soup with bacon. Your brother Alexander is coming over later, and you know how he's always hungry."

Abigail had three older brothers: Alexander was the youngest of the three. She was the youngest sibling and the only girl. Her two oldest brothers, Peter and Richard, left

Nantucket to move to Hudson, New York, about ten years before, where they started a lumber mill. Neither of them was interested in the whaling industry, and they found island life to be too confining. Abigail missed them terribly as did Phebe.

THERE WAS A very strong connection between Nantucket and Hudson ever since the first Nantucketers moved there in 1783. By the end of the Revolutionary War, whaling was in ruins, decimated by the war. Eighteen families from Nantucket, called the Nantucket Navigators, had had enough; they saw their livelihoods destroyed by war and knew that the risk would always be there as Nantucket's harbor was easily accessible to friend and foe alike. To protect their futures, they looked for and found a location that allowed easy access to the ocean yet would be difficult to attack. It was a Dutch farming community in New York State called Claverack Landing, and it fit the bill perfectly. Being one hundred miles from the sea, it was protected from attack. It was surrounded by forests and farms that could support a growing ship-building trade. The Nantucket Navigators moved everything—including their houses, which they took apart and reassembled in their new location. New houses were built in the lean-to style typical of Nantucket. Shortly after settling there, the Navigators renamed Claverack Landing "Hudson," though there was a contingent lobbying for "New Nantucket" as its new name. By 1802, this remote outpost of Nantucket was thriving as a whaling port.

"I NEED TO see him today," said Abigail. "The *Omega* just came into port, and we need to review the orders for her next voyage. I imagine she'll sail again within the fortnight as I expect them to take one more voyage this season."

Abigail and Alexander had been running the family shipping business, Gardner & Sons, since their father, William, had died seven years ago. Their father had inherited the shipping business started by his grandfather, Phineas, and over the years had grown it to be the most successful shipping agency on the island. The Gardner family had been in seafaring businesses since their ancestor, John Gardner, arrived on the island in 1672. He was enticed to move to Nantucket from Salem, Massachusetts, to fish for cod, which the island used to pay its annual tribute to its mainland controller, New York. Nantucket didn't become part of Massachusetts until twenty years later in 1692, a fact that most of Abigail's peers didn't know and, frankly, didn't care about. The only reason she knew about it was because of her ancestor and from her father. From the time she was a young woman, William had included her in the family business as he did her brothers. In teaching her and her brothers the ropes of the family business, William was meticulous in explaining the reasons for their financial success. He had explained to her that the change of mainland control was a big financial boon for their family; Massachusetts did not tax whale oil and New York did, thereby giving Nantucket whalers a huge financial advantage over those from eastern Long Island.

Abigail liked working with her brother. Not surprisingly, they shared the same vision of how the business should be run and had settled naturally into the division of duties. Alexander was responsible for getting new business and negotiating with the ship owners. He hired the captains and crews, scheduled voyages, and most importantly, knew how to grade oil. Abigail did all of the accounting, kept the ledgers, assessed monetary exchange rates, and determined when was the best time to ship oil and whalebone to market. In addition to running the family business with Abigail, Alexander had a thriving sheep farm just outside of town and produced a lot of the wool used by Nantucketers for their cloth and yarn. It was not unusual for families to have several businesses as the whaling industry was very unpredictable.

"I'll tell him to stop by your house after the midday meal," said Phebe. "Will you be home this afternoon?"

"Yes. I'm going now. I was going to have tea, but I'd better get home. We left bread in the oven, and it should come out in fifteen minutes." Abigail was eyeing the grandfather clock in the hall. As she turned to leave, she reminded Sarah that she needed to work on her embroidery when she got home.

She walked east on India Street to Center Street, passing the stores selling fabric and notions. If she hadn't taken over her father's shipping business, she would have loved to open a yarn shop on Petticoat Row, as Center Street was informally known. She didn't like to sew, which is probably why she insisted Sarah practice her needlework so she wouldn't be as bad at it as Abigail was; but she loved to knit, especially for little children, because the tiny sweaters took no time at all to finish. She walked briskly down Main Street to Union Street, nodding to her many acquaintances that were out and about. A returning ship would keep town streets full of activity for days.

Entering her house on Union Street by the back door, she could smell the baking bread and thought that there was nothing better than stepping into a house warmed by bread baking. She hung up her hat and cloak and went downstairs to the cellar, basket in hand for carrying the loaves up to the kitchen.

"Mother, I'm home!" came a shout from upstairs. "Is there something to eat?"

Abigail smiled. How does he do it? Actually, both of her children were masters of fortuitous timing—Sarah in timing her baking and Thomas for picking the opportune time to eat.

She climbed the stairs and met her son, Thomas, in the kitchen. He was very tall for his age, taking after both her and Matthew. Although he was only eight, she could already picture the man he would become. Where Sarah was her serious child, Thomas was Sarah's exact opposite; he had a sunny disposition, was quick to laugh, and wasn't above playing silly practical jokes, especially on his sister, who would good-naturedly ignore him most of the time.

"You'll get something to eat once you've built up the fire in the kitchen."

"Mother, I'm hungry now!"

"Thomas, you're always hungry. Now go. It's starting to get cold in here."

A knock on the back door startled both of them. Turning to look, they saw Samuel, Elizabeth and Michael's sixteen-year-old son. For a moment, Abigail was speechless because the twelve-year-old boy she remembered was now a full-grown man.

"Samuel, come in! I hardly recognized you!"

"Hello, Mrs. Starbuck, Thomas." Samuel removed his cap and wiped his feet on the mat before coming in.

"My mother sent me straight over. There's a letter for you." He handed the envelope to Abigail. "Is Sarah around?"

Her heart leapt, and even though she knew that the news would be several months old, getting a letter from Matthew was always a happy occasion.

"No, Samuel. I'm sorry. She's not. She's at her grand-mother's. I expect her home shortly though."

Samuel looked crestfallen; clearly he had hoped to see Sarah. Michael and Matthew spent many nights teaching their two children about astronomy and, surprisingly, both Sarah and Samuel developed a keen interest in the subject. The children would often stay out in the backyard stargazing long after Matthew and Michael finished their lessons. When Michael and Samuel went to sea, Sarah seemed to lose interest in stargazing. She had halfheartedly kept it up with her father but then stopped altogether after he left. At the time, Abigail thought it was because she missed her father. But now, seeing Samuel's downcast face, she reconsidered, wondering if Sarah and Samuel were more than just child-hood friends. Impossible! They were children when Samuel left for sea. Except for her brothers, Abigail hardly knew what a boy *was* at Sarah's age. After a moment, she dismissed the thought; her imagination was running away with her.

"Do you want me to send her over after the evening meal? She has chores to do this afternoon."

"Thank you, Mrs. Starbuck, that's not necessary. I'll see her tomorrow." Samuel left by the back door and crossed their backyard into his own.

Thomas had finished adding wood to the kitchen fire, which was now blazing nicely. Abigail could feel the warmth creep back into the kitchen.

"I'm going to sea as soon as I can!"

"You will go to sea when your father says you're ready."

Abigail turned her head so Thomas could not see the look of dismay on her face. She wasn't ready to add "Thomas being at sea" to the list of things she already worried about. Like most sea captains' wives, she worried every day about Matthew and the dangers that could befall him. Whaling was dangerous and extremely difficult; loved ones had good reason to worry. She wished that Thomas was more interested in farming or the family business, like his uncle Alexander, so she could keep him safe on Nantucket forever.

She put Matthew's letter into her skirt pocket and started preparing the midday meal for herself and Thomas. She knew that Sarah wouldn't be hungry when she got home as she just had hot chocolate and bread at her grandmother's. She would have loved to tear the letter open immediately, but she also wanted to read it when she could savor it and reread it several times, imagining Matthew by her side speaking to her, instead of two-dimensional on paper.

"After I eat, can I please go down to the wharf?"

"Yes, that's fine. But before you go, please make sure that we have enough firewood in the house to get through the evening, and be home at dusk. We have Bible study tonight."

Thomas's normally happy face clouded over at the mention of Bible study. He would rather do anything outside, even cleaning the chicken coop, than study the Bible.

Abigail ignored his crabby face. "Please get bowls and spoons from the cupboard. We're having fish stew."

TWO HOURS LATER, with Thomas out of the house and Sarah sitting quietly by the kitchen fire working on her sampler, Abigail went upstairs to her bedroom and climbed into bed, pulling the feather comforter around her, feeling decadent to be in bed during the day. She reached into her pocket for Matthew's letter. It was dated September 1842. As she carefully broke the wax seal on the back of the envelope, she could imagine him at his table on the *Young Hero*, quill in hand, concentrating as he wrote. She often visited the *Young Hero* while the ship was in port, because when he was away she liked to visualize him on the ship, going about his duties. In her mind, she could picture how he looked as he wrote her this letter: his dark brown hair would be pulled back and tied with a leather strap, the thick ponytail skimming the top of the collar on his immaculately pressed captain's uniform. He was fastidious about his appearance while in command. She imagined him with a small smile on his clean-shaven face as he thought about her and the children, softening his normally stern and serious countenance that was part of a captain's daily life while at sea. With happy anticipation and holding Matthew in her mind's eye, she took two sheets of paper out of the envelope and unfolded them.

My darling Abigail,

I hope this letter finds you and the children well and that the winter has not been too harsh on our island. I just arrived in Maui in the Sandwich Islands, and I will sail for Pitcairn within the week. Our hold is still only half full. I fear that the whales have learned where we are and can cleverly avoid us. There are hundreds of whaling ships off the west coast of South America, and we've not been one of the lucky ones. Each whale has been yielding only twenty barrels of sperm oil, so our progress has been slower than I had hoped. I hope to get our quota in the South Pacific, and if not, I will have to wait until March and sail north to the Kamchatka Peninsula of Russia where I understand the whaling has been excellent. It's too late in the year to sail north now; it would be too dangerous with the sea ice, and you know that I will not take unnecessary risks. As of now, I hope to be home by October 1843.

I'm happy that I have been able to get this letter to Michael; he's on his way back to Nantucket with a nearly full hold. It was good to gam with our neighbor and to share a few evenings talking about home. He was in Maui stocking up on provisions before sailing for Nantucket.

I can picture the look on your face when Samuel delivered this letter. He's grown into a man on this voyage, and Michael is so proud of his son, and rightly so! He's definitely no longer the little boy who spent evenings stargazing with Sarah. I'm sure she will be very surprised when she sees him as well.

While it was great to see Michael and Samuel, I have to say that seeing how much Samuel has grown has made me feel a little sad. I realize that Sarah and Thomas will also have changed dramatically during my voyage, and I have missed it. Dear wife, I put a tremendous burden on you, which I know you take on willingly, and for that, I am so grateful. You have to be mother and father to our children. Since I was a young boy, I have never wanted to be anywhere but on the sea. But these feelings have changed for me on this voyage. As I face being away for at least another thirteen months, I am questioning my love for the sea. Is being a sea captain worth what I have to—nay, what we have to give up to hunt whales? You, our life together, and our children—these are dearer to me than anything.

Tell the children that I miss them and think of them every day. Tell Thomas to be good at his studies—I know how much he dislikes school—but remind him that he needs reading, writing, and math if he wants to be a ship's captain one day. Tell Sarah how much I appreciate all that she does to help you. She's such a good daughter! Tell her I will bring her something very special from the South Pacific.

My darling wife, I know this letter is not bringing you good news or comfort, and for that I'm sorry. I wish I had better news. I miss you and the children. You are in my heart, now and always.

Your loving husband,
Matthew

She reread the letter four times. She realized that her earlier estimate of July was wrong and that he wouldn't be home for seven more months. She felt sad, not only for herself and the children, but also for him. He had never been unhappy about being at sea before. She knew that he missed her and the children, but this was the life they signed up for. He first went to sea at thirteen. He was a first mate on his father's whaling ship when she married him sixteen years before, and she knew that the sea was his life. His love for the sea was as much a part of him as his dark blue eyes. *We're getting old and sentimental,* she thought, smiling, as she got out of bed to go downstairs, wondering if their family was reaching a turning point in their lives.

2

Abby and Matt

March 2008, Boston

*S*tepping out of the taxi into the pouring rain, Matt silently swore as a gust of wind drove his umbrella inside out and cold March rain poured down his neck. He looked at his watch as he walked into the lobby of 30 Rowes Wharf, happy that he had left his hotel early to account for the awful weather. He checked in with the security guard who directed him to the nineteenth floor.

Matt stepped into the elevator. *OK, buddy, time to focus,* he said silently to himself as the elevator ascended. *You can do it!* His business, Starbuck Enterprises, had been wooing Gardner & Sons for months, and he had finally gotten a meeting with its CEO, Abby Gardner.

"Matt Starbuck, from Starbuck Enterprises, here to see Abby Gardner."

As he approached the beautifully dressed, attractive, middle-aged woman sitting at the impressive mahogany reception desk, he saw that her name was Caroline Gardner.

"Good morning, Mr. Starbuck. You can put your coat and umbrella in the cloakroom and then, please, have a seat."

Caroline pointed to the leather chairs by the window with a full view of Boston Harbor, which was obscured by the pouring rain.

He stepped into the cloakroom, trying not to leave a trail of water as he hung up his soaking coat and placed his useless umbrella on the floor under it. He was fifteen minutes early and glad to have the extra time to gather his composure before meeting Abby Gardner. He was more nervous than usual before a big sales pitch. At thirty-five, Matt was the third-generation CEO of Starbuck Enterprises, and he was afraid he'd be the last. He had a lot riding on this meeting— probably the fate of the company if he were to be really honest with himself. The software industry was increasingly competitive, and Starbuck Enterprises had struggled in the last three years to win big, long-term contracts. But while Matt was not normally a pie-eyed optimist, he was also not a doom-and-gloom pessimist. Yes, the fate of his company could be significantly influenced by this meeting—but even if this meeting didn't go well, he would figure something out. He knew it would do him no good to walk into the meeting feeling desperate. To distract himself, he tried to guess the relationship between the receptionist and the CEO. He wondered if they could be sisters. As Caroline appeared to be in her late forties, this was the most likely relationship. He had googled Abby Gardner and Gardner & Sons, but as a privately held company it wasn't obliged to provide much information to the public. He could only find a short, cor- porate biography with Abby's credentials and information about the company and its services. *Funny*, he thought, *that your sister would be the receptionist when you're the CEO of the firm.* He couldn't imagine either of his sisters as his recep- tionist; both of them would insist on being vice presidents! Maybe the last name was purely a coincidence.

"Mr. Starbuck, Ms. Gardner will see you now." Caroline opened the large door behind her to her left.

Matt walked through the door into a large room with floor-to-ceiling windows on two sides and a wall of bookcases centered around a wood-burning fireplace on the third side. Caroline softly closed the paneled mahogany door behind him. For a moment, he lost his bearings. While the floor-to-ceiling windows were a modern effect, the furnishings, the fire in the fireplace, and the rich wood accents all combined to give the impression of a room from long ago. He noticed the carved scrimshaw and sailors' valentines on the shelves, both art forms from the whaling years of the 1700s and 1800s. The art, furnishings, and antique oriental carpets on the floor combined to create an atmosphere of another age. For a second, he thought he was back in his ancestor's house, one of the Three Bricks on Main Street on Nantucket, built in 1838 by Joseph Starbuck for his son George.

He snapped out of his fog and looked at Abby. For all of his preparation for today's meeting, he could have never prepared himself for the impact of seeing Abby Gardner for the first time. At first, he had trouble seeing her clearly as the light from the windows backlit her. As she stepped from behind her desk toward him, right hand extended, his breath caught in his chest. When his eyes adjusted, he froze and only raised his hand to meet hers at the last second before he would appear to be a world-class idiot. *I know her*, he thought, dazed. He knew her really, really well—nearly as well as he knew himself—but how could this be possible?

Abby was a bit puzzled by Matt's slow reaction. She knew her office was beautiful, but she didn't think the setting was intimidating. She had deliberately furnished it to resemble a room she saw in a book about Nantucket's golden age of whaling, whaling captains, and their homes. Until she was sixteen, she spent two weeks every summer at her family's home in Codfish Park on the eastern end of the island. Starting at seventeen, she didn't join her parents as she was working at Gardner & Sons and couldn't get the two weeks off. Her father, Bill, was insistent that she treated her summer job seriously.

EIGHTEEN YEARS EARLIER, Abby had started in the family business as a summer intern at fourteen, and yes, it was in the mailroom, cliché as that sounded. Her father insisted she start in an entry-level position, and for the next three summers, she continued working in the most junior roles in his organization: mailroom, cafeteria, and when she was eighteen, as a janitor. She remembered complaining to her father the year he told her she was to be a janitor.

"Really, Daddy? A janitor? Emptying garbage and cleaning toilets? Isn't there some advantage to being a Gardner?"

"With that attitude, young lady, you may find yourself coming back next summer as a janitor as well. I could not be more disappointed in you than I am right now." She had never seen her father so angry.

"But, Daddy, I don't know anything about being a janitor. It's not my lifelong ambition!" Abby was not backing down, but she was clearly flustered.

Bill took a deep breath and realized this was a teaching moment for his daughter.

"Let's think about it this way: when you come into the office, and everything is clean and in its place, how does that make you feel? Ready to work? Productive? Our janitors take pride in what they do. Not every office in Boston is as well cared for as ours are. You will learn a lot from them this summer if you keep an open mind. I expect you to do your best, including cleaning toilets."

Finally, at nineteen, after her freshman year at Boston University, he allowed her to work in accounting, reconciling bank statements. If her father hadn't died unexpectedly three years ago in a freak sailing accident at the age of fifty-three, Abby was quite certain that he would have passed the CEO reins on to her when she was forty, not when she was twenty-nine. She joined the firm full-time at twenty-one, immediately after she graduated from college with a dual degree in computer systems engineering and business administration. She had worked at Gardner & Sons on every school break; she was definitely not raised to feel entitled to a position at the firm—she earned it. Like her, most of the seven hundred employees at Gardner & Sons had been with the firm their entire careers; they had seen her in the mailroom and as a janitor and accepted her as one of the team.

BEFORE MATT ARRIVED, Abby too, had prepared for their meeting, giving herself her own pep talk. She thought about her career progression at Gardner & Sons and reminded herself that she was an experienced business-woman running a successful business. She had no reason to be intimidated by Matt Starbuck though she had heard that he was not easy to work with. As she stepped around her desk to greet him, several thoughts raced through her head. She realized that starting where she did in the firm was probably why the employees accepted her as CEO at twenty-nine even though she wished that she had had at least ten more years of her father's coaching and guidance. What was it called? A battlefield promotion? And why was she thinking about this now? Maybe she was a little nervous; she needed Starbuck

Enterprises' software, and she hoped that he was not going to be difficult to work with.

Shaking off her momentary insecurity, she greeted Matt. "Mr. Starbuck, very nice to meet you. I'm sorry you're experiencing one of our cold, blustery March days."

"Please, it's Matt, Ms. Gardner. And trust me, we get days like this on Nantucket as well."

"It's Abby. Thank you, Matt. Please have a seat."

She directed him to one of two leather couches placed perpendicularly in front of the roaring fireplace. She sat across from him and pointed to a sterling silver coffee pot on the table between them.

"Coffee?"

She deliberately started business negotiations in this setting. In a way, it was a test. Many people were uncomfortable with the informality of the setting and others too comfortable. She evaluated every new business partner with one simple criterion: can I work with this person and organization for the next thirty years? She learned this from her father. Most of their clients, business partners, and suppliers had been working with Gardner & Sons for more than twenty years. Long-standing partnerships were a cornerstone of the firm's traditions; her father and grandfather believed that this principle made their firm stronger and more successful. Like her father, she was not interested in short-term profits or relationships. As long as Gardner & Sons stayed privately held, Abby was insistent on establishing relationships as she saw fit. The "couch test," as she called it, was her favorite way to get a sense of the person she was considering doing business with.

"Do you come from a family of psychoanalysts?"

Startled, Abby replied, "Why do you ask that?"

"You have two big couches that are clearly old and well-worn. I thought they might be family heirlooms from private practice days."

She laughed out loud. "Mr. Starbuck—sorry—Matt, you're the very first person to make this observation about my couches. No, no psychoanalysts in the family. I come from a long line of entrepreneurs."

Matt smiled. "That's good. I'm not sure my psyche is up for in-depth analysis. I'm a WYSIWYG kind of guy—what you see is what you get."

Abby added cream to her coffee and sat back on the couch, suddenly awkwardly aware that she had been leaning toward Matt during this conversation. She wondered what she was doing—now she was the one who was too comfortable in this setting.

It's déjà vu all over again, thought Matt, cringing that he was channeling the Yankee manager, Yogi Berra. As he sat on the couch, having coffee with Abby, it seemed to him as if he'd been here before, but definitely not in this lifetime. It had to be the similarity to the formal living room in his family's former house on Nantucket, the East Brick at 93 Main Street. He ignored the sensation of having met her before; prior-life stuff was just too weird to think about, and he needed to stay focused.

With the weather and coffee out of the way, Abby got straight to the point. "What can I do for you, Matt?"

You can place the largest profitable order Starbucks Enterprises has ever had, he thought, while saying, "It's what Starbuck Enterprises can do for you, Abby. We have a new software that would be a perfect fit with StarTaker."

StarTaker was a technologically advanced navigational device used by a broad range of customers: from hobby sailors to the US Navy. It was a modern-day astrolabe; it charted the position of the vessel by its relative position to

the stars with a high degree of accuracy, eliminating the
need for satellites. It used a series of complex mathematical
equations and software algorithms to provide position information.

"I didn't know that we needed new software. StarTaker
has been the flagship of our operation for over one hundred
years. I wasn't aware that it needed improving."

She took a bold position to start the meeting while in
the back of her mind she knew that StarTaker was starting
to lose market share for the first time in fifty years. If they
hadn't deeply discounted it for the last nine months, the
decline would have been even more precipitous. But there
was no way Matt could know this; their revenues weren't
public. In fact, this was her biggest challenge as the CEO;
she was getting a lot of pressure from her advisory board to
go public to get an infusion of capital to shore up declining
profits.

"Just hear me out. StarTaker has been the market leader
for one hundred years. My software can ensure that it's the
market leader for the next hundred. Your competition is
moving aggressively into next-generation automation, and
so far, you've gotten lucky. They're bad at it, and they're not
working with us."

"Let me get this straight." Abby bristled at his comments
about being lucky. "You think that understanding your
market, having outstanding relationships with your customers, and working harder than everyone else—you think *this*
is getting lucky?"

She knew she shouldn't have taken the bait—losing her
composure was not going to help—but she was afraid that
he was right and she was, frankly, not in a good negotiating
position. She needed Matt, and as predicted, he was proving
to be difficult to work with. She had been with him for all of

ten minutes, and he was already irritating her; this was not a good omen.

"Abby, we're getting off on the wrong foot, and I apologize. I know your company's success has nothing to do with luck. Let's start over."

Matt forced himself to smile and look relaxed. *Wow,* he thought while taking a deep breath, *that was a YouTube moment titled: "How not to sell something."* If he didn't dial it back, he'd be kicked out of there in the next five minutes.

"My goal is to form a long-lasting partnership with Gardner & Sons, so that both of our companies can build on our long histories and be successful for the next one hundred years, as I said earlier. I think you and I are in a unique position to form a partnership that will outlive both of us."

"If this is such a good idea, why hasn't it happened before? Why haven't our families' businesses worked together before now?"

"Would you believe me if I said that I think it goes back to the Half-Share revolt on Nantucket in the late 1670s? Look, as you might know, Starbuck was one of the original nine families who settled on Nantucket, each one having a full share of ownership of the island in what was called the proprietary. They were called 'full-share men,' who quickly realized that they were missing skills needed for a thriving community, so they offered half-shares to craftsmen and tradesmen to entice them to move to the island from the mainland. In principle, this was a good idea—men and their families, who were willing to take a risk, became landowners on Nantucket when they would not have had the same opportunity on the mainland. Your family, the Gardners, were 'half-share men.' It all went wrong when the original nine families created a two-tier society: full-share, with all rights in the proprietary, and half-share, with severely diminished rights, such as not being able to acquire more land on the island. After time, the half-share families, such as yours, understandably grew resentful of not having equal rights on the island, and they staged their own minirevolution. The two main protagonists were John Gardner, who I assume was your ancestor, and a man named Tristam Coffin. Our two families weren't going directly head-to-head at the time—luckily, I'm not a Coffin—but we were still on opposite sides of the conflict. After the revolt, things settled down pretty quickly, but the animosity between the full-share families and half-share families remained. It only ended when Jethro Coffin married Mary Gardner in 1686, but I think it never went away completely."

Matt paused to drink his coffee. "I know you probably think this seems silly. I'm sorry for going on about the island's history, but it has always fascinated me, and while I don't think our two families carried a grudge for 350 years, I'd offer that it set us on separate paths right from the beginning."

Abby watched him as he was talking about Nantucket's history and thought it was a little weird. If someone had told her that morning that she would be discussing events that had happened 350 years ago in a business negotiation, she never would have believed it.

"This is all very interesting, and I am fascinated by the island's history too. But I still need help to understand what you mean by a partnership between Gardner & Sons and Starbuck Enterprises. Are you suggesting that we merge our firms?"

"No, Abby, sorry! When I referred to a partnership, I was referring to the strong mutually beneficial relationship that I believe our firms can have. I did a little digging and learned that you have long-standing relationships with your suppliers. Like you, most of our suppliers have been with us for at least ten years and many, more than twenty." He grinned. "But if you'd like to consider a merger, I'm in."

As Matt said this, he was again struck by the eerie sense that they had been business partners before. *This is distracting,* he thought. *I need to stay focused.*

"If it's OK, I'd like to tell you more about our software and what I think it can do for StarTaker."

He spent the next thirty minutes describing the functionality of his software and how he imagined it could benefit StarTaker. As her background was computer systems engineering, Abby caught on quickly and saw that, while working with him might be a pain in the neck, his software was potentially a good fit for her flagship product.

"OK, let's do this. I am intrigued by your software and also by the idea of two long-standing businesses working together for the very first time. It could be potentially interesting for our company. I suggest that our next steps would be to engage our technical people to review the fit of your software with StarTaker, and after this review, you and I meet again to continue our discussion. Say, four weeks from now? Can you make your technical development team available starting in the next couple of days? If yes, I'll get Legal to draw up the nondisclosure agreement and send it over to you by end of day today. After your lawyer reviews it, we can sign it and our folks can get started."

"Sounds good, Abby. I look forward to seeing you in early April. I'll schedule it with Ms. Gardner on my way out. By the way, are you related, or is the last name a coincidence?"

"She's my mother." Abby was amused by the startled look on his face. "You're wondering why the CEO's mother is her receptionist and personal assistant?"

He regained his composure and looked her directly in the

eye. "Yes, frankly, I am. I can't imagine my mother working for me. It'd have to be the other way around."

Abby smiled and then grew serious. "When my father died so unexpectedly three years ago and I took over our firm, both my mother and I felt lost. I don't know if you ever met my father, but he was a force of nature. Losing him, the way that we did, was overwhelming. There was little time to grieve, as I had to step in as CEO immediately. My mother had always been my father's top advisor though never formally. In the first weeks after his death, she came with me into the office every day, originally to help sort the papers in his office. After a month, we both realized that this worked very well for us, and as my mother's never been a 'lady who lunches' type of woman, she's been my right hand ever since. And she's an excellent judge of character. Her first impressions tend to prove true over time."

As she said the last sentence, she watched him squirm, just a bit. "Now you're wondering if you did something odd while you waited for me, no?"

Matt laughed out loud. "I stopped worrying about that long ago, Abby. If I worried about people thinking I was odd, I would never leave my house."

He stood up to leave, and just before he opened her office door, he turned to face her. "I know this will sound trite, but I just have to ask, have we met somewhere before? You seem so familiar to me."

"No, Matt, I don't believe so. I'm not perfect at remembering names, but I'm great at remembering faces, and I'm 100 percent certain that we haven't met before." With his thick dark brown hair and startling blue eyes, he was one of the handsomest men she had ever seen. Abby was quite sure she would remember having met him.

"I guess it was in a previous life," Matt blurted, wondering to himself why in the world he just said that. He didn't believe in people having past lives, but it was the first thing that popped into his head.

"I'm sure that must be it." She returned his warm smile as she closed the door behind him, although she didn't believe that people had past lives.

If that's true, thought Abby as she walked to her desk, *I wonder if he was any easier to deal with then.*

3

Matthew and Abigail

October 1843, Nantucket

"Captain," shouted Billy Coffin, the first mate, "land ho!"

"Mr. Coffin, all hands to stations to bring the ship to dock!" Matthew shouted the command with lightness in his voice.

He brought his spyglass up to his right eye to get a better view of the land off the starboard side of the *Young Hero*. He could see the saltbox houses on the western shore of the island. He had sailed around the island so often as a boy that he knew every inch of the shoreline. Thrilled to be home, he put his spyglass away and hurried to the bow; this was no time to be reminiscing about boyhood sailing excursions—the currents between Tuckernuck and Nantucket were unpredictable at the best of times. Now that he was so close to home, Matthew prayed that the winds would stay favorable until they reached the dock. *That would be just my luck,* he thought, as he watched as the crew reached their stations and prepared for docking, *that we'd have to tack offshore for hours waiting for the wind to change after being away for four years.*

The winds stayed favorable, and the *Young Hero* was able to sail directly to an open position on Old North Wharf. As usual, there was a large crowd of townspeople gathered at the wharf, waiting for the ship to dock. Matthew could sense the excitement in his crew; each man was looking forward to being reunited with his family.

I thank the Lord that we don't have any deaths to report this voyage, he thought. There's nothing worse than giving sad news to a family who has waited so long for their loved one to return. They might not have gotten as much whale oil as he had hoped, but everyone was safe, so that was a blessing.

"Captain, this is your home?"

Matthew turned to see 'Ailani and his wife, Anuenue, standing by his side. He met the young couple at a prayer meeting while in Maui, one of the Pacific Sandwich Islands. He spoke with them several times during the week while he was in port and 'Ailani surprised him with a request to join his crew just before the *Young Hero* was due to set sail. 'Ailani was the youngest son of the local chief, Ewelani. He told Matthew that he and Anuenue wanted to see the world; they knew that others from their island had also joined whaling ships in the past. Matthew remembered their conversation as if it were yesterday, although it was more than thirteen months ago.

"Are you really sure, 'Ailani? Nantucket is beautiful, and I love her, but she's not like your island. The weather can be terrible and very cold. We often have days and days of fog when we don't see the sun. It is so different from here."

"Yes, Captain, I am very sure. Both Anuenue and I want to see the world and make our fortune. We are both very good at making things with our hands. I am sure that we can find work. We will work very hard on your ship to pay for our passage."

"If you leave here, you may not get a chance to ever come back. There's no guarantee that you will find a ship that can bring you back to the Sandwich Islands if you don't like Nantucket. You're both only twenty years old. Are you really sure that you want to leave your home and possibly never come back? You'd never see your family again." Matthew persisted because he was worried that the young couple would be unhappy.

"We're willing to take that risk. Captain, I know that you're trying to protect us, but we're very certain about our decision. We've prayed about it, and we trust the Lord to guide us and keep us safe."

"Then, let's do this. You'll work on the crew for the remainder of the voyage at the direction of my first mate, Mr. Coffin. Anuenue can help our ship's cook. When we get to Nantucket, you can stay with my family until you find work and a place of your own. You can agree with my wife, Abigail, as to how you pay for your room and board with us. Are these terms acceptable to you?"

"Yes, Captain! Thank you so much, Captain! I must run home and tell Anuenue to pack."

"Be at the *Young Hero* by 0800 tomorrow. We sail with the tide."

COMING BACK TO the present moment, Matthew looked at the couple standing by his side and smiled. They were wearing cloaks that were cobbled together from old flour sacks on the ship. *Welcome to Nantucket*, he thought. It was only October and already they were freezing—just

wait until January. He was not unkind, so he held back the
bad news about the winter weather.

"What do you think of your new home?"

'Ailani and Anuenue were silent, having seen the coast-
line go by with no palm trees, no flowers, and very little
green in sight.

"You were right, Captain, this is very different than our
island," said Anuenue. "But I am certain the Lord brought us
here for a very good reason."

Matthew knew one reason. They both had helped him
tremendously during the last part of this voyage; their
wonder at seeing all of the new things reminded him, in
a way, of his children. He was a lot less homesick than he
thought he would be. What started out as a simple kindness
had turned into something deeper and more personal during
the remainder of his voyage. He wondered what Abigail
would think when she met them. He hoped that his generos-
ity in the Pacific would be as well received at home.

"Well, as much as I would like it, the Lord won't help
dock this ship, so if you'll both excuse me, I must get back
to my duties." Matthew noticed the stricken looks on their
faces after his nearly blasphemous comment about the Lord.
He added a bit more gently, "Be sure to stay out of the way
of the crew as we navigate to port. It's always tricky in these
waters."

An hour later, the crew of the *Young Hero* had finished
securing the ship and were waiting on deck at the head of
the gangplank, eager to leave the ship.

"Permission to disembark, Captain!" shouted Billy who
was smiling ear to ear having spotted his wife, Mary, on the
wharf.

"Permission granted. All ashore!"

After the crew left the ship, Matthew, 'Ailani, and Anuenue made their way down the gangplank. He, too, had seen Abigail and the children thirty minutes before as he was completing his docking duties. Abigail looked exactly the same as the day he left, but he was astonished at how grown-up his children looked. It took all of his patience to keep from sprinting down the gangplank and throwing himself into their eagerly waiting arms. A sea captain has to maintain a certain amount of decorum, or so he told himself, so he settled for a warm but brief hug with his wife. He was more exuberant with Sarah and Thomas.

"Abigail, who are these children? Where are Sarah and Thomas? I mean, these are pretty good-looking children, but they are way too big to be ours."

"Father, Father, it's me! It's Thomas! Can't you see? I'm now big enough to go to sea with you. When are you sailing again? Can I go with you this time?" Thomas was beside himself with joy at seeing his father and was circling Matthew like a golden retriever puppy, looking for a good place to chomp.

"Thomas!" Abigail said his name in a loud whisper—only the large crowd of people in the vicinity kept her voice low and prevented her from giving him a good whack around the ears. "Your father has been on land for all of three minutes."

While Abigail was scolding Thomas, Sarah quietly reached for Matthew's hand and asked in a serious voice, "Father, don't you recognize me? I'm Sarah."

"Of course I recognize you, my darling girl! I was just teasing you and your brother."

His eyes met Abigail's over Sarah's head; yes, his little daughter was just as serious at thirteen years of age as she was at nine. She shrieked, though, as he lifted her off her feet, giving her a big hug.

"Family, I want to introduce you to two friends I made on this journey: 'Ailani and Anuenue. They come from a magical place where it's sunny and warm all year long with palm trees, parrots, and amazing flowers." 'Ailani and Anuenue stepped forward and solemnly shook Abigail's, Thomas's, and Sarah's hands.

"Why are you here? Why didn't you stay in your magical place? And what are you *wearing*?" Thomas, who always said precisely what was in his head, blurted out exactly what Abigail was thinking.

"Thomas! Where are your manners?" Ignoring her son, Abigail smiled warmly at 'Ailani and Anuenue. "Welcome to Nantucket, I am honored to meet you. I look forward to getting to know you."

"That will be easy, Abigail, as they will be living with us until they find a place of their own in New Guinea," said Matthew nonchalantly, as if it were completely normal to bring home two Pacific islanders every day. New Guinea was the section of Nantucket just west of the Starbucks' home on Union Street where other Pacific islanders, as well as the Portuguese and Africans, had established their own community.

Abigail, though startled by the news, took it in stride. "In that case, let's go home and get you settled. I'm sure you must be tired, hungry, and cold."

They had plenty of room for their guests; the house had four bedrooms in addition to the kitchen, dining room, and two reception rooms. Matthew's cousin, Thomas Starbuck, who had run a very successful millinery business, built it on Union Street in 1795. He was married for thirty years but never had heirs of his own. When Thomas's wife died in 1820, he changed his will and generously left his house to Matthew. Sadly for Matthew, who dearly loved his cousin,

Thomas died shortly after he married Abigail and never got to meet his namesake.

LATER THAT EVENING, when their guests and the children were in bed, Abigail and Matthew sat in their favorite chairs by the dying fire in the kitchen. She looked at her husband and wondered about his life over the last four years. Seeing how tired he looked, she decided it was not the time to ask about it. There would be plenty of time in the days to come.

"Come, my dear husband, let's go to bed. You're tired, and there's no need to stay awake any longer."

Matthew gazed at her, his heart full. For a moment, he was overcome by his feelings. He couldn't have spoken even if a team of horses were dragging it out of him. His thoughts were so muddled; he always suffered during the transition from the sea to the land, never feeling as if he belonged in either place. He was reminded of the saying: "One foot on the boat and one on the dock" as he climbed the stairs to their bedroom. This last voyage was the worst; he couldn't remember a time when he had longed to be home on Nantucket more than he did on this past trip. He felt physical pain in his heart. Yet now that he was home, he didn't feel as happy as he expected to feel. He attributed it to being tired and overexcited by the homecoming.

THE NEXT MORNING dawned clear and bright. There was frost on the ground, which would melt with the midmorning sun. Matthew walked the children to school on Fair Street, promising to pick them up when the school day was finished. Thomas, in particular, liked showing off his sea captain father to his friends.

He walked east on Main Street to Federal Street, trying

to decide if he should go straight home or to check on the *Young Hero*. He decided that, after being gone for four years, he'd better head home. Five minutes later, he entered the house to see Abigail speaking to 'Ailani and Anuenue who were dressed in his and Abigail's clothes.

"Oh, good, Matthew, you're back. Did the children get to school without a problem?"

"Yes, Abigail, I remembered the way to the school on Fair Street." Matthew smiled at his wife.

Abigail laughed. "That's not what I meant. You know how popular you are when you're first home. I thought you might have gotten sidetracked by one of your friends."

"Good morning, Captain," said 'Ailani.

"Good morning, 'Ailani, Anuenue. Did you sleep well? I see that Abigail has gotten you appropriately clothed for our weather."

"Yes, we did. Thank you, Captain," said Anuenue. "I will sew us some proper clothes right away."

"I told them that they were welcome to keep these clothes. They just told me that they are very anxious to find work. I was encouraging them to take a few days to explore town and get their 'land' legs, but they seem to be eager to start working."

"Yes, Captain, Mrs. Starbuck is correct. We would like to find work right away. We don't want to be a burden to you." 'Ailani was adamant.

"Abigail, what do you think about my asking Cousin Eunice if she needs help?" Eunice Starbuck Hadwen was Matthew's first cousin, and while they didn't see each other very often, they were close. Eunice was a very generous and kind person, known for helping her family and friends. She shared her home at 100 Main Street with her sister, Eliza; Eliza's husband, Nathaniel Barney; and their children, Joseph and Sarah. It was one of the biggest houses on the island and often the center of society events.

"I think that's a great idea, Matthew! Why don't you pay her a visit before you pick up the children from school this afternoon? Today is her normal 'at home' day to receive visitors, and I can imagine having her sea captain cousin stop by unannounced will thrill the ladies calling on her. You'll make her the talk of the town for the rest of the week." She smiled at the thought of the looks on the ladies' faces when the dashing sea captain appeared in his cousin's reception room.

FOR THE REST of the morning, into the early afternoon, Matthew puttered around the house, feeling at loose ends. There was so much to do every day on a ship, and it was odd for him not to have a full day. He picked up and put down the *Nantucket Inquirer* a half a dozen times, unable to concentrate on what he was reading.

Abigail walked into the kitchen, a basket of washing balanced on her hip, and saw her husband, who quickly snatched up the newspaper, trying to appear engrossed in his reading. She knew that he was staying home for her sake—and she loved that he was so thoughtful—but she also knew it was hard for him be in one place after four years on the open sea.

"Matthew, please go. Get out of the house. Have you checked on the *Young Hero* today? Aren't there friends you'd like to see? 'Ailani and Anuenue are walking around town. If you run into them, you could give them a little tour before you go to Eunice's."

"I thought, having just gotten home yesterday, you'd like

me to stay home today at least." He looked a little sheepish at being caught pretending to read the paper.

"Of course I love having you here. And thank you for considering my feelings, but I'd love it even more if you weren't underfoot as I'm trying to get my chores done. Off you go. I'll see you later this afternoon."

Relieved, he put on his coat and hat and stepped out into the midday sunshine. While the day had started with a chill in the air, by noon it was almost too warm for a coat. He walked north on Union Street until he reached Main Street, trying to decide if he should walk to Old North Wharf to check on the *Young Hero* or if he should go to his family's shipping agency, Starbuck & Co., to check in.

He saw that a lot had changed in the last four years as he walked west on Main Street, deciding to stop by the *Young Hero* after walking through town. He crossed the intersection at Federal Street and continued walking north. He didn't remember there being so many clothing stores on Main Street before. He looked at the woman's fur coat hanging in the window of one store, marveling that such an item was available on Nantucket. Clearly, the whaling business had created a lot of prosperous citizens. But unfortunately for him, that wasn't true for his last voyage. He knew that his 1,000 barrels of whale oil was not considered a successful voyage; his quota had been 1,500 barrels. But when he was three and a half years away, he decided to cut his losses and sail home, unwilling to be away even longer and still end up with a poor outcome.

He turned right onto Center Street and nearly walked straight into Lyndon Wright.

"Captain Starbuck!" exclaimed Lyndon, who was the

editor of the *Nantucket Inquirer*. "I heard that the *Young Hero* docked yesterday, but I was too busy getting the newspaper out to go to the wharf to greet her. Welcome home, Matthew! I was just on my way to my dinner. Would you join me?"

"Yes, thank you! I can catch up on the Nantucket news."

"What? You haven't been keeping up with the *Nantucket Inquirer* while you were away?" Lyndon laughed.

"As you can guess, the delivery has been a bit sporadic. But I have to say, when I would gam with other Nantucket whaling ships, it was always one of the most prized possessions to exchange."

They reached the tavern and quickly found a table. After ordering their meal and a pint of beer, they launched into the topics of the day.

"How was your voyage? Was it as successful as you planned?"

"Hmm . . . Are you asking as the editor of the *Nantucket Inquirer* or as my friend?"

"Matthew, this entire conversation is between friends only, but you know that a returning ship is always news, so I hope that we can have a more formal exchange before next week's issue."

"I'd be happy to, Lyndon. No, I didn't get my quota on this voyage. I came up five hundred barrels short. After three and a half years away and at just over breakeven, I had to decide: stay out at least another year or sail for home, hoping to encounter more whales on the return voyage. I decided the latter and wasn't lucky. With one thousand barrels, I did a little better than breakeven, but as you can imagine, the crew was very disappointed with their lay."

New England and Nantucket whalemen were paid differ-

ently than other countries' whalemen: they got a percentage
of the catch, which was called a lay. The percentage was tied
to the position the man held on the ship with the captain
taking the biggest lay, on down to the oarsmen, who were
traditionally the lowest rank on the ship. Matthew knew that
the responsibility for the voyage's success rested solely on
his shoulders.

"You know the old saying: one good year in seven more
than makes up for six bad years, but I would rather have the
reverse," said Matthew.

"At least Gardner & Sons is doing well, or so I hear."

A dark look crossed Matthew's face, which, luckily, went
unnoticed by his friend. He didn't need reminding that his
wife's business was successful. He was happy for Abigail, of
course, and he was very proud of her business acumen, but
hearing about her success right now made him feel inade-
quate as the family provider in light of his mediocre result
from his recent voyage.

He changed the subject. "Tell me, what's the news on
Nantucket? Catch me up on the past four years."

"Oh, you only want the news for the last four years! Sadly,
I have to go back to work this afternoon. How about I give
you the highlights? You are more than welcome to come to
our offices and go through the archives."

Lyndon went on to give Matthew the highlights of
1843: more than 150 ships; 1,100 brigs; 8,200 schooners;
and 3,500 sloops had sailed into Nantucket Harbor. It was a
lucky year; no ships or seamen were taken captive by priva-
teers. The encroaching sandbar at the mouth of the harbor
was continuing to be a challenge for the larger ships, which
were avoiding the problem by sailing to New Bedford on the

mainland instead of Nantucket. Politically, the news was about Nantucket's increasingly public support for abolishing slavery on the mainland.

Since the 1700s, Nantucket was against slavery, strongly believing that all men are created equal, due mainly to its widespread Quaker population. In 1769, Nantucket's most prominent whaling merchant and owner of the *Friendship*, William Rotch, insisted that Captain Elisha Folger pay Boston Prince, a black man, his lay directly and not to John Swain. This was unusual because Boston Prince's father had been owned by John Swain's father and John Swain believed that he owned both Boston Prince and any money that he had earned. Rotch's meddling made Swain furious, and he took the matter to court, losing ownership of Boston Prince in the Court of Common Pleas. Swain appealed the first court's decision to the Supreme Court of Massachusetts but ultimately dropped his appeal because Rotch promised to hire John Adams as the lawyer to represent Boston Prince. As a result of this highly publicized case, Nantucket, followed by Massachusetts, abolished slavery nearly eighty years ahead of its abolition by the federal government.

Matthew and Lyndon said good-bye, promising to catch up later in the week.

AS HE STEPPED into the waning afternoon sun, Matthew realized that he would have to hurry to squeeze in his stop at Eunice's house before picking up the children at school.

Eunice's front door was opened by her butler, Thaddeus, who frostily informed him that madam was in the front reception room with her guests.

"Is she expecting you?" asked Thaddeus with a disapproving look on his face. Family or not, there was a specific protocol for calling hours, and Matthew was ignoring it on two counts: he was a man, and he hadn't sent his visiting card beforehand.

He smiled at Thaddeus's disapproval. "Thaddeus, you've known me since I was born. As I just returned yesterday from four years at sea, I was hoping you could overlook my lack of manners this one time."

"Yes, sir. Of course, sir. Right this way." Thaddeus acquiesced but was clearly not thrilled.

Opening the double doors to the front reception room, Thaddeus announced, "Captain Matthew Starbuck, Mrs. Hadwen, ladies." He stepped out of the room and closed the doors behind him.

"Matthew, what a surprise!" exclaimed Eunice, extending her hand to her cousin as he crossed the room to greet her. "I had heard that a ship had arrived yesterday. I didn't know that it was yours. Welcome home!"

"Cousin Eunice, thank you for seeing me. Ladies, I hope that I'm not interrupting."

Eunice jumped in before her two guests could answer. "You're not. Misses Macy and Coffin were just leaving."

After a few minutes of polite good-byes, Eunice and Matthew were alone. He declined her offer of tea, saying that his visit had to be brief as he had to pick up the children at school. She studied his face, noting how tired he looked.

"I didn't mean to scare away your guests."

"Nonsense. We see each other several times a week, and I haven't seen my darling cousin for four years. I am so happy to see you, but I expect the reason for your unusual visit is that you want something?" Eunice and Matthew shared a common family trait: directness.

"Yes, Eunice, I do. I've a favor to ask you. I brought home two Christian Pacific islanders, 'Ailani and his wife,

Anuenue, who want to see the world and earn their fortune. I've spent the last thirteen months with them on the *Young Hero*, and I can recommend their characters without reservation. They're staying with us until they find a place of their own. They're both very eager to find work right away even though we've urged them to explore Nantucket for a bit before starting to work. I'm here to ask you if you might have a position for Anuenue? She's young, energetic, and very fit. She was a tremendous help on the *Young Hero* from cooking to sewing. She's an excellent seamstress."

"Matthew, no need to persuade me further! If you would like me to hire Anuenue, I will. I'm happy to do this for you. As it happens, I have several sewing projects for the winter, and she can help with these."

"Thank you so much, Cousin Eunice! I must be off. I'll tell Anuenue to stop by tomorrow afternoon."

As she called Thaddeus for Matthew's coat, she stood up and surprised her cousin with a quick hug. "Take care of yourself, Matthew. You are precious to me."

Startled, he awkwardly hugged her back. He wondered what that was about as he took his coat from Thaddeus. His cousin Eunice was not normally so demonstrably affectionate.

"Leaving so soon, sir?" Thaddeus continued to make his disapproval known to Matthew.

Matthew nodded. "Thank you, Thaddeus, and I bid you good day."

As he walked down the steps of 100 Main Street, he felt oddly reassured by Thaddeus's criticism; not everything had changed during his four years away. He met the children in front of the school, who ran to him with outstretched arms, and the three of them walked home.

THE FOLLOWING DAYS and weeks were spent establishing a new routine in the Starbuck household. Six weeks before, if you had asked any member of the Starbuck family what they wanted most, each person would answer: for Matthew to be home safe and sound. Yet when he was first home, he disrupted their routine tremendously. Abigail was accustomed to making all of the decisions needed to run the house. The children understood that their mother was the final call on all decisions while their father was away. But now, overnight, there was father to consider; and like all children, they knew which parent to ask to get the answer they were hoping for. While Matthew was sensitive to this dynamic, he was also a sea captain and very used to giving orders that were followed without question. When he was at sea, he would consult with his first mate before making a big decision, but normally the day was filled with many little decisions that required no consultation. Unfortunately for Abigail, this practice continued on land. It didn't occur to Matthew to ask her opinion about whether Thomas could go out to play with his friends, not realizing Thomas was ducking his Bible study. Add two strangers, 'Ailani and Anuenue, to the household, and it was not surprising that it all came to a head about a month after Matthew's return.

"I'M SO FRUSTRATED with Matthew." Abigail had stopped by Phebe's house for a visit. Even though she was closer to her father when she was growing up, ever since her marriage only Phebe could comfort her when she was unhappy.

"He's normally not a bossy person, but he's struggling

with the fact that he's not 'captain of the house.' He's giving the children, and especially Thomas, either one of two things: orders or everything they ask for. For the latter, I think he's trying to compensate for missing so much of their lives in the last four years. I understand, and sympathize, but he rarely consults with me. And sometimes, the children can't have what they want. Thomas hasn't studied the Bible once in the last four weeks. I bite my tongue ten times a day as I don't want to seem unhappy that he's home, but I'm telling you, I'm at my wit's end!"

Phebe looked up from her embroidery and gazed at her daughter. This was a very familiar theme on Nantucket. Women, who had so much responsibility while their husbands were at sea, often struggled with the nearly overnight shift back to "first mate." The traditional roles were reversed while the men were away and somehow were expected to magically revert immediately when they stepped ashore. It often caused resentment between husbands and wives with both parties feeling guilty that they were not happier to be reunited.

"And another thing, he's encouraging Sarah to spend so much time with Samuel. He and Michael take them out star-gazing every night. She's not interested in stargazing. She didn't do it once in the last four years. I think she has a crush on Samuel. She's too young to be interested in boys. She's a serious, quiet girl, not a frivolous boy chaser!" Abigail was clearly agitated, and Phebe could see that her eyes were filled with tears.

Phebe put down her embroidery, walked over to Abigail, and put her arms around her. While she longed to make all of her worries disappear, as she hated to see her daughter unhappy, she knew that this was something Abigail would have to solve on her own. She gave her a quick hug, pausing for a moment to think of how to best help her.

"So tell me, my darling daughter, what's really the problem?"

"Oh, Mother, I should be so happy that Matthew's home and that he's safe. But I'm frustrated and miserable, which makes me feel guilty, and then I feel even worse. I know that he appreciates what I do to raise the children and keep the house running while he's away, but I also feel like he takes it all for granted. I may not be a ship's captain, but I have important work too. Running Gardner & Sons with Alexander is not a hobby. And by the way—and I would never say this to him as it would hurt his feelings—but Gardner & Sons has been much more successful than his last voyage was. He barely broke even. It's my work that's keeping the family afloat financially."

Phebe paused for a moment before answering Abigail. "Matthew loves you with all of his heart. He has from the first day he saw you. I know. I was there. Your father always used to say that negotiating the terms of a marriage is a lot like negotiating a business deal. You have to find a way for both sides to win and feel good about the deal. It's scary to tell someone you love what you need and what you want from them, but if you don't, well, it results in what you're feeling at this moment."

"Mother, what should I do?" Abigail's voice cracked, her anguish showing through.

"Oh, Abigail, I can't give you advice. You have to do what you think is right for the both of you. I can only say that I truly believe that you and Matthew were ordained by God and that you both are strong, kind, good people. You'll work it out. Besides, you know the old saying: no one knows what goes on in a marriage except for the two people in it, and half of the time, one of them doesn't even know."

Abigail was indignant. "My life is falling apart, and you think a funny platitude is the answer!" She knew that her mother was right, but she wasn't ready to let go of her hurt feelings just yet.

"Actually, my darling, I do. I think humor is the first casualty when hurt feelings arise between two people. I think it's worth remembering that humor can be a healing balm. You've always had a good sense of humor. Use it to help you over this rough patch with Matthew. Now, go home and talk to your husband. You won't fix this sitting here with me."

ABIGAIL LEFT HER mother's house and stepped outside into the cool fall air; the sun had shone all day, and she could feel a warming breeze blowing up from the harbor, bringing the familiar salty sea air smell. She was hoping for a mild winter this year: sunny, warm days would definitely improve her state of mind. As she walked home from her mother's house, she thought about what Phebe had said and knew that she was right, as much as she hated to admit it.

Abigail hated being wrong. She was always fine if other people were right too, but she really needed to be right. Smiling to herself, she decided that she could blame this character flaw on her mother for raising her to have such strong opinions.

Starting to feel a little better, she thought back to the moment she first saw Matthew. She hardly noticed him though he said later that the moment he first saw her, he knew that he would marry her. They met at church on a lovely September day when she was seventeen and he was twenty. It was not surprising that they had not met when they were younger; he was often at sea, and her family had just converted from attending the Friends Meetings to the First Congregational Church on Center Street. While her family had been Quakers, also known as Friends, for generations, her father and mother did not like the direction the Friends were taking and felt that the congregational community better reflected the relationship that they wanted to have with God. When Abigail was sixteen, the family started attending services at the newly built First Congregational Church.

One Sunday after services, the Gardners were standing outside of the church, chatting with their friends, when William saw Captain Jonathan Starbuck coming out of the church with his wife, Sybil, and son, Matthew. William called to Captain Starbuck, who came over, happy to see his good friend and business rival. The Starbucks, in addition to being sea captains and ship owners, also ran a shipping agency similar to Gardner & Sons.

"Captain Starbuck! I heard that you were back." William smiled as he shook his friend's hand.

"Yes, it's great to be home. So much has changed after three years! Mrs. Gardner, very nice to see you." He nodded hello to Abigail's brothers and asked William, "Is this the Abigail I've heard so much about? I hear she's your new right hand at Gardner & Sons."

Abigail blushed, uncomfortable being the center of attention. Normally not shy, she felt awkward under the scrutiny of this larger-than-life sea captain.

"Yes, this is Abigail." William turned to his daughter, taking her by the elbow to propel her forward. "Abigail, where are your manners? Please say hello to Captain Starbuck, but don't be too nice to him; his family is our fiercest competitor."

Abigail politely shook Captain Starbuck's hand and

nodded to Mrs. Starbuck. She gently shook off her father's hand and stepped to the side, back to the safety of her brothers' proximity. She didn't know why she felt so intimidated—maybe it was because Captain Starbuck was very tall and his voice was booming; he was very different from her own father.

Captain Starbuck laughed. "Come now, William, there are more than enough whaling ships to go around. I think both of our family agencies can share in the bounty. I don't think you've met my son, Matthew. He was my first mate on the last voyage."

Matthew stepped forward to shake William's hand, unable to take his eyes off of Abigail. He thought she was the most beautiful girl that he had ever seen, and he decided that very minute he had to marry her. Abigail was unaware of Matthew's attention; she was chatting with her mother and brothers. While she might not have noticed Matthew, Phebe's sharp eyes caught the look on his face when he saw Abigail. She knew that the Gardner family would be seeing a lot of First Mate Starbuck in the coming months.

AS ABIGAIL REACHED the corner of India and Federal Streets, she saw the Nantucket Atheneum, the town library, directly in front of her and decided to get a book. She entered the imposing Greek Revival–styled building and greeted her friend, Maria Mitchell, who was sitting behind the large desk to the left of the entryway. Maria was the first librarian of the Atheneum, a position that she held since she was eighteen. Abigail and Maria knew each other for years, having joined some of the same study clubs started by women on the island to satisfy their intellectual curiosity. They both enjoyed studying on their own as they had keen intellects: Maria focused on science, mathematics, and especially astronomy; and Abigail's interests covered a wide range of topics from Shakespeare to gardening. Abigail was a little jealous of Maria because she had access to the Atheneum's books at any time. She thought it would be a luxury to be able to read all day and learn new things as part of your work. She was very happy in her family's business, but it was a long time since she had learned something new at work.

"Abigail, so nice to see you! You must be thrilled that Matthew is home." "Yes, we thank the Lord every time he comes back safe and sound." Abigail remembered that a returning ship is big news for weeks after its homecoming.

"I heard that he brought home more than whale oil. Didn't I also hear that he brought back a married couple from the Sandwich Islands? How are they adapting to our climate? It must be a bit of a shock."

Maria, unlike others whom Abigail would accuse of asking just because they were gossipy, was truly interested in 'Ailani and Anuenue. To her, they were a source of first-hand knowledge about the Pacific and the Sandwich Islands and, because of this, were fascinating to her.

"Their names are 'Ailani and Anuenue. They are lovely people. They're so young! I don't remember ever being so young. Everything about Nantucket enchants them. I thought they would be a little more homesick than they are, especially with the weather getting colder, but they're not. They've already made friends in New Guinea, and they've found work. Anuenue is working for Matthew's cousin, Eunice Hadwen, at her lovely house on Main Street. She's an excellent seamstress—you should see what she did with flour sacks on the *Young Hero*—and 'Ailani is working with a local Portuguese basket maker in New Guinea. He makes the most beautiful baskets. They're still staying with us, but I expect they'll move out once they find a suitable accommodation in New Guinea. Would you like to meet them?"

"I would, thank you! I could come to your house Sunday after services. Would this suit you?"

"It's fine for me. I'll check with them tonight when they're home from work. I'll ask Thomas to stop by the library tomorrow after school to confirm. By the way, when you see him, maybe you could also remind him how important mathematics are—that boy and mathematics are not a match made in heaven. His father keeps telling him that without mathematics, he can't be a sea captain, but he's nine and doesn't understand why mathematics are important. Nothing seems impossible when you're nine, except maybe geometry."

Maria laughed. "You must think me a miracle worker, Abigail! I'm sure the sea will be the best motivator for Thomas once sailing with Matthew becomes more of a likelihood." As she said this, Maria noticed the sad look that passed over Abigail's face. "I'm sorry. Did I say the wrong thing?"

"No, Maria, you didn't. I just hate the idea of my baby—who's no longer a baby—going to sea and being away for years at a time. Sea captains go back six generations in both of our families, so the chance that Thomas will be a farmer is nil. While I'm resigned to the idea, I can't be happy about it."

Abigail shook her head and smiled. "I'm not going to worry about it today! Help me find a new book to distract me from my cares. You always know exactly what I want to read."

TWENTY MINUTES LATER, with Shakespeare's *Much Ado about Nothing* in hand, Abigail walked up to her back door and, through its window, saw Matthew sitting by the fire, reading the *Nantucket Inquirer*. For half a second, she forgot her irritation with him and her heart skipped a beat at the sight of her husband, whom she adored. However, the happy interlude didn't last; her annoyance came back in full force because she had hoped to come home and have the house to herself for a little while. While she loved having 'Ailani and Anuenue stay with them, the number of members of her house had doubled with Matthew's return, and it was rare that the house was empty.

Taking a deep, calming breath, Abigail stepped into the house and forced a happy tone into her voice. "Guess who I just saw."

Matthew looked up from the paper. "Your mother?"

"Yes, I did see Mother, but I also saw Maria Mitchell at the Atheneum. I stopped for a book on my way home from Mother's."

"Is she still scouring the heavens from the Pacific Bank roof every night?" Matthew had a small smile on his face.

"Yes, she is. Her passion for the stars is equal to yours for the sea." Abigail answered bluntly, still feeling out of sorts and not willing to be quite so lighthearted as her husband.

The smile faded from Matthew's face. "Abigail, we need to talk."

While talking to Matthew was exactly what Phebe had recommended that she do, now that it was actually happening, she was reluctant to start. To stall for a moment, she took off her cloak and hat and put them away in the cupboard by the back door. Finally, unable to delay any longer, she sat in the chair by the fire opposite his. She waited for him to begin, searching his serious face for a hint of what was to come.

After a very long pause, Matthew began. "All my life, my love was the sea. Some of my earliest memories are of longing to go to sea with my father and feeling so sad when he sailed without me. Finally, at twelve, he took me with him, and it was as wonderful as I thought it would be. The crew told me that I would be afraid when we rounded Cape Horn, but I wasn't scared. It was all too exciting to be scary, and I knew that my father would keep us safe no matter how large or violent the waves."

Abigail sat silently, watching her husband as he paused again, collecting his thoughts.

"This trip was different. I've been hunting for whales for twenty-five years, and a lot has changed during this time. When I started, it was—I'm not sure how to characterize it—more civilized? It's brutal now. Hunting whales has always been a brutal business, but the character of the ships' crews seems to have changed a lot in this generation of whale hunters. Awful things happen in port in the South Pacific that you can't even imagine, and I would never tell you about them; they're too cruel and un-Christian. Often, it's the officers' behavior that is the most appalling. I used to look forward to being in port during the voyage, but now I mostly stay to myself as I can't abide what happens between the crews and the local people."

Matthew paused a second time, clearly struggling to keep his composure.

"Matthew, I've heard what happens in the South Pacific; it's not a secret here on Nantucket. It does you justice that you won't speak of it, but I know there are captains who take native 'wives' during their voyages, using spirits and trinkets as a lure for these innocent women. I know that there are men in our community who behave as fine, upstanding Christian men when they're home, only to behave abominably when they're away—not only with the natives—but also with their crews. I thank the Lord every day that you're the good man that you are."

"It discourages me, and I'm starting to hate being at sea because of it. I never imagined that I could hate being at sea."

Abigail looked at her husband and saw the pain on his face; it broke her heart to see him suffer so. All of the frustration of the last four weeks melted away. In that moment, she knew that their difficulties with his transition from sea to land were insignificant compared to the melancholy he was facing. She wanted to say exactly the right thing to comfort him, but she wasn't sure she had the words. She was inclined to be kind, yet she knew in the pit of her stomach that this wasn't what he needed.

"Matthew, I would love it if you never went to sea again. If I were a truly selfish person, I would use your malaise to convince you to give up the sea and keep you home with us. I would play on your sense of honor and tell you that I can't run Gardner & Sons without you and that it's your duty to me and your family to stay on Nantucket, never to sail again."

Matthew stared at his hands in his lap. He couldn't look at Abigail while she was talking because her comments shocked him. He never knew that she felt so strongly about his chosen life—learning this made him feel even worse.

"Matthew, look at me."

He raised his eyes and found her love looking back at him.

"This is not about what I would love—or need—this

is about what's important to you. And what's important to you is the sea. I knew this about you when we married. You were away at sea from the time we became betrothed until we married. I signed up for this life, willingly and happily. I said what I said to shock you. I said these things to remind you that you need the sea like you need air to breathe. And if you need the sea, then our family needs the sea too. None of us can be happy if you're unhappy. What will it take, my husband, to make you happy again?"

Matthew stood up, reached for a log near the fireplace, and added it to the dying flames. Using an iron poker, he stoked the coals and waited until the fire was blazing again. Then he looked at Abigail, who was waiting silently.

"I don't know. I don't know how to get back my love for the sea when I feel so conflicted about life at sea and about leaving you, Sarah, and Thomas. The sea has become a mistress whose demands are too high."

"Didn't you say the *Young Hero* needed significant repairs?"

"Yes, she does."

"How long will she be out of commission?"

"It depends on the weather, but I'd estimate at least four months."

"Then we don't need to decide anything today, do we? Let's see how you feel in February when she's seaworthy again. Until then, I could use some help at Gardner & Sons. Alexander is very busy with the farm and is leaving more and more of his duties to me."

"As always, Abigail, you have the right answer." Matthew felt better for having gotten his troubles off his chest.

"Now that's what I like to hear! You know how much I love being right."

"Yes, I know. It's the curse of marrying such a clever wife. I only get to be right on the deck of the *Young Hero*."

With the change in Matthew's mood, Abigail debated with herself about bringing up her topic. In comparison to his unhappiness, she felt it was less urgent and maybe now was not the time to add to his troubles. At the same time, she knew that she couldn't be a good partner for him while her unspoken resentment festered.

"Matthew, as we're talking, I, too, have something to talk to you about."

He waited, curious.

"You know that I willingly do all that I do for our family—when you're here and when you're away. When you're away, I'm 'captain of the house,' so to speak. I make all of the decisions and the children live by my rules. I also work at Gardner & Sons, and in addition to running our house, this keeps me very busy."

Matthew waited, wondering where this conversation was going. He wisely realized it was not a good time to interrupt her.

"We're thrilled that you're home. But you've been away for four years—our routine in the house has changed while you were away. You can't help it, but you disrupt our routine. We've been living without you, and how can I say this without sounding ungrateful that you're home, you've walked back into the house as if you are 'lord and master.' Our home is not the *Young Hero*, and we're not your crew."

Matthew couldn't stay silent any longer. "Abigail, you know I don't think that way about you and the children!"

"I'm sorry to be so blunt, but sometimes there's a difference between your actions and your words. I know it's not intentional, and I know you're not old-fashioned in your views of marriage. I also know that you're not trying to be unkind or bossy. That's why I've held my tongue until now. Let me give you an example: Thomas has avoided Bible study for four weeks because, when he's supposed to be studying the Bible, he asks you if he can go out and play and you say yes. He knows that if he had asked me, I'd have said no. While it seems like a small thing—and I know it is—you should tell Thomas that you give him permission as long as I also agree. I know that as a sea captain, you make many bigger decisions all day long without consulting anyone, so I understand why you don't check with me for something as simple as Thomas going out to play, but it's important that you do. Do you see my point?"

"Yes, and I'm so sorry. I like that the children come to me for their questions. I thought I was taking some of the burden off you as you had to be mother and father for so many years. I had hoped that I was helping you. My intention was to be helpful, not to cause discord or to walk around the house as—how did you phrase it—as lord and master. I feel terrible. How long have you felt like this? Why didn't you say something sooner?"

Abigail decided that she had said enough and she knew—putting herself into Matthew's shoes—that she would have behaved exactly the same way without thinking of the consequences.

Rather than answering him directly, she said, "I wanted your homecoming to be happy with no bad feelings. I felt guilty that I was feeling resentful, so I decided not to say anything at first. Mother convinced me today that I was being unfair by not talking to you about how I felt. Let's put it behind us. For me, it's finished and forgotten."

"Thank you for telling me, my darling, and I will try my

best going forward. And can I count on you to remind me?" As he said this, he smiled.

As Abigail laughed, they heard a knock on the back door; it was 'Ailani and Anuenue coming home after work. She opened the door for them, urging them inside to get out of the cold.

"You don't need to knock. This is your home too."

"You're very kind, Mrs. Starbuck, but we can't take advantage of your generous hospitality. We would not feel comfortable just walking into the house without knocking."

"Anuenue, could you help me prepare supper? I expect the children soon, and as we all know, Thomas will be hungry. Thomas is always hungry."

AFTER THE EVENING meal, 'Ailani and Anuenue excused themselves after helping Sarah clear the table and clean the dishes. The children sat quietly in front of the fire, finishing their lessons for school the next day. Matthew sat with the unopened *Nantucket Inquirer* on his lap and watched his wife as she read *Much Ado about Nothing*. After all of the emotions of the day, he felt exhausted but peaceful. As always, Abigail had helped him see what was important, and while he was still a little frightened and nervous, he was more optimistic about the future. As he gazed upon his wife's serene face, he knew that he was blessed. *Besides*, he thought, *how hard can running a shipping agency be?*

"Father, are we stargazing tonight?" Sarah had a hopeful look on her face.

"Do you want to?" Matthew remembered the earlier conversation with Abigail and quickly added, "Are your lessons done?"

"Yes! I'll go get Samuel and Mr. Coffin." Sarah leapt to

her feet and grabbed her cloak and hat from the cupboard by the back door.

After the serious conversations before the evening meal, Abigail tried to keep her tone light. "Sarah seems to be newly inspired by the stars since you've come home."

"She's good at astronomy. She catches on very quickly. I think she would make a very good navigator one day."

"Is Samuel equally as keen?"

"He is. He learned a lot from Michael when they were away." Matthew was oblivious to the implied question in her voice.

"Well, if Sarah's serious about studying astronomy, I can ask Maria for some study tips. She's coming to the house on Sunday after services to meet 'Ailani and Anuenue."

LATER THAT EVENING, as they got into bed, Abigail asked Matthew what she really wanted to ask him earlier but didn't because Thomas was in the room.

"Matthew, are you sure that Sarah is really interested in astronomy?"

He looked at his wife, puzzled. Didn't they just have this conversation two hours before?

"Or is she more interested in spending time with Samuel?"

"What? She's thirteen! She's my little girl! How could she possibly be interested in Samuel? They've been friends since she could walk. I think you're misreading the situation." Matthew, like most men, could not imagine his darling daughter ever leaving him for another man, at least not until she was thirty.

"Sarah had no interest in astronomy for the last four years. This might come as a shock to you—but I think that her motivation to study the stars is to spend time with

Samuel and not you. Just keep an eye on the situation, will you please? I fully agree with you. She's much too young to be betrothed to anyone, even someone we love as dearly as Samuel."

Abigail couldn't resist being a bit mischievous. "Though, having her right next door would be pretty handy. As Samuel's an only child, I expect that he'll inherit his parents' house when the time comes."

Matthew was speechless. Today was a whirlwind of emotions for him, from being called "lord and master" to learning that his baby girl was about to get married. *For all of its hardships, life was definitely more straightforward on the* Young Hero, he thought, as he blew out the candle, kissed his wife good night, and drifted off to sleep.

4

Abby and Matt

July 2008, Boston and Nantucket

bby got off the elevator on the nineteenth floor at 7:30 a.m., Starbucks coffee in hand.

"Good morning, Mother. What a glorious day. I'm sorry. I didn't think you'd be here already, or I'd have brought you a coffee."

"Yes," replied Caroline, "the weather gods are kind to us this week: blue skies, low humidity, and temperatures in the low eighties. We should be at the beach. By the way, you know that Matt is not *that* Starbuck, right?"

"Funny, very funny. Let me know as soon as he arrives. We have a lot to do today before this afternoon's press conference."

Caroline was about to ask Abby how the meeting with the advisory board had gone the night before but got distracted by an incoming call.

After Abby and Matt's first meeting in March, the collaboration between the two companies proceeded very quickly.

Almost immediately, it was clear that Starbuck Enterprises's software would give Gardner & Sons' StarTaker a strategic competitive advantage for at least the next ten years.

I'd have never imagined that four months ago we'd be here today, thought Abby as she walked to her desk and turned on her personal computer before sitting down. Based on their first ten minutes together, she'd have predicted the opposite.

She remembered her conversation with her mother after Matt left their March meeting. Her mother surprised her, saying she thought that Abby and Matt would have a long, profitable relationship spanning many years. How her mother could have known this after spending ten minutes with the man was a mystery to her. *Mother's always right,* she thought. *At least, that's what she tells me every day.*

The elevator doors opened, and Matt burst out of it like a Tasmanian devil, three Starbucks coffees in hand. "It's a glorious day, Caroline, and all the more so because I start it seeing you!"

Caroline laughed, now accustomed to his exaggerations. "Good morning, Matt. You're in fine form this morning."

Matt handed Caroline one of the Starbucks coffees and winked at her. "You know I get a percentage of each one of these coffees, don't you? Don't tell anyone my secret, but I'm one of *those* Starbucks."

"Nice try, but I do my homework. You're as related to Starbucks Coffee as I'm the mayor of Boston. Go right in. Abby's expecting you."

Abby looked up as Matt walked into her office. "I have the press release here. Both of our legal and communication teams have vetted it. I think we're good to go. Take one more look at it. We'll release it today at noon as we agreed."

"And good morning to you too." Matt crossed the floor and handed Abby her coffee. "Thanks for bringing me a coffee, by the way." He eyed the Starbucks cup on her desk.

A look of irritation passed over her face. Although they were getting along much better, he still had a knack for pushing her buttons.

"Thank you, Matt, both for reminding me to breathe and for bringing me a coffee. I'm sorry. I really didn't think you'd be here this early, or I would have brought you one too. If it's any consolation, I didn't bring one for my mother either."

Abby was tired. She was in the office until 9:00 p.m. the evening before in a very cantankerous meeting with her advisory board. She wished that her father and grandfather had never put the contingency clause in the board bylaws that transformed the advisory board from a purely advisory role into one with oversight and veto powers for Gardner & Sons. She realized that they were protecting the company and her, but she was certain that they didn't know it would turn out like this. She was very sure that the board was behaving opposite to what they expected, and especially the chairman, Peter Coffin.

Like most larger-than-life chief executive officers, William Gardner, who went by Bill, had assumed he'd live forever. His father, Thomas, retired as CEO of Gardner & Sons at sixty, handing the baton to forty-year-old Bill. Gardner & Sons was a privately held company with the family owning 43 percent of the equity, making them the single largest shareholder. Because they were privately held, they didn't need a formal board of directors to oversee the company, which had its pluses and minuses. To compensate for one of the minuses—not having a group of seasoned businesspeople as advisors for the company—Thomas created an advisory board of his peers in the business community, who, in return for a small equity stake in Gardner & Sons, would convene quarterly to review the business, focusing on new strategies. Thomas had handpicked the seven board members and had appointed Tristam Coffin as the chairman of the group. He found their advice invaluable, as it was rare that the people in his company would challenge the CEO. First, most employees were too afraid to tell the boss that he was wrong, and second, people genuinely liked Thomas; they wanted to support him and his ideas even if they might be bad ones. Once the advisory board was in place, Thomas had an intelligent, commercially savvy group of people who he could turn to for honest feedback. He never intended for the advisory board to operate beyond his term as CEO, but as he got closer to retirement, both he and Bill saw the value of keeping it in place.

Just before Thomas retired, he and Bill made three changes to the board bylaws. The first one was that advisory board positions were hereditary: if any board member wanted to retire, and he had an adult son or daughter who could step into his shoes and be effective, then the heir of the existing board member could take his place. As Gardner & Sons had been in business for over one hundred years, both Bill and Thomas valued the continuity and sense of tradition. This also had an unintended outcome: the original advisory board was all men, but Bill's board had three women on it. Bill welcomed the gender balance on his advisory board; after all, wasn't his daughter, Abby, the CEO-in-training? He was happy for her to have strong, powerful businesswomen as role models. The second was a contingency measure to protect the business in the event of the CEO's untimely death before the planned succession date; before any significant new business strategy could be implemented, the advisory board had to approve it by a four-to-three majority.

Neither Bill nor Abby ever expected that this contingency clause would be triggered. Bill expected to retire at sixty like his father, which meant that Abby would take over as CEO when she was forty-one, thereby nullifying the amendment to the bylaw.

However, Thomas and Bill unknowingly made one mistake in their third change to the bylaws by also making the chairman's role hereditary. Because of this, Peter Coffin became the chairman when his father, Tristam, retired. At the time, it seemed like a good idea, and there was no foreshadowing of the problems to come. Bill and Tristam's families were very close, and Bill treated Peter as a protégé and like the son he never had. Peter was seven years older than Abby, and he often took on the role of surrogate big brother while they were growing up. While Bill was alive, Peter thrived under his tutelage and guidance, especially after his own father died. After Tristam's death, Peter took over managing the Coffin family's extensive business interests, in addition to chairing the Gardner & Sons advisory board. Abby knew that her father enjoyed coaching Peter and was never jealous of the time that he spent with him. Neither Bill nor Abby had any reason to distrust Peter because, on the surface, everything was fine, but underneath his easygoing manner there was a dark side to Peter that he kept carefully hidden—until Bill died. He was not the man his father was; he was much more insecure and always acted as if he had something to prove. During Bill's lifetime, Peter played his cards close to his vest, never giving a hint of the power-hungry chairman that he was to become. Once Bill died, the mask came off. It was quickly apparent that Peter had been biding his time to make his move. While he had no legal recourse for ousting Abby and appointing himself CEO of Gardner & Sons, he could make her life very difficult, which he did at their very first advisory board meeting after her father's death.

In her first three years as CEO, Peter challenged every strategy she brought to the advisory board, forcing her and her team to do more research and analysis in order to get the votes that she needed to proceed. This delayed implementing the new strategies by three to six months and was having a negative effect on the business; they were getting outpaced by their competitors! It was time-consuming and frustrating for Abby. He always claimed that he was just doing his best to protect the company, but his frequent challenges were very disruptive to Gardner & Sons' business as well as to her authority. Compounding the problem, she had her own doubts about the decisions she was making in her first months as CEO. She didn't feel confident enough to directly confront him, especially as he always had a plausible reason for his challenges, and he had been her father's protégé. At the beginning, Peter had the board on his side because they knew him longer and they were concerned about Abby's inexperience as a leader. He manipulated this situation to his benefit by assuring her the additional analysis and delays would lead to a better outcome for the company. She believed that her father would have removed Peter as chairman if he could have known how he was going to act, but unfortunately the wolf was wearing sheep's clothing at the time of Bill's death.

ALL OF THIS history came to a head in the meeting the previous evening and tap-danced on the boardroom table like a bad vaudeville act. By now, Abby had invested time to get to know the advisory board members individually and for them to get to know her. She had developed strong relationships with most of them. Because the new venture with Starbuck Enterprises was so important to Gardner & Sons, she reviewed the strategy with each board member as soon as the technical teams confirmed its viability. Three of the board members were very supportive, two were opposed, and two, including Peter, were leaning toward more study and analysis before giving their opinions. The prior night's meeting was to take the final vote needed before Abby and Matt would sign the letter of intent the following morning followed by the afternoon's press conference. She had hoped that one of the two board members on the fence would swing to her side, making the meeting quick, but that was not the case. Peter called the meeting to order, and after thirty minutes Abby wished that the windows on the nineteenth floor opened as she was ready to push him out even with witnesses in the room.

"Abby," said Peter, "I believe you're rushing to an answer and not doing the proper due diligence about this collaboration with Starbuck Enterprises. I don't see how we, as the trusted advisors appointed by your father, can take such a risk with the company your father left in our trust."

Abby sat there, not trusting herself to speak. *If he brings up "trust" and "my father" one more time . . .* she thought, scouring her mind for the appropriate torture that would satisfy her rage.

She took a deep breath, pausing for a moment before replying. "I know my father would be very happy to know that his daughter's advisory board chairman was so diligent in his duties. I also know that he would want you to act in a timely fashion. We all know that the situation with Star-Taker is urgent and, factoring in development time, even if we start tomorrow we're at least a year from a market-ready product. I suggest, Mr. Chairman, that we end the debate and call for a vote."

Peter acquiesced and called for the vote. As she expected, the vote was split three in favor, two opposed, and two abstaining, one of whom was Peter. All the board members spoke at length about why they voted the way that they did and, after an hour, the discussion was over.

"Abby, you don't have your four-vote majority needed to proceed. I'm afraid this will have to wait until our next meeting in October. That will give you plenty of time to do more analysis and to present a more detailed proposal for our review." Peter stood up and started gathering his papers.

"Sit down," Abby said it quietly, but there was no disguising the steel in her voice.

"Excuse me?" Peter was incredulous that Abby would speak to him in this manner in front of the other board members. Who did she think she was?

"You heard me. Sit down." Abby took another deep breath and paused before continuing. "I checked with our lawyers today, and you're right, I need a four-vote majority to proceed. But as CEO, I have the power to override the advisory board's vote once in a fiscal year. My father had added this clause to the bylaws a year after he took over from my grandfather. Unlike in Grandfather's time, my father saw that this board could potentially undermine the CEO's ability to steer the business, so he built in this protection. Up until now, I haven't played this card. But this deal is too important. I'm not willing to do more analysis, so I invoke my right of override. Ladies and gentlemen, I will sign the letter of intent in the morning, and we will announce it tomorrow afternoon."

"I know nothing about this!" spluttered Peter. "Did the rest of you know about this?" The remaining board members reluctantly nodded their affirmation. "I want our lawyer here now!" Peter shouted, clearly furious with the turn of events.

On cue, the firm's general counsel, Michael O'Malley, came through the boardroom door, papers in hand, having anticipated Peter's challenge. He gave one page to each board member and pointed to the highlighted clause in the board bylaws. Michael was careful not to meet Abby's eye while he walked around the board table as he was gloating at Peter's comeuppance. He was afraid he'd start grinning ear to ear.

"Listen here, young lady. You might have won this round and think you're so very clever, but you're not. You will not treat this board in this manner going forward. You have not heard the end of this, not by a long shot." After reading the document, all of Peter's pretenses of acting professionally were gone.

The other board members were shocked; while each one of them held a private opinion that Peter was full of himself, his behavior was still startling. Peter stuffed the papers in his briefcase and stormed out of the room, slamming the boardroom door as he left.

The room seemed be holding its collective breath until Michael broke the silence. "Well, other than that, how did you like the play, Mrs. Lincoln?"

"ABBY, ABBY!"

Startled, Abby came back to the present moment and looked at Matt, who was staring at her with concern on his face. "Where were you? You were a million miles away."

"No, I was just reliving last night's meeting. Sorry, Matt, last night was the worst advisory board meeting of my life, and I'm sure I've created a powerful enemy in Peter. I did the right thing and saved our collaboration, but I'm not sure at what cost."

"Can I do anything?" Matt was concerned by how distant Abby looked. They both had a lot riding on today, and he needed her to be at the top of her game.

"Could you have him killed?" Abby remembered how Michael's dark humor the night before had diffused the tense moment. She wasn't normally so blunt, but she was physically and emotionally exhausted after yesterday's debacle of an advisory board meeting.

Matt looked startled—of the two of them, he was always the one crossing the line between the appropriate thing to say and the totally inappropriate thing to say. He thought that must have been one epic battle last night. He would have loved to have seen Abby the Warrior in her finest hour.

"Well, I'm sorry, Abby. Today's fully booked. Get back to me early next week, and I'll see if I have an open appointment."

She laughed and the tension from the prior evening disappeared. She picked up the phone and called Michael O'Malley and her press officer; it was time to get started.

BY THE END of the day, Abby and Matt were exhausted. Once the official press release went out, both companies were deluged with requests for interviews from reporters from the financial press and local Boston television stations. Gardner & Sons had the lead on the communication strategy, which was well prepared in advance of the announcement. They followed the strategy, sticking to the key speaking points: first, that the two firms each had a long, successful history as industry leaders in their respective fields and this new version of StarTaker, StarTaker 2.0, married the long-standing success of both firms. Second,

StarTaker 2.0 would revolutionize the industry and be well ahead of Gardner & Sons' closest competitors. And last, they were especially happy to build on their respective families' history, which had started in Nantucket in the 1650s. Because of their Nantucket roots, they took the unique step of giving the Nantucket *Inquirer and Mirror* the exclusive right to their announcement before launching it to the general media. This was very unusual as the *Inquirer and Mirror* was published only weekly—on Thursdays—and while the paper covered business topics, it was definitely not the *Wall Street Journal.*

"I don't think the *Inky Mirror* editor, Debora Johnson, will forgive us for giving her the exclusive." Matt was sitting on one of Abby's couches in her office. The *Inquirer and Mirror,* which had started out on Nantucket in 1821 as the *Nantucket Inquirer,* was affectionately called the *Inky Mirror* by local Nantucketers.

"Why is that?" Abby was shutting off her computer and tidying her desk. Even after such a long day, she hated to leave the office before she had cleaned her desk.

"She rarely gets breaking news, and even if she does, it usually isn't timed with her publishing date, so the story is old news by the time she publishes it. She and her team were inundated with calls from financial and sailing reporters worldwide. I'm guessing I'm going to get an earful when I get back to Nantucket tomorrow. I think I'll lay low for a couple of days."

"Chicken. Wait. You're going back tomorrow? I thought you were staying in Boston."

"No, there's no need to stay, and I get antsy when I'm off island for more than three or four days. Over the last few months, I've been here more than I've been home. I need to get home. Don't you feel the same way about Boston?"

"No, not really. But to be fair, I don't travel that much,

maybe one week a month at most, and it's always to see customers. When I'm on the road, I'm so busy that I don't get time to miss being home."

"I'll tell you a secret, Abby: when I'm too many days away from Nantucket, I feel physical pain. My heart hurts. This has been true since I was a little boy. I don't know where it comes from, but I have this strong sense that leaving Nantucket means leaving more than just the island behind. Before you say anything, I know it's weird, but as we're now officially business partners, I thought I'd let you in on one of my deep dark secrets. TLN."

Abby laughed. "TLN?"

"Too late now. You're stuck with me."

They cleared a few last-minute items and agreed who would do what over the next few days. Now that StarTaker 2.0 was public, it would be much easier to get the development team up and running. Because it was an easy commute between Nantucket and Boston, they agreed that the team could decide among themselves as to how they wanted to work and where. Eva Mueller, Abby's head of research and development, would be the project lead. Eva had been with the firm ever since Abby was a little girl. Now in her early sixties, Eva was a physicist and mathematician by training. She had her PhD and both teams called her "Dr. Eva" though Eva herself rarely used the title. Abby had complete confidence in Eva. She had done a great job in leading the technical evaluation of Starbuck Enterprises's software. Plus, both teams loved her; she was everyone's favorite grandmother who wielded authority with a velvet glove. No project of Eva's would run behind schedule, come in over budget, or fail to meet specifications.

"Are you and I still on for dinner tonight?" asked Matt.

"Would you mind terribly if I took a rain check? To be

honest, I'm running on fumes since last night's advisory board meeting."

Abby saw the disappointment on Matt's face and felt a twinge of guilt. "How about we do this? You're staying at the Four Seasons, right? Why don't we have a quick drink at the Bristol Lounge Bar? My house is on Joy Street, just off Beacon, and I can walk home after our drink. It's a lovely night, and the walk home across Boston Common will do me good."

"IT'S A NICE bar." Matt looked around as the waiter served his Sam Adams Pale Ale and Abby's glass of Sonoma-Cutrer Chardonnay 2012. They were seated at a table by the window, which looked out onto Boston Common.

"Yes, I like it. I don't get out too much, but this is always a favorite when I do. Sometimes Edward and I stop here after going to the theater."

"Edward?"

"My boyfriend, Edward Fanning." Abby was very aware that she and Matt had not shared too much personal information up until now. So far, every conversation had been about the weather and their business collaboration—the few times that they had departed from these two topics, they talked about the Red Sox.

"What does he do?" Matt was amused by the uncomfortable look on her face. She clearly regretted bringing up Edward.

"He's a lawyer with a local firm. He specializes in maritime law."

Matt had one hundred more questions that he wanted to ask Abby now that she had cracked open the door to her personal life, but he decided to put her out of her misery and moved on to more neutral topics. They chitchatted about their favorite restaurants in Boston for about fifteen minutes and then Matt asked, "Have you lived on Beacon Hill long?"

"My whole life. I live in the carriage house behind the house I grew up in. My mother lives in the front house though she keeps threatening to sell it and move into a condominium in Tudor on the Park. I know that she'd never be happy with one-third of the space she has now. She complains the house is too big for one person, but I also know that she'd never get rid of all the treasures she collected traveling the world with my father.

"What about you? I know you live on Nantucket, but that's all I know. Where do you live on Nantucket?" As Abby asked Matt this, a strange look came across his face, as if he were far, far away. He didn't answer her immediately.

"Like you, I live in what was my family home. It's been in my family for nine generations. I live at 15 Union Street, which is right in the center of town. It has a long and storied history that I would be happy to share with you when we have more time. Unless you want another drink, I think we should call it a night."

Abby was a bit surprised by his abrupt ending to their evening, seeing as they had originally planned to go to dinner, and it wasn't late; in fact, it was still light out. She hid her surprise, and they chatted about nothing important for a few more minutes as they finished their drinks and paid the bill. She wondered what she had said to elicit such an abrupt response.

Matt walked Abby to the main entrance of the hotel,

offering to walk her home, which she declined. He watched her cross Boylston Street and enter Boston Common, disappearing from sight.

"I need to get to the water," said Matt out loud to no one in particular. "I need sea air."

The doorman hailed a cab, and Matt directed the driver to the New England Aquarium on One Central Wharf. He had visited it as a teenager with his school class.

"Abby must think I am barking mad," Matt spoke to the seagulls swooping around him as he leaned against the railing behind the Aquarium, looking out to the harbor. "And right now, I would agree with her. I can't believe I got so spooked when she asked me where I lived."

He walked north to Harborwalk, standing on Long Wharf for several minutes, remembering what had just happened at the bar. When she asked him where he lived, she appeared vividly in his mind. He saw her sitting by the fire, in a chair in his kitchen, across from a man who looked a lot like him. They were talking to each other and smiling; they looked so happy together. The man had the *Nantucket Inquirer* on his lap, and he could see the date; it was Thursday, October 3, 1839.

After commenting to her in their first meeting that they must have known each other in a previous life, Matt knew that telling her that he just saw her sitting in his house in 1839 would have confirmed her opinion that he was crazy. As they would be working closely together for many years to come, he didn't want her to think that she'd just signed on with some "nut job."

He continued to walk around the waterfront, watching the sky change colors as the sun set. The breeze from the harbor was soothing; the salt air restored his sense of equilibrium, and the unsettled feeling that had come over him in the Bristol Bar faded away.

The sense that he knew Abby before got stronger each time he saw her. She clearly did not have the same thoughts about him. He didn't know if he should say anything to her or just let it go. He almost brought it up again while they were having drinks—his vision was so real, it felt as if he were looking at a photograph—but it just didn't feel like the right moment to say anything. He was kind of surprised that it disturbed him so much.

He decided to walk back to the hotel. He liked this part of Boston with its proximity to the ocean and how it was surrounded by history. He walked past Faneuil Hall, which was full of people enjoying the restaurants and shops on a warm summer's night, and he was happy to be out among people and not completely alone with his thoughts. But he also knew that it was time to get home; he needed to be back on the island.

WHILE MATT WAS at the Aquarium, Abby was walking across Boston Common. She reached into her purse for her cell phone and dialed Edward.

"Hey there! How did it go today? How's my favorite business mogul? I had Bloomberg on in the background all day but didn't catch any news."

"It went fine, surprisingly well, considering the advisory board meeting last night." She had a grimace on her face as she spoke to Edward. "We had a busy day with the financial and sailing press, and I guess you might see more news tomorrow. While our deal is important to us, it's hardly breaking news for the financial markets."

"Where are you now? I thought you were having dinner with Matt?"

"No, we changed our plans. We just had drinks at the Bristol Bar, and now I'm walking home."

"Should I come over? Would you like some company?"

"I'm so tired. If you don't mind, can we skip it? We're on for dinner tomorrow night, right?"

"Sure, no problem. Look, I'll let you go, and I'll see you tomorrow. Sleep well and I love you."

"You too. Good night."

As she reached Beacon Street, she turned right up the hill to Joy Street. She thought, *Why didn't I say "I love you" to Edward? Would it have killed me?*

Ever since the abrupt ending to her drinks with Matt, Abby was feeling out of sorts, and this feeling extended to Edward as well. To be honest, she was feeling out of sorts with Edward more and more lately. She attributed it to the stress of the business deal with Starbuck Enterprises, but now that the deal was signed and announced, this should not have been the case tonight. She was sure she would feel better after a good night of sleep and she walked the last few blocks toward home.

ABBY AND EDWARD had known each other for five years; they met at a conference for firms in the shipping business and, at first, got together occasionally on a professional basis. Over time, it evolved into something more. She loved him, no question, but she was still holding something back. A year before, she asked her mother what she thought about Edward.

"He's a smart, kind person with a very big heart."

"Mother, you could be describing a golden retriever. What do you think about Edward and me?"

Caroline danced around the elephant in the room. "In what way?"

"Are Edward and I a good match?"

"I think you enjoy his company, and he's very kind to

you. He's thoughtful and he's supportive of your career as you are to him."

"That's not what I'm asking." Abby was still reluctant to clearly state what she had on her mind.

Finally, Caroline couldn't take it anymore. "Are you asking me if you should marry Edward?"

While that was exactly the question Abby was asking, she was shocked to hear it said so bluntly.

"We've been dating for four years, and we've known each other for five. Wouldn't it be logical that we should be thinking about marriage?"

Caroline looked at her adored daughter's face and wished that Bill were still alive; he was the romantic in the family and would have known exactly how to counsel Abby.

"From the day I met your father until the day he died, he made my heart skip a beat. I know it sounds trite and cliché, but I was always happiest when I was wherever your father was. I'd walk into a room and feel a flutter of excitement because he was there. He was the love of my life, and I couldn't imagine what my life would have been like without him. Is this how you feel about Edward?"

"Not all of us have relationships with fireworks exploding in the sky!" Abby felt defensive; why couldn't her relationship with Edward be just as happy even if it didn't have the passion her parents shared?

"That's not what I'm saying, and frankly, if you don't want my opinion, you really shouldn't ask me." Caroline was equally defensive and a little bit irritated.

"Mother, I'm sorry! I just feel like Edward and I should be moving toward something, and I'm not sure that's what we're doing. It feels more like we're treading water."

"Do you want to marry him?"

"I really don't know. He is all those things that you described—he's kind, thoughtful, and funny—and we get along really well. We like the same things. When we spend time together, it's easy. I'm not sure I'd ever meet a better fit for me than Edward."

"You had a year with Edward before you lost your father and took over as CEO. Your relationship with him wasn't very far along before your world was turned upside down. You've had a lot on your plate the last three years, and Edward's been a tremendous help to you. He was patient when you worked eighteen hours a day in the beginning and never pressured you. As we said, he's a very kind person. In my opinion, while four years seems like a long time to be treading water, as you called it, I think the reality is that you haven't been able to deepen your relationship with him because of everything that's been going on. Getting married doesn't have a fixed timeline. It's up to the two of you to decide if and when you want to get married. It doesn't matter what anyone else thinks."

Abby remembered this conversation with her mother as she climbed into bed and turned off the light, falling into a dreamless sleep.

EARLY THE NEXT morning, Matt stepped off the Gardner & Sons corporate jet onto the tarmac of the Nantucket airport. This was definitely a perk of doing business with Abby's firm. He didn't mind taking the nine-seater propeller plane from Logan, but coming by private jet was definitely easier. The rest of the day was filled with meetings and organizing the work needed in the coming weeks. Now that the deal was public, it was much easier to get things done. By 6:00 p.m., Matt was shutting off his computer and getting ready to leave for the day. He was having dinner at the Galley with Debora Johnson.

As always in July, the Galley was heaving at 7:00 p.m. when Matt walked in. People were three deep at the lovely wooden bar and the outside patio was full, except for one table closest to the beach with a Reserved sign on it. The hostess, Sally, greeted Matt as he walked in.

"Hi, Matt! Have you been off island? I haven't seen you for a week or so."

"Hi, Sal." He leaned in to give her a kiss on the cheek. "Yes, I was in Boston. We announced our deal with Gardner & Sons this week."

"I heard about that. Great news for Starbuck Enterprises." Sally's brother Todd was a programmer at the firm.

"Yes, it's exciting—a lot to do—but exciting. Is Debora here?"

"No, you're the first to arrive. I reserved your favorite table, but I've had to fight people off with a club to keep it free for you. Tonight's 'inducement' to give up your table was $500 from the guy in the neon green pants. See how much I love you?"

Matt laughed. "Sal, you're the best. I'll let you get back to work. See you later."

"I'll send Debora over when she arrives."

He navigated through the crowd, glancing at Mr. Neon Green Pants as he made his way to his table. He knew that Nantucket thrived because of all the money the summer people spent on island, but some of them had as much class as a drunken sailor on shore leave. *Patience*, he thought, *most of them will be gone by Labor Day.*

He sat at his table—the sun wouldn't set for at least another two hours—but he was pretty sure the folks around him wouldn't make it to sunset at the rate they were downing Dark & Stormies and pomegranate martinis. He smiled to himself, remembering the not-too-recent past when he would have kept up with them, and wondered when he got to be such a responsible citizen.

"Hi, Matt. Have you been waiting long?" Debora pulled out the chair opposite his.

"No, just got here. Sally saved our table, but if you want to make a quick 500 bucks later, Mr. Neon Green Pants has been lusting after our prime spot. You could sell it to him and make a nice little profit."

Debora snorted. "Summer people. Can't live with them, can't shoot 'em. Hey, how does it feel to be a big tycoon?"

Matt laughed. "Yup, that's me, tearing up the software world. Look out, Steve Jobs. I'm moving Silicon Valley to Madequacham." The irony wasn't lost on Debora as Madequacham was the part of Nantucket covered in scrub pine and small ponds, hardly a spot for the next Silicon Valley.

"All joking aside—congratulations! This is a very big deal for Starbuck Enterprises and for Nantucket. It's great to have a business on the island that's not dependent solely on tourism."

"Thanks, Debora. But Abby Gardner is really the star of this deal. Did you know that she took over Gardner & Sons at twenty-nine when her father died unexpectedly? She's been single-handedly running the business ever since and, in my opinion, doing all of the right things—including signing with Starbuck Enterprises, of course."

"I don't know much about her or Gardner & Sons. There's very little public information available."

"You really should get to know her. She's just like you: funny, smart, and of course, very business savvy. She had to battle her advisory board to get this deal done, and she took them on without backing down one inch. I wasn't there, but from what I heard from her mother, Caroline Gardner—who's her right hand by the way—is that Abby was a warrior!"

Debora skipped over his blatant compliment and watched his face light up as he was talking about Abby. *Oh boy*, she thought, *he has it bad*. She'd bet that he didn't even realize that he was falling for her. She hadn't seen him like this since he lost Lizzie six years ago.

MATT AND LIZZIE Mitchell went to kindergarten together, and since they were eleven, they were best friends and inseparable. They ate lunch together, studied together, sat together on school trips, and, when they were freshmen in high school, started "officially" dating. They were both very active in school sports. Matt played football and was the quarterback of both the junior varsity and varsity squads. Lizzie was a national-level champion swimmer who, when she was a junior in high school, missed making the 1988 US Olympic team by one one-hundredth of a second. Oddly enough, Lizzie was not bitter about not making the Olympic team. She and Matt attended Bowdoin College in Maine; it never occurred to anyone that they would go to separate colleges. Lizzie came back to Nantucket after college to teach science at Nantucket Middle School and to coach the junior and senior swim teams. Matt joined his family business. Many parents wanted Lizzie to give their children private swimming lessons, hoping for their own national-level athletes, but Lizzie was happiest working with all kids, not just the elite. She had been a lifeguard at Surfside beach since she was sixteen and returned every summer throughout college. Right after college, she was promoted to director of the lifeguards, a position she took very seriously. Because she was a teacher, she was able to do both because the two roles overlapped by only about a month.

That's what made Lizzie's accident so tragic, thought Debora as she half-listened to Matt's blow-by-blow description of the day before. No one could understand how she could drown, especially in waters she'd been swimming in for over twenty-five years.

SIX YEARS BEFORE, it was a beautiful July day, just like the weather they were having now. The Nantucket Police report still didn't make sense to anyone who knew Lizzie; it seems that she had gotten up just before sunrise and decided to have a quick swim before the beach officially opened at 8:00 a.m. Her normal routine was to check all the lifeguard stations on the island before they opened, and occasionally, she would sneak in a swim, time permitting. The police speculated that she arrived at Surfside a little before sunrise and the beach was deserted; no one saw her go in the water. As well as they could determine, she must have gotten caught in a rip current, causing her to plummet to the bottom of the ocean where they believed she hit her head on a large rock, knocking herself unconscious. Tourists walking the beach found her body later that morning. In his autopsy, the coroner in Hyannis noted a large lump on her forehead and water in her lungs and ruled accidental death by drowning. The entire island was in mourning for months, as Lizzie was beloved by all. Matt was beyond consolation. After her funeral, he didn't leave the house for a month, and as far as Debora knew, he has never been back to Surfside beach.

"DEBORA? HAVE YOU heard anything I said in the last fifteen minutes?"

"Yes, Matt, I heard it all." She prayed he wouldn't ask her what he had said. She didn't want to admit she was thinking about Lizzie. She quickly changed the subject. "So when will I get to meet Abby the Magnificent?"

Matt laughed. "Hey, as an editor, aren't you supposed to avoid all hyperbole? I don't know. She hasn't been to Nantucket in years. She spent two weeks every summer at their family cottage in Codfish Park until it got washed out to sea during the No Name Storm. I get the impression that she's been nearly 100 percent focused on work since she was seventeen, except for the occasional family vacation. She's not very forthcoming on private topics."

"A workaholic at seventeen? That seems odd."

"Each time I suggest that she come over, she always has a good excuse to stay in Boston, and as she sends the company jet for me, I don't push it."

"Well, if she does come over, let me know, and we can grab dinner."

Debora and Matt changed the subject to local gossip, catching up on their mutual friends and how the summer was going for local businesses. The island was booming: houses were selling at unprecedented prices, inventory was low, and the competition for the good ones was fierce. The construction industry was also having a great summer. The Historic District Commission and Zoning Board couldn't keep up with all of the applications for new houses and renovations. As the saying goes, a rising tide raises all boats, and business owners on Nantucket were enjoying a prosperous, albeit work-intense, summer.

ABBY AND EDWARD sat at a window table in the front dining room of No. 9 Park, one of their favorite restaurants. She felt good; she finally had a chance to do some personal pampering and had spent the afternoon at Bliss, her favorite spa in Boston, getting a full "tune-up" as she called it: facial, manicure, pedicure, haircut, wash and blow-dry, and last, a professional makeup application.

"You look lovely tonight."

Abby blushed. She never was completely comfortable with compliments about her appearance, and while she knew she was attractive, she thought lovely was a stretch.

"I love this weather. I feel like I've missed most of the summer getting ready for the deal with Starbuck Enterprises."

At that moment, the waiter appeared with an ice bucket, two glasses, and a bottle of Cuvée Rosé Laurent-Perrier champagne, her favorite.

"What are we celebrating? The deal closing? I'm not sure it warrants Laurent-Perrier."

Edward just smiled and stayed silent while the waiter popped the cork and poured the champagne into the glasses. After he left, Edward lifted his glass in a toast to Abby. "To you, my darling, and to us."

She clinked her glass against his. "To us? I don't understand."

Edward took a deep breath. "Abby, I love you. I've loved you since I first met you. You are perfect for me, and I hope that I am perfect for you. I know you appreciate directness, so here goes . . . Will you marry me?"

As he said this, he slipped out of his chair, dropped to one knee, took a small black Tiffany box out of his pocket, and opened it, revealing a lovely two-carat diamond solitaire in the classic Tiffany setting.

Abby felt her breath catch in her chest; she had had no idea that Edward was planning to propose. Had she been so wrapped up in her business that she missed the signs? She tried to compose herself, unable to say anything.

Edward started to laugh as he squirmed, waiting for her answer. "Abby, darling, can you give a guy a break here? I'm on one knee on a hardwood floor." Clearly, Edward was sure that Abby was going to say yes, so it didn't occur to him that making a joke might not be in the best of taste.

She reached her hand out to coax him back into his chair. "Edward, you've caught me completely by surprise! I don't know what to say."

"Try 'yes.'" Edward attempted to smile and was starting to feel awkward. The Tiffany box in his hand was turning radioactive with each passing second.

She looked at the longing in his eyes, and it broke her heart. She knew, in that moment, that she couldn't say yes, and she also knew she didn't want to let him go—she loved him. Maybe, with time, she would change her mind.

"Edward, I love you. I love sharing my life with you. We get along so well. It's easy with you," she spoke softly, aware that all of the tables around them were watching them surreptitiously.

"I think you're describing a golden retriever." He tried to salvage the moment with humor. It had never occurred to him that Abby would not immediately say yes.

She smiled, matching his attempt to lighten the awkward moment, before turning serious. "Well, you know that's my favorite dog, so that's not necessarily a bad thing. I need more time. I love you—I don't want to be with anyone else—but I don't know if I'm ready to be engaged."

Edward slipped the Tiffany box back into his pocket. He was upset and hurt, but he also was a very kind person, so he didn't fault Abby for being honest with him.

"Let's save it, shall we? Or did I get the ring wrong too?"

"You got the ring exactly right, and knowing you, I'm sure it would fit perfectly. When the time comes, I'll be thrilled to wear it."

"Do you want to leave?"

"No, do you? We have this lovely bottle of champagne. And, Edward, I meant it—I do love you, and I love being with you. If you're OK, I'd like to stay and have dinner."

AFTER DINNER, EDWARD walked Abby back to her house, leaving her at her front door. While they managed to salvage dinner, they both instinctively knew it was better to spend the night apart. She opened her front door, went straight to her bedroom, and put on her most comfortable pajamas. As she looked out her bedroom window, she saw her mother's bedroom light on and, acting on impulse, threw on her robe and slippers. She crossed the courtyard and let herself in the back door of her mother's house. Not wanting to scare her, she called upstairs, "Mother, it's me. Are you still awake? Can I come up?"

"Yes, Abby, I'm just reading. Why don't you bring us two glasses of port when you come?"

Abby went to the sideboard in the dining room and poured two glasses of Taylor Fladgate's Chip Dry White Port, a favorite of both of theirs since their last family vacation together in Porto, Portugal, when she was eighteen. She climbed the stairs and walked into her mother's bedroom.

When Bill died, Caroline left the bedroom as it was for nearly two years. In her grief, she couldn't bear to change anything in the house. Then, slowly, she started making small changes as her grief lessened. The first room she changed was their bedroom. Bill normally left the decorating decisions to Caroline with two exceptions: his study and their bedroom. As a result, the bedroom was decorated with strong, vibrant sea colors, reflecting Bill's love of the sea. It was both dramatic and beautiful, but it was not restful or soothing. Caroline redecorated the bedroom, still using sea colors, but instead of the dramatic blues and greens, she picked softer shades of turquoise, sand, and off-white. Abby loved the transformation, and it was her favorite room in the house.

Caroline was sitting up in bed as Abby entered, and she scooted over to make room for her. She handed her mother both glasses of port as she kicked off her slippers and climbed into bed.

"Can't you sleep?" Caroline handed Abby her glass of port, knowing that she would tell her what's wrong in her own time. "I can't either, and I have this fabulous book by Eric Jay Dolin, *Leviathan*, that I just can't put down."

"What's it about?" Abby was relieved that her mother was giving her a chance to make small talk.

"It's about the history of whaling in America, and it's so well written. It reads like someone is telling you the most fascinating story instead of writing about history. You can borrow it after I'm finished. I know you'll like it."

"Edward asked me to marry him tonight."

Caroline's eyes immediately went to Abby's left ring finger and saw that it was bare.

"As you can see, I said no. Well, I actually said, 'I'm not ready to be engaged.' Mother, I was so shocked that he asked me! I had no idea it was coming."

"How did you leave it with Edward? Will you still see him?"

"Yes! I love him. I do. But when he asked me, to be honest,

I just couldn't see myself marrying him right now. I hedged and said that I needed more time." Abby's voice rose as she said this to her mother.

"Do you really need more time, my darling? Or did you say that to be kind to Edward? I think you know in your heart that you will never marry him."

"Do I? Do I know that? I'm not sure. I just know I can't say yes right now, but I also can't definitively say no either. I don't want to hurt him. And what if, with time, I could see us getting married? Isn't it better to be cautious now?" Abby's eyes filled with tears.

Again, Caroline wished that Bill were still alive. She knew that Abby would never marry Edward, but it wasn't up to her to give her daughter the answer. She had to find the answer on her own.

"You are my lovely, strong, and kind daughter. I'm sure that you did exactly the right thing tonight. You don't need to second-guess your decision though I can imagine when you didn't say yes it must have been very awkward. Did he have a ring?"

"Yes, a lovely ring from Tiffany's. I was tempted to put it on. It was so beautiful! Awkward is an understatement. At one point, he said that I was comparing him to a golden retriever."

"Ha!" Caroline was triumphant. "I knew it! If I remember correctly, you yelled at me when I made the same comparison a year ago."

"Yes, Mother, as always, you are right." Abby felt comforted by the conversation with her mother. "I think I'll sleep here with you tonight. I'm too lazy to go back across the courtyard."

She snuggled under the covers and was soon fast asleep. Caroline sat for a while, watching her daughter sleep. She had been observing Abby and Matt together for months, and she knew, with her mother's intuition, that they were becoming more than just business partners. She wondered when Abby was going to realize that she would never marry Edward because she was in love with Matt.

5

Abigail and Matthew

July 1844, Nantucket

By the following summer, Matthew had been home for seven months. In February 1844, when the *Young Hero* was seaworthy again, he declined to captain her, giving his first mate, Billy Coffin, the opportunity for his first command. Billy had earned it, and Matthew was holding good to his promise to Abigail to make a go of it at Gardner & Sons. 'Ailani and Anuenue had found a little house in New Guinea and had established their own dry goods business with 'Ailani's baskets and Anuenue's original clothing designs. Abigail and Matthew saw their friends less frequently, which saddened both of them. Eunice also missed Anuenue, but Anuenue compensated by offering her the first choice of her new designs and promising to make only one of a kind for her. Sarah and Thomas settled back into the routine of having both of their parents around, with Thomas quickly losing the ability to play one off the other to avoid Bible study. Matthew dangled the carrot that sea captains often led their crews in prayer, so Thomas was a bit more enthusiastic about Bible study than he was before. In spite of Abigail's worries, Sarah and Samuel's stargazing didn't appear to go beyond a platonic friendship; and because of this, she stopped insisting that Matthew accompany them every night.

As they agreed in November, Matthew joined Abigail at Gardner & Sons, and he didn't take on any new captain commissions though several ship owners had asked him in the last seven months. He took over some of Alexander's responsibilities at the firm and found that, while he was not sure whether he liked the work of a shipping agent, he did like working together with Abigail because he enjoyed spending more time with her. It wasn't easy; he had a lot to learn about running a shipping agent's business, but both Abigail and Alexander were patient with his mistakes. He had expected it to be easier; he had been a sea captain for many years, but his commercial experience was limited to the shipboard aspects, and he understood very little about the financing, insurance, and risk management details. He tried his best and felt embarrassed when he made mistakes, even though neither Abigail nor Alexander ever blamed him. Oddly enough, he found that his days on land were less predictable than those on the sea. He never imagined that business topics could be more intimidating than facing the turbulent weather at Cape Horn or dealing with a rogue whale that was trying to ram his ship. His moods were also less predictable on land, and he was often in a bad mood, which he tried to hide from his family. He couldn't explain why he was frequently unhappy or out of sorts; he attributed it to missing the sea, even though he knew this was probably not the complete answer. Abigail sensed his unhappiness but didn't ask him about it; she understood the transition from sea to land would be difficult for him. She tried to keep things as normal as possible, hoping that he would share his concerns with her when he was ready. She desperately wanted him to be happy on land.

"Did you see Captain Swain when the *Hero* arrived yesterday?" asked Abigail as they sat together in the Gardner & Sons' offices on Straight Wharf on the second floor above the warehouse. "How was his trip? Do you know how much whale oil he brought back? Did he bring back baleen? Is he going back out soon?"

Matthew looked at his wife and bit his tongue. He wanted to say to her that until he answered her first question, there was no need to ask him the other questions. But as they had had many tense moments in the last seven months, he decided to let it go. He looked out the office window and could see several ships in the harbor. The wharves were full of barrels of whale oil and bales of baleen, all neatly laid out in symmetrical rows radiating outward from the ships that brought them. One of his tasks was to meet the captain on his return and inventory the barrels and bales. This inventory was used to calculate the profit of the voyage for the ship's owner and formed the basis of the lay for the crew.

"No. I just missed him. I'll see him today."

She looked at him and hesitated before speaking. If this was any other employee, she would be much more direct with her next statement. She hated to criticize him as she knew that he had been unhappy for months.

"Captain Swain is not always so easy to work with. When he's returned from other voyages, Alexander has observed him speaking to other agents before checking in with us. He suspects that he might be looking for a better deal, even though he's legally beholden to us and the *Hero's* owner, John

Franklin. It's really important that you see him as soon as you can." She looked down at her ledgers as she said this, hoping that appearing casual might soften the criticism.

"I'm going now." He stood up, picked up his hat, and walked out of the office without looking at her or saying good-bye, barely able to control his irritation. She could hear his heavy footsteps on the staircase as he left the building, each thud reverberating in her heart.

She felt tears prick her eyes. She knew this wasn't working, but she still clung to the hope that he could learn to be happy in her family's business. She stood up and walked to the window, watching him as he strode angrily across Washington Street to the wharf.

He took in a deep breath as he walked to where the *Hero* was docked. As always, the sea air calmed him, and he regretted his abrupt departure from the office. He knew it wasn't her fault that she had to remind him of his obligations. He just wished that he had more of an affinity for the family business. He was so conflicted; he loved being at home, but he desperately missed being at sea. He was very happy to have more time with Abigail, but he disliked that she was his boss—nothing was worse than making a mistake in front of your boss, especially when your boss was your wife.

"Captain Swain!" shouted Matthew as he reached the *Hero*, seeing him on the deck. "Permission to come aboard?" Old North Wharf was full of activity—the *Hero* was the fourth ship to arrive this week—and as nearly half of the island's population was employed in the whaling industry, the wharf was a beehive of activity.

"Permission granted, Captain. Make it lively. I have things to do."

Matthew walked up the gangplank and took his second deep breath of the morning; after his tussle with Abigail, he was in no mood to be scolded by Swain.

The two captains shook hands, and Swain gave Matthew the captain's log and inventory list. Unlike most captains, who would offer their quarters for the agent's review of the documentation, Swain left Matthew standing on deck, which was an added insult as they were peers. Matthew read through the documents, which he did quickly, albeit uncomfortably. He spent the next hour taking a physical inventory. It was his job to take an inventory of all of the whale oil, ambergris, and baleen before they were off-loaded from the ship. As a general practice, agents also reviewed the captain's log to determine if there were any discrepancies between the inventory and the captain's log. Because he was a captain himself, it was easy for him to ascertain that, while Swain might be difficult to work with, the inventory was accurate. He would sign it off and go as soon as Swain reappeared.

He walked to the starboard railing of the *Hero* and looked around. He could see the *Rose*, the *James Loper*, and the *Three Brothers*. The *Hero* still had her tryworks blazing as she was lucky enough to kill a whale a day's sail from Nantucket. Whale blubber turned rancid after six weeks, so in the 1750s, ships' owners put their blubber processing plants, called tryworks, onto the ship, which enabled the ship to stay out to sea much longer. The *Hero* was one of the best and most successful ships in Nantucket's whaling fleet, and at 313 tons, she was also one of the largest. She had five whale-boats that would hold thirteen men each and regularly sailed with a crew of nearly one hundred men. She consistently brought back sperm oil as her crew was very experienced and had sailed together for many years; they were not intimidated about attacking the aggressive sperm whale. On this voyage alone, they had 1,200 barrels of the more valuable sperm oil and another 1,000 barrels of whale oil, making it a very successful voyage. Matthew continued to watch the activity in the harbor, wishing Swain would hurry up. The harbor smelled bad most of the time, but standing next to a stationary tryworks was just awful. He could feel the smoke from the oily blubber coating his nose and throat. Just as he was about to go look for Swain, he reappeared.

"Everything in order, Captain Starbuck?" barked Swain, clearly impatient to get Matthew off his ship.

"Yes, Captain, it is. If you would just sign the inventory sheets, I'll be off." Matthew remembered his duties as a representative of Gardner & Sons and grudgingly congratulated Swain on a successful voyage.

"That's what happens when you sail with Nantucketers and not a bunch of Coofs," Swain remarked as he signed each page of the ten-page inventory list. "Coofs" referred to anyone who was originally from Cape Cod. It was later expanded to describe anyone from off island. It was not a term of endearment.

Matthew's cheeks turned red. On his last voyage, the majority of his crew came from New England as the *Young Hero's* owner decided to sail late in the season—most of the experienced Nantucketers were already at sea. His crew was all experienced whalers, but he still cringed at the implication. Nantucket was a very small town; everyone knew everyone's business, especially in relation to whaling. He knew that the insult from Swain was intended.

He shook Swain's hand and hurried down the gangplank, happy that this was over. He knew that he should go back to the office to turn in the inventory so Abigail could start the accounting work, but after the morning he had had, he was not in a hurry to go back. He tucked the inventory list into the inside pocket of his coat and took off at a brisk pace toward Brant Point. Fifteen minutes later, he reached the small spit of land that jutted out into the harbor. The breeze coming off the harbor was warm, and he took off his coat, being careful not to drop the inventory list as he folded it over his arm. He was in a bad mood, triggered by his meeting with Captain Swain, though if he were really honest with himself, he would have blamed his bad mood on his curt words with his wife. In his heart, he knew that his discontent wasn't her fault. The last several months had been very difficult for the entire family, and he didn't know how to fix it. For a fleeting second, he wished that they had lived during an easier time. In the early 1700s, whaling ships sailed from November to March. Each of the voyages was six weeks long at most due to the abundance of whales in the North Atlantic and the fact that there weren't tryworks on ships yet. He realized that modern advantages, such as floating tryworks, also brought disadvantages. He sat down on his haunches and watched the waves as they gently lapped against the shore, hypnotizing him as he sat there, and bringing him some peace. He sighed—he might not have any answers, but he always had the sea, even if it was only from shore. With his bad mood eased, he stood up, brushed the sand off his pants, and headed back to the office.

OVER THE NEXT couple of weeks, Matthew acted more like his old self though he still had dark moments. He felt happier because his work had gotten a bit easier as most of the returning sea captains appreciated working with one of their peers. He took the opportunity to live vicariously through their adventures, and from some of their stories was reminded of why he had chosen to stay home. He also spent a lot more time with Sarah and Thomas. Sarah was doing better and better in astronomy and would soon be more advanced than Matthew. Luckily, Maria Mitchell had taken Sarah under her wing, and he expected that Sarah would be teaching him astronomy by September. The summer's night skies were crystal clear, and they stargazed nearly every evening. Thomas showed no interest in stargazing; having just turned ten, he was most interested in anything that floated and would spend hours with his friends rowing an old whaleboat around the harbor. No matter how unhappy he was about not being at sea, Matthew was thrilled to spend so much time with his children. As work got easier, he and Abigail were also getting along better; they were nearly back to the relationship they had had before his last voyage. He found that he wanted to spend more of his free time with her, which he didn't want to do shortly after they had first started working together. He had gotten better at separating "Abigail his boss" from "Abigail his wife," and they did more things together.

ONE STEAMY AUGUST evening, after their meal, Abigail and Matthew were walking to the Atheneum to meet 'Ailani and Anuenue for a lecture by Frederick Douglass who had just returned to the island after a two-year absence. Abigail had heard Douglass speak the first time he was on Nantucket in 1841, but Matthew missed his lecture because he was at sea at the time. Even though Nantucket had long abolished slavery, it still had its struggles in integrating African Americans into society. The schools were still seg-regated, which dismayed both Matthew and Abigail. Because of their deep friendship with 'Ailani and Anuenue, they wanted to visibly show their support for integration. As they entered the speaker's hall on the second floor of the library, they saw many familiar faces. They took four seats in the fifth row, saving two for their friends, who had not yet arrived. They greeted their friends and neighbors, noticing that the audience reflected the current state of things on Nantucket— there was no intermingling of whites and African Americans in the audience; each stayed to their own kind.

Quietly, Abigail said to Matthew, "I think we're going to start a little revolution tonight," referring to the seats they were holding for 'Ailani and Anuenue.

"Abigail, it's two chairs, not muskets."

"That might be so, but look around. Do you see anyone else sitting with their African American friends?"

"'Ailani and Anuenue are Pacific islanders, not Africans."

Abigail was exasperated, both with Matthew's logic and his stubborn refusal to see her point.

As before, Douglass mesmerized the room with his rhetoric, which had gotten even more powerful and persuasive since his last visit. Like the stoic people that they were, the Nantucketers' applause after his lecture was polite but hardly enthusiastic. Abigail knew that Douglass's success was not in getting rousing applause, but in having a full speaker's hall. She made a point to tell him this after the lecture.

She stepped outside and saw Matthew, 'Ailani, and Anuenue standing together off to one side, quietly talking while waiting for her. While all of the other people were greeting each other and exchanging pleasantries, no one approached her husband and her friends. This made her furious. How could people attend a lecture on abolitionism and then act this way? She quickly made her way over to them and was about to loudly express her frustration when she felt a light touch on her right forearm.

"Cousin Abigail, so nice to see you!" Eunice Starbuck

Hadwen stood by Abigail's side. "Hello, Matthew, 'Ailani, Anuenue. Did you enjoy the lecture?"

"Hello, Cousin Eunice. Yes, we did. Did you?" 'Ailani and Anuenue nodded their agreement.

"Yes, I did. Mr. Douglass is a passionate, persuasive speaker. I am sure he opened the minds of many of our neighbors tonight."

Abigail was not as optimistic, but she was not about to contradict Eunice. She knew that Eunice's gesture of speaking to the four of them would be noted by all of the gossips in town. What Eunice Starbuck Hadwen did mattered in society, and Abigail understood that even small gestures could make a significant difference. She was happy she was related, even if it was only by marriage, to this principled, fearless woman. Feeling mollified, she took Matthew's arm, and they walked home.

THE NEXT DAY, a simple sailing trip turned into a pivotal moment in Abigail's and Matthew's lives. Having gotten up with the sun at 5:30 a.m., Matthew bounded up the stairs at seven and woke Abigail.

"It's a glorious day, and the winds are perfect for sailing. Come with me, Abigail. I want to be out on the water with you today."

"Matthew, I have so much to do. I don't have time. Why don't you take Thomas? You know that he lives for sailing with you."

Abigail got out of bed, stretched, and started cataloging in her mind everything she had to do that day. By item number ten, she seriously considered getting back into bed and pulling the sheet over her head. But she stood up and was heading for the water closet when she heard the change in Matthew's voice.

"I really need time alone with you. I want to sail with you, not just eat our meals together," he spoke softly as he watched her walk away from him.

Abigail couldn't remember the last time Matthew said that he needed something from her. Sure, he asked for a second cup of tea or another piece of chicken or if his favorite shirt was washed and ironed, but the tone of his voice as he asked her to go sailing got her attention. She stopped and turned toward him, and the look on his face was all that she needed to defer her list to the following day.

"Then, sail we shall! When do you want to leave?"

"We should go soon. The wind and the tide are both favorable right now."

They dressed quickly, had a quick cup of tea and a slice of bread with butter, and headed to the harbor where Matthew had a small, fifteen-foot sailing sloop tied to the wharf. It was his very first boat, and he was sentimentally attached to it. He kept it to give lessons to Thomas and his friends. It was a perfect size for two people to enjoy a couple of carefree hours on the water.

"Permission to come aboard, Captain!" Abigail was getting into the spirit of the day.

"Permission granted, First Mate Starbuck!"

Abigail settled into the stern and left the sailing duties to Matthew. Before long, they were in the middle of the harbor, tacking upwind. Once their direction was fixed, he sat next to her, the main sheet in his right hand, tiller in his left. Even in a little boat, it was thrilling to her to be on the water. She could fully understand his love of the sea; she felt a freedom on the water that she never felt on land. She understood how much he was giving up to stay on land.

They sailed northeast toward Great Point. After an hour, they both felt more relaxed than they had in months.

She tilted her head toward him to capture the rays of the sun and to enjoy his physical proximity. It had been a long, cold winter in more ways than one. She wondered how they could have drifted so far apart. They had always been of one mind, but the last six months had been especially difficult. The last few weeks had been a little better, but she still felt as if there were a wall between them that she couldn't break through. She knew that he missed the sea, and although he didn't complain, she also knew that he disliked working at Gardner & Sons. She had tried several times to talk to him about what was wrong. But whenever she asked him about what was bothering him, he always said that he was fine even though he clearly was not. He was moody, which was unusual for him, and she and the children often tiptoed around him rather than upset him. It made her both angry and sad, and all she knew to do was to act as though everything were normal. After making several attempts to talk about his feelings in the last few months, she finally decided to let it go, hoping that he would talk to her when he was ready. For the moment, in the July sunshine with the lovely summer's breeze drifting over her, she forgot their difficulties and just enjoyed the day.

"Abigail, look out!" Matthew shouted as a gust of wind heeled the boat to starboard and the boom swung around, hitting her squarely on the back of the head. She fell to the floor of the boat like a bag of rocks, unconscious.

He raced to secure the boom and the tiller and moved to her side. He cradled her in his arms and felt the back of her head, where a lump was beginning to form. He took a handkerchief out of his pants pocket and reached over the side of the boat, soaking the handkerchief in the cold salt water. He wrung it out and wiped it across her brow but to no avail. She didn't wake up.

"Abigail, can you hear me?" Matthew was shouting, unsure of what to do next. If she didn't wake up quickly, he would have to leave her lying on the floor of the sloop to navigate back to town. "Abigail!" Every second she was unconscious made him more anxious.

Abigail was dreaming, or at least she thought she was. She could see Matthew out at sea, with no land in sight, but the picture was all wrong—he wasn't on a whaling ship, but rather a long, white, shiny boat with three masts. This wasn't the only thing wrong; while she was quite sure it was Matthew, he looked odd. His hair was very short, and he was wearing the strangest clothes of bright yellow and dark blue. His captain's uniform was black; what was he wearing? Her confusion continued. His shoes looked as if they were made out of cloth, with white blubber on the bottom, but how could this be? She noticed that he was alone, which was also strange; she couldn't imagine him sailing a boat this big by himself. He looked worried; he kept going below and coming back on deck with a piece of paper, which he would look at and then scan the horizon to the south. Far off in the distance, she could see that the sea and sky merged into one ominous black object. She couldn't make out what it was. A few seconds later, she could see the object clearly and it terrified her. She gasped. It was the largest wave she had ever seen, easily twice the height of her three-story home, and it was heading straight for Matthew, who had his back to it as he was intently scanning the southern horizon. Couldn't he hear the roaring water?

"Matthew, look out!" Abigail screamed in her dream, but her warning was too late; and even if he had heard her, there was nothing that he could have done. In less than a second,

Matthew and his boat were swallowed up by the rogue wave! After it passed, it was as if he wasn't ever there.

"Matthew, Matthew, I've lost Matthew," she was mumbling and sobbing at the same time, coming slowly back to consciousness, but still in the throes of her dream.

"Abigail, come back to me this instant!" She had been unconscious for about five minutes, but to Matthew it felt like a lifetime.

Abigail could hear his voice and was confused. She just saw him go down with his boat; how could he be calling her name? After a moment, she fully regained consciousness and her bearings; she remembered sailing with him into the harbor that morning but could remember nothing else, except her terrible dream. She sobbed and burrowed more deeply into his arms, unable to shake the terrible premonition that she would lose her husband to the sea.

"My darling wife, are you all right?" He was shaken to see her so distraught as this was very much out of character for her.

"Matthew, I had the most terrible dream. You were sailing a huge shiny white boat by yourself and had very short hair and a bright yellow jacket and the soles of your shoes were made out of blubber. Before I could warn you, a three-story wave swallowed you and your strange boat. And after it passed, you disappeared, like you were never there." She got it all out in a rush without pausing for breath or punctuation.

Matthew had always heard that blows to the head could cause temporary insanity but felt that this was not the time to mention it to her.

"Hush, my darling, you took a hard blow to the head. I'm afraid you'll have quite the headache for a few days. Just relax and I'll take us home." He settled her onto some blankets in the stern, tucking them around her to stop her from shivering.

He was thankful that the next hour was uneventful, and they were back at the wharf by early afternoon. Even though she felt a bit unsteady, Abigail was able to walk the short distance home, and Matthew insisted that she go straight to bed.

"It's one in the afternoon! I can't go to bed!" She felt both sheepish and exasperated at the same time. Her "I can do it!" attitude always surfaced in times of crisis.

"Yes, you can, Abigail. As much as I know how you loathe this, I am appointing myself lord and master of the house, and I command thee to bed!"

She giggled and acquiesced. "Ouch. I guess I'll be sleeping on my side for the next few days." She winced as her head and its large lump met the pillow.

She drifted off to sleep, mercifully spared from a rerun of her dream. When she woke, the room was dark; it was after nine in the evening. She had slept eight hours. She got out of bed and went downstairs to the kitchen where Matthew was reading the paper.

He leapt to his feet and went to her side. "Steady. You don't need a matching lump on the front of your head." He led her to the chair opposite his. "Can I get you anything? A cup of tea? Are you hungry? How's your headache?"

"A cup of tea would be nice. Thank you, Matthew. My head hurts, but it's better than it was this afternoon."

He prepared her a cup of tea, adding an extra spoonful of sugar. As she drank it, he tried to make light conversation. "Your dream was pretty crazy. Do you remember any of it?"

"I remember all of it, Matthew, and I know what it

means." He looked at her skeptically. He didn't believe that dreams meant anything; they were just simply dreams.

"I realized that my dream must be a premonition of the future. How else can you explain all of the strange things I saw: the boat, your clothes, and your short hair? None of it is anything like anything we know from history or the present time, so it must represent the future. I am sure it was a premonition: a terrible, awful premonition. The only comfort that I have is that I will not be the one losing you to the sea in this life. If that were true, I would have seen you go down on the *Young Hero.*"

"Abigail, don't take this the wrong way, but I would like to add some rum to your next cup of tea, strictly medicinal."

"Don't make fun of me. I am very serious."

"I know you are, my darling, but you have to admit—predicting the future? It is a bit unbelievable."

"My reasoning skills are superb. Therefore, if none of the things I saw are from current times, or the past, they must come from the future. And how could I possibly imagine what the future would look like? I can't. Therefore, by deduction, it was a premonition and not a dream."

Matthew tried to lighten the mood and knew that he couldn't argue with her unassailable logic.

"I hope I fare better in your next premonition. I don't like how this one ends. Next you'll be telling me that Mocha Dick eats me."

Mocha Dick was a mythical seventy-foot white whale who lived off the west coast of South America and, as stories had it, terrorized and attacked whaling ships and crews for years, never to be caught.

"That would be impossible. Mocha Dick was sighted just

two months ago and I saw the future, as fantastic as that sounds. You're safe from being Mocha Dick's supper."

Abigail never believed in premonitions before today and the realism of hers made her feel very unsettled. *Whoever loves Matthew in the future,* she thought, *is in for a terrible loss.*

6

Abby and Matt

November 2008, Boston

*D*espite the season, Abby thought it was hard to be thankful when gale-force winds were whipping through Boston, driving freezing rain down the back of her neck. It was the day before Thanksgiving, and she had given her employees the day off. She was on her way to the office to get some things done before the four-day holiday and was looking forward to the peace and quiet of an empty office. She stepped off the elevator, unlocked the main office door, and headed straight for the Nespresso machine in the small kitchen. Double espresso in hand, she unlocked her office and turned on the lights and her personal computer. She took a pad out of her desk drawer and began her to-do list for the day, intending to write down all of the things that she felt she had to accomplish before meeting Edward later that afternoon. They were driving to his parents' house in Lenox, Massachusetts. He had called her at 7:00 a.m. to remind her that they needed to get on the road before 3:00 p.m. or Interstate-90 West would be a parking lot. After fifteen minutes, Abby stopped writing even though she could think of twenty more items she could have added to the list.

The development team working on StarTaker 2.0 was doing well. Eva was keeping the project on track and the team was in good spirits in spite of the long hours. The extra day off for Thanksgiving was a good morale boost for the team. As with most software projects, new requirements appeared as the software was tested. The new features were definitely useful, but Abby worried that changing the initial scope would delay the October 2009 release date. She was tackling the first item on her to-do list, which was to review and sign off on the latest changes to the specifications when her phone rang. It was Matt.

"Abby, it's Matt. We have a problem."

She sighed. Would a "hello" kill him?

"What's up?"

"I'm in the office reviewing the latest specs, and I think there's a mistake in the software's logic, but I don't know enough about navigation software to determine if it's a big problem. Can you talk?"

For the next two hours, Abby and Matt worked on the new specifications, comparing the planned changes to the prototype they were using for testing. While his abruptness continued to irk her from time to time, they had established a good way of working together when they were focused on the product, its technical designs, and its functionality. By 10:00 a.m., they were both happy with the proposed changes, which Matt would give to the software developers on Monday.

"What are you doing for Thanksgiving?" asked Matt.

"We're going to Edward's parents' house in Lenox. My mother decided at the last minute to visit some friends in Boca Raton. You?"

"I'm staying on island. I signed up for the Turkey Plunge."

The Turkey Plunge was held on Thanksgiving morning every year, and it was Nantucket's equivalent of the Macy's parade in New York City. Hundreds of people jumped into the harbor at Children's Beach to raise money for a local charity. The water temperature would be about forty-five degrees Fahrenheit, so only the brave or the crazy attempted it. Hundreds more came to watch and cheer on their neighbors and friends.

Abby laughed. "Better you than me. I don't like going in the water in June!"

After wishing each other a happy holiday, they hung up. Abby picked up her to-do list and saw that she had ticked off only one item. She consoled herself with the fact that it was the number one item and the most important. Impulsively, she decided that she had worked enough for one day and would go home earlier than she had planned.

SHE CALLED EDWARD when she got home, saying that she could be ready to leave anytime after 1:00 p.m. Instead of being happy that she could leave earlier, Edward's reaction was snippy; he had scheduled back-to-back meetings until 2:45 p.m. assuming that she would not be ready before three, so he was stuck in the office until then. Ever since his attempted proposal in July, Edward was sometimes curt with Abby, which he had never been before. For the most part, she ignored it. She put herself in his shoes and let it go. Besides, with everything happening in the financial markets since the collapse of Lehmann Brothers in September, she had bigger things to worry about.

While the financial market collapse affected Gardner & Sons—their customers delayed payments—it had a much

larger impact on Starbuck Enterprises. Many of Matt's customers had ties to the financial and insurance industries,
and he had several large contracts canceled on short notice.
He was scrambling to find other work to keep his software
developers working, but it wasn't easy. Every week, he was
either in Boston or New York or Hartford, trying to get new
contracts with little success. He held up his end on StarTaker
2.0, but he was looking more and more tired each time she
saw him. He was starting to get gray hair and was losing
weight. She had introduced him to several of her long-standing customers and suppliers, and he had presented them with
proposals, but nothing had materialized yet. She reminded
herself to call Leo Drumm, CEO of Gardner & Sons' insurance provider, when she got back after Thanksgiving, hoping
to speed up the decision process for Matt's sake.

At 7:00 P.M. that evening, Abby and Edward were
finally at the Lenox exit off Interstate-90 West.
He had been in a foul mood the entire trip, and the traffic
didn't help. It was bumper-to-bumper for the first two hours.
Abby didn't say a word for most of the drive and hoped that
the entire weekend wasn't going to be like this. They were
spending Thanksgiving Day with his family. On Friday, they
were treating themselves to a spa day at Canyon Ranch,
which they often did when they visited his parents. As they
both had crazy work schedules right now, they planned to
drive back to Boston after breakfast on Saturday. Abby loved
being in the Berkshire Mountains during this time of year. It
had been a mild fall; many of the trees still had their leaves
and the colors captured by their headlights were beautiful.
They drove up the half-mile driveway to Edward's childhood
home: a large rambling farmhouse that was built in 1820 and
thoughtfully renovated over the years.

Entering the kitchen by the back door, they were immediately engulfed in hugs and hellos from Fanning family members. The fireplace was blazing, and the scene was straight out of a Norman Rockwell painting: loving family, comforting food on the table, and a sense that all was right in the world. They got glasses of Tignanello, Abby's favorite red wine, and joined the family in the living room. There were Susan and Tim, Edward's parents; his older brother, Nathan, with his wife, Betsy; and their fourteen-year-old daughter, Daisy. Edward's younger sister, Anne, and her family, were spending the holiday with her in-laws in Hudson, New York. It was just the seven of them for the holiday. As it was often only Abby and her mother at holiday events, even just seven people seemed like a lot to her. The conversation was light and casual, ranging from how the Patriots were doing to what was new at Edward's firm. Abby sat back and enjoyed the happy family scene; it was a lovely respite, especially after the tense drive from Boston.

THE NEXT MORNING dawned sunny and bright. Abby woke in her room at 8:30 a.m. and lazily stretched before getting out of bed. She and Edward always slept in separate rooms when Daisy was in the house though everyone, including Daisy, knew this was an unnecessary gesture. Abby liked this old-fashioned gesture; she thought she would set the same standards for her own children. She dressed in jeans, a soft blue cotton T-shirt, and a fisherman's knit sweater and went downstairs to the kitchen. She could smell the turkey roasting as she entered where everyone but her was already at the big farmer's table, making plans for the day. As Thanksgiving dinner was well in hand—Susan had been up since 6:00 a.m.—the group decided it was a perfect day for a walk to stimulate their appetites. The Fanning house was surrounded by twenty acres of forests; and when they were children, Edward, Nathan, and Anne had marked several hiking trails throughout the property.

Eight hours later, the family was back in front of the fire in the living room, each person as stuffed as the turkey had been. Abby and Daisy were talking about the pointer, Cookieland Seasyde Hollyberry, who was the winner of the National Dog Show presented by Purina and hosted by the Kennel Club of Philadelphia. The family watched it every year and everyone chose—incorrectly—the dog they thought would be best in show. Abby and Daisy were sure that their favorites should have won. The rest of the family looked on in amusement as they argued the merits of their picks.

Abruptly, Daisy turned to her uncle, Edward, and asked, "Mom told me you bought Abby a ring from Tiffany's in July. Why isn't she wearing it?"

"Daisy!" Betsy was exasperated at her daughter's thoughtless comments. She had had a quiet talk with Edward on the walk and learned a few more details about his awkward proposal. She felt sad for her brother-in-law who was clearly madly in love with Abby. Like the rest of the family, she knew that Abby had said "not now" in July, and they were all hoping that she'd be wearing her engagement ring at Thanksgiving. When they saw that she wasn't, they respected the couple's privacy and, until this moment, weren't going to talk about it. Unfortunately, they forgot to caution Daisy, who adored and idolized Abby.

Edward was startled by Daisy's question, and it rubbed him the wrong way. He was not in a generous mood, so he decided to make Abby squirm, just a little. "I don't know, Daisy. Why don't you ask Abby?" Susan looked at her son, surprised that he would be so unkind.

Abby gave a choked little laugh and tried to lighten the moment. "Why, do you have a bridesmaid's dress that you're desperate to wear?"

Daisy, who was now suffering under the glaring looks from both her mother and grandmother, said, a bit defensively, "I just thought she forgot her ring! I wanted to see it. No one told me that she didn't say yes!"

Susan jumped in, ever protective of her middle child, and Abby, whom she had grown to love like a daughter. "It must be movie time! Daisy, help me in the kitchen with the popcorn. And, Tim, can you get *It's a Wonderful Life* out of the bookcase?"

A collective groan went up. No one could imagine eating one more thing, and this was their twentieth viewing of *It's a Wonderful Life*. To lighten the moment, Abby moved closer to Edward on the couch who reluctantly let her snuggle up against him. The rest of the evening went without incident, and they miraculously managed to scarf down the big bowl of popcorn. Everyone said good night after the movie; it was an early night in the Fanning house.

THE NEXT MORNING, Abby was up with the birds, whose cacophony drove her out of bed. She wondered how anyone could sleep past 5:00 a.m. in Lenox. She realized that she must have been exhausted two nights before to sleep through the birds' chatter. In dire need of coffee, she tiptoed downstairs to the kitchen, not wanting to wake the others. Susan was sitting at the farmer's table, nursing a cup of coffee and a half-eaten slice of pumpkin pie. She looked at Abby with love and sadness in her eyes. After last night, her mother's instinct told her that Abby would never be her daughter-in-law.

"I'm sorry," began Abby, both for disturbing her and

also wanting to explain why she hadn't accepted Edward's proposal.

"No, dear, you don't need to be sorry, and you don't need to explain. I understand."

"I don't know how you can! I hardly understand it myself." Abby's eyes filled with tears.

Susan got up from her chair and walked over to Abby, who was leaning stiffly against the white porcelain farmer's sink. She put her arms around her and held her close, neither of them speaking for a long minute. Once Abby started to relax, Susan released her embrace and held Abby by the shoulders, looking into her eyes as she said, "Sweetheart, I think you do understand, even if you're not ready to accept it. I know that you love Edward, and you would do anything to avoid hurting him. But it's kinder to tell him it's over. I know my son. I can see that your delay in accepting his ring is killing him inside even if he keeps telling you that he's fine."

Abby gently pulled away from Susan and sat down. Her legs could no longer support her, and she was afraid that she'd fall down.

"I don't know how to tell him. It just feels so cruel, and I really do love him. But you're right. I don't love him like I should love my future husband."

Abby was relieved to finally say out loud what had been in her heart for months. She was fully aware of the irony of the situation: telling her boyfriend's mother that she didn't love her son enough to marry him and then looking to her for comfort and consolation. She felt like she was taking unfair advantage of Susan's love for her.

"I never told you this, but when Nathan was in kinder-garten and Edward and Anne were still toddlers, they had a younger sister, who was stillborn, when I was six months pregnant. We named her Abigail. We don't talk about it in our family because after losing our Abigail, I was clinically depressed for a very long time. It's not a time our family wants to remember."

"After two years, I slowly started getting better. Tim did so much during this time—never giving up on me even when there were weeks when I refused to get out of bed. Once I felt strong enough, I got professional counseling. By the time Edward and Anne were in school, I was nearly back to my old self."

Abby sat quietly. She instinctively knew not to interrupt even to say how sorry she was.

"So when we first met you, I immediately felt a bond with you because of your name even though I know this sounds silly now. You were—in a small way—a part of our family right from the beginning. My Abigail had come back to me."

"Why are you telling me this now?" Abby's voice caught as she spoke. She felt terrible before this conversation started, and now she felt close to despair. Not only would she never marry Edward, but she would also never be the replacement for the Abigail who broke Susan's heart.

"Because you're not the Abigail we lost—you're *you*. We grew to love you for who *you* are. And while the selfish part of me wants you to be part of our family forever, we will always love you whether you are a Fanning or not. You will always be our Abigail, the one we were meant to have." Susan smiled as she said this, reaching her hand across the table to take Abby's, whose eyes were filling up again. While Susan hated that Edward was going to have his heart broken, she knew she didn't want to lose a second Abigail, whom she had grown to love nearly as much as the first. She hoped that her story of overcoming a devastating loss could help Abby make the break with Edward. Abby felt as though a tremendous weight had been lifted off her shoulders. She realized that she had underestimated Susan's love for her.

Abby smiled sadly in return, knowing that there was nothing more that needed to be said. "Any chance there's more pie?"

"That's my girl. Everyone knows pie is the answer!"

At that moment, Edward walked into the kitchen. "If pie is the answer, what's the question?" he said it lightheartedly, but there was a deep sadness in his eyes. Susan looked at her son and realized that he must have heard most of their conversation. She hugged him and excused herself, leaving Abby and Edward alone.

Abby spoke first. "Edward, I'm . . ."

"Please, Abby, stop. There's no need to say any more. I'm just very sad, and I know you are too, but let's not drag this out. I really don't think that there's anything left to say."

While Abby wanted to say something to erase the hurt from his eyes, she knew that, short of turning back time and accepting his proposal, there was truly nothing more to say.

They canceled their spa day at Canyon Ranch; neither one of them was in the mood to relax in the presence of others. Abby managed to convince Edward to drop her off at the train station, and she caught Amtrak back to Boston. He decided to stay in Lenox until Sunday, and she was happy that he would be with his family. It was times like these that she wished that her family was more than just she and her mother.

MATT JERKED AWAKE at 3:00 a.m., covered in sweat. This was the third time this week he had had the same dream. He'd been having the same dream for months, but the frequency was increasing; he now had it several times a week. His stress level was through the roof ever since the market collapsed in September. Nearly 40 percent of his contracts had been canceled, and he was scrambling to keep his employees employed. If he didn't get more contracts soon, he'd have to start laying people off. The only bright spot was the collaboration with Gardner & Sons, so he thought maybe that was why Abby featured so prominently in his dreams.

In his dream, he and Abby were married and living in colonial Nantucket. He wasn't sure of the exact time period, but he guessed it was the 1800s. He knew enough about the history of Nantucket to recognize the things in the dream as being from that time period. He could see both of them as clearly as if he were watching a movie, which unnerved him. Before he met Abby, he could hardly remember any of his dreams; and because of this, he had always assumed that he didn't dream at all. It always started the same way: it was evening, and they were sitting in front of the fireplace in the kitchen—his kitchen at 15 Union Street—and quietly talking about their day. They looked happy. He could also see two other vague images, and he wondered if they might be children. This also freaked him out—it was startling enough to see him and Abby in a domestic scene from two centuries before—but kids? They had kids? The dream had small variations as to how long they talked or if 1800s-Matt read the paper and 1800s-Abby did needlework, but they always ended the same way—with them going upstairs to bed. Then, the screen in his head mercifully went blank. He absolutely didn't need a visual of him and Abby in bed together; it would make it impossible to work with her. He knew that he wouldn't sleep any more that night, so he got up, went downstairs, put on a heavy jacket, and walked out into his backyard.

The stars were dazzling. The night was cold and clear, and Matt was reminded of the ancient Persian saying

inscribed on one of the very first navigation devices, an
astrolabe: "The world is decorated with stars." He sat on an
Adirondack chair and tilted his head back, taking in the spectacular heavens that were a hallmark of Nantucket; he could
even see the Milky Way. Still cold from the Turkey Plunge
that morning, he reminded himself that every year he swore
he would never do it again. He thought about Abby—how
could he not as he was dreaming about her multiple times
a week—and wondered if she enjoyed Thanksgiving with
Edward's family. She didn't sound too keen on the phone
the day before, but like most things about women, he didn't
spend too much time speculating on the reason. It wasn't
that he was insensitive; he just lived by the philosophy of
Alf, the TV character from the 1980s, who once said: "Find
out what you don't do well, and don't do it." He knew that he
would never be good at understanding women; it had started
with his sisters and continued throughout his life until now.

Thinking about his sisters, Lilly and Emily, brought a
smile to his face. As every year, dinner was at Lilly's house in
Madaket and the house was full—with all the in-laws, nieces,
and nephews; they were thirty people altogether. Lilly
wisely gave up cooking everything herself years ago; she
only cooked the turkey. Everything else came from Bartlett
Farms. There would probably be a revolt if she ever did try
to cook anything—being a notoriously bad cook—but she
was an excellent hostess. Matt realized that being a disciple
of the Philosophy of Alf must run in the family. After an
hour, Matt went back inside, made coffee, and turned on his
laptop. With the state his business was in, he could use every
available hour for work.

A WEEK LATER, Matt met Abby at the Nantucket
Memorial Airport. He had convinced her to come

over for a working day at his office and to stay for Christmas Stroll. She had never been to Stroll, so he used it as an inducement to get her to the island. After months of his weird dreams, he felt that he had to tell her about them, and he had to tell her on Nantucket. He couldn't explain why; he just knew that it was important. Her plane landed at 8:00 a.m. They had a quick coffee at Hutch's, the airport coffee shop, agreed on the schedule for the day, and drove to his office.

This was Abby's third trip to the island since July, and the software development team was happy to see her. They spent the day in project reviews and both of them were pleased with the team's progress. They finished the day with a meeting with Dr. Eva. They agreed on the work schedule for the upcoming holiday weeks, glad that they were slightly ahead of schedule, and could give the team a much-needed break. If they had to, they would have asked the team to work between Christmas and New Year's, but luckily, they wouldn't have to.

At 6:00 p.m. they were ready to leave the office. Matt had gotten tickets for the Annual Christmas House Tour and had made reservations at Company of the Cauldron on India Street for dinner at 9:00 p.m. He drove Abby to the Union Street Inn where she checked in and quickly changed her clothes before they set off together on foot for the house tour. This year, most of the houses were on Darling Street. Each year for Christmas Stroll, the Nantucket Island Chamber of Commerce asked homeowners to allow the general public to tour their decorated antique homes. They always had more homes than they needed.

"I'm amazed at how many people are here!" Abby exclaimed as they stood in line at 8 Darling Street, waiting to tour the house.

"It's the busiest weekend of the year. The local merchants rely on it. It's their last chance to make their numbers for the season. Wait until tomorrow when we watch Santa Claus arrive at Straight Wharf by Coast Guard cutter; you'd think George Clooney was arriving!"

Abby laughed, enjoying the festive evening and the holiday atmosphere. She realized that she and Matt had never done a social activity together before. Sure, they had had dinner together several times in the last nine months, but those dinners were always an extension of their business meetings. She was unexpectedly enjoying herself.

They toured from house to house and, of course, nearly everyone knew Matt. He introduced her to all with a raised eyebrow as "one of *those* Gardners," which everyone found hysterically funny, even Abby, though she had no idea why it would be.

After the tour, they walked to the restaurant, one of Matt's favorites. Company, as the locals called it, looked magical. Outside, the windows were framed in tiny sparkling white lights, and the window boxes were filled with a variety of greens and magnolia leaves with seashells tucked in among the branches. Strung fresh cranberries were hung on the greens like a festive holiday necklace, completing the Nantucket Noel effect. Abby was enchanted. Inside, the magic continued. As they took their seats at the table, she looked around, admiring the lovely decorating touches that made the restaurant look as if they were eating in someone's well-loved home. It was very romantic, and if she didn't know better, she would think they were on a date. She blushed.

"Something wrong?" Matt was concerned about the flush on her cheeks. "Do you feel OK?"

Abby blushed again, embarrassed about being caught

blushing. "Yes, Matt, I'm fine. It's a little warm after being outside in the cold air."

They ordered two glasses of champagne, and Matt ordered a bottle of Stag's Leap Cabernet Sauvignon to go with their meal. Company had a set menu every night, and they were in for a real treat; the Christmas Stroll menus were always fabulous. He nodded to more people he knew in the restaurant but didn't leave the table to speak to them. Abby thought that if Nantucket were ever to have a mayor, he would be a shoo-in. As they ate their appetizer, they chatted about the houses that they had seen, and Matt told Abby about the other events that would be happening on the weekend. She wanted to go to the Crafts Fair at Preservation Hall to find something for her mother, who loved handmade items, and she was really looking forward to seeing Santa Claus arrive at Straight Wharf.

They continued their easy camaraderie throughout dinner, both of them a little surprised at how much they were enjoying each other's company outside of the office. Because they were getting along so well, Matt decided to tell Abby about his dreams from the prior weeks.

"Do you remember your dreams?" Matt asked casually, trying to sound like this question was the same as asking Abby to name her favorite movie.

"Sometimes. I have really complicated dreams—thousands of characters doing many things in multiple locations. It's as if Cecil B. DeMille is filming an epic in my head. Do you remember yours?"

Matt took a deep breath, still unsure how to tell Abby about his dreams and reluctant to break the lovely mood of the evening. He stalled, pausing for a moment. "I do now. I never did before. In fact, I would have sworn that I didn't dream."

"That's unusual. I'm wondering why you've started dreaming now? Or do you think that you've always dreamed before, but you're just remembering them for the first time now? When you wake up, can you remember them?"

"Yes, I can. They're actually very vivid even after I wake up. It's like watching a TV show in my head."

"What are they about?" Abby's curiosity was piqued. She laughed then added, "Can you tell me, or would it be TMI?"

Matt looked at her, puzzled. "TMI?"

This time, it was Abby's turn to have some fun with acronyms. "Too much information. I don't need to know all of your deep, dark secrets, Matt."

Matt forced an awkward laugh and decided to launch in. "I see us, Abby. I see you and me, sitting in my kitchen on Union Street."

"Oh. Considering how much time we spend together, I guess . . ." While she was surprised by Matt's revelation, she didn't want to overreact to it.

Matt interrupted her. "I see us sitting together in my kitchen *in the 1800s.*" He paused, taking in the confused look on her face and then decided to swing for the fences. "In my dreams, we're married, and we appear to be very happy. It's always the same time of day—evening. We're sitting by the fireplace. We're either talking to each other or I'm reading the paper and you're doing needlework. And there's more. We have two children, though I can't see their faces as clearly as I can yours and mine." He felt relieved to finally tell her, but after seeing the look on her face, his relief was short-lived.

Abby wasn't sure how to answer Matt. She could see the serious look on his face, so she knew that making a joke wouldn't be appropriate. But really, this was crazy to her! Married to Matt in the 1800s? With children? She knew that many people believed in people having prior lives, but she had never met anyone who did. Sure, people sometimes joked about prior-life stuff, but Matt was definitely not making a joke. He looked very serious and, at this moment, a little ill.

"Matt, I just don't know what to say. Did I understand you correctly? You think that we were married in a prior life?" Abby tried to keep her voice level and her tone nonchalant.

"Yes, that is exactly what I'm saying. For months, I've been having these dreams three or four times a week."

Now it was Abby's turn to look ill. One dream was odd, but weeks of the same dream—the dream he just told her about—was creepy. There was no other word for it. She didn't have to say anything to him; the look of horror on her face said it all.

"Listen, Abby, hear me out. I know that I've just made you very uncomfortable. Heck, it makes me uncomfortable. I don't believe in all this prior-life stuff, never have. But these dreams are so vivid! I wish I could tape one for you to watch. If you saw what I saw, you'd understand why I had to tell you about it."

Being an innately kind person, Abby tried to stay calm because she didn't want to hurt Matt's feelings. She could see the concerned look on his face, which she knew came from his being vulnerable with her. She imagined herself in his shoes and shuddered; she didn't think that she could have told Matt what he just told her.

"You're right. I am very uncomfortable with the fact that you're having so many dreams about us from the 1800s. It's a little weird. I don't know what to tell you. I don't have any dreams like this."

"Abby, to be honest, I'm just not sure anymore that they're dreams."

"If they're not dreams, what are they? What do you

mean?" She was perplexed; this conversation was getting stranger and stranger.

"Look, here are the facts. I've never dreamt before in my life. Now, I'm having twenty dreams a month, and they're nearly exactly the same every time. I don't dream about anything else. I don't know what to call it either, but I don't think this is dreaming."

"Matt, I just don't understand." Abby's voice was low, but insistent. All of the goodwill of the evening had evaporated, like an early morning fog in August. "Are you saying that you're having *visions*? And even if you are, what could it possibly mean?"

"I'm saying that I think my dreams aren't dreams at all. I think they're visions of us having shared a prior life." If Matt thought telling Abby about his dreams was hard, saying this to her was excruciating. But as he was never one to back down from things that were hard, he plowed on. "There's nothing to 'do' about it, Abby. I just needed to tell you."

"Well, I agree with that point! I don't know what we would 'do' about it in any case. I'm hardly going to marry you in this life." She tried to make a joke, but it fell flat.

At that moment, the waiter handed Matt the bill, bringing a welcome interruption. Abby tried to reach for it, but he held it away from her. "You're my guest." He handed his credit card to the waiter. "You can pay when we're in Boston."

"Thank you, Matt. It was a lovely dinner." She tried to salvage the evening. He smiled briefly at her, signed the check, and asked for their coats.

They left Company and walked south, zigzagging their way to the harbor on the way back to her hotel. In trying to return to their earlier mood, Matt kept the conversation light, pointing out different sights that marked the holiday season, such as the Christmas trees lining Main Street or the floating Christmas tree in the red Killen Real Estate rowboat in the harbor between Easy Street and Old North Wharf. After twenty minutes, they reached the Union Street Inn and said good night, agreeing to meet at 10:00 a.m. the following morning.

ABBY WOKE AT 7:00 a.m. to the sun streaming in her window. She had slept well in spite of the awkwardness of the evening before, but she awoke feeling unsettled and uneasy. In the daylight, Matt's visions didn't seem as upsetting as they were at dinner, but she still felt uncomfortable, as if there were a piece of food between her teeth that dental floss just couldn't reach. She lay on the bed and stretched, thinking about the upcoming day's events of Santa Claus, the Crafts Fair, and, most importantly, spending the entire day with Matt. With a start, she realized that she couldn't do it. She couldn't spend the entire day with him. While she felt a little better about their prior night's conversation, she also knew that she didn't want to have the same conversation again today. She worried that if they picked up where they left off, they would damage their professional relationship, and she had too much riding on their collaboration to risk it. She called Gardner & Sons' pilot, who told her they could be wheels-up in an hour. She dressed, packed her bag, ate a quick breakfast, and forty-five minutes later was in a taxi to the airport. She sent Matt a text as she rode to the airport, thanking him for the lovely dinner and telling him that something had come up, she had to leave, and she would call him on Monday. She didn't really want to talk to him again this weekend; she hoped that her text would discourage him from calling her. As her plane took off, she looked out over the island and was struck by its beauty. The crystal-

clear blue sky and surrounding waters contrasted sharply
with the browns and grays of the island, creating a dazzling
visual effect. She felt calmer as she watched the waves break
against the south shore beaches as her plane banked to the
left and flew north toward Boston.

MATT ALSO WOKE up early and was happy to see the
sunshine. He was looking forward to the day. After
talking to Abby the night before, he slept better than he
had in weeks—no dreams, no visions, and no insomnia.
After a cup of coffee, he decided to get in a quick workout
at the Nantucket Health Club before he met Abby. It was
such a beautiful day that he rode his bike to the club, feeling
virtuous that he was getting in a double workout. He came
home, showered, and was just about to leave the house to
meet Abby when he noticed the text alert on his phone. His
good mood vanished as he read her text. At first he was
angry. How dare she sneak off the island without having
the courtesy to say good-bye in person? His second thought
was kinder and his anger evaporated. He knew that she must
have been freaked out to leave without saying good-bye. He
also knew that she was looking forward to the day's events,
so she must have felt really uncomfortable to bolt like she
did. His next thought was to call her, but after rereading
her text, he realized that she probably wouldn't answer if
he did. He instinctively did what he always did when he was
troubled: he left his house and headed for the water.

As he walked to the harbor, he noticed it was an unseason-
ably warm day. *The temperature must be nearly 55 Fahrenheit*, he
thought. He turned around and went back to his house, collected his cold-weather sailing gear, and headed back to the
harbor, this time straight to his Sunfish sailboat, *The Lizzie*,
that he kept tied up at the town pier off season. He had had

The Lizzie since he was fourteen. In fifteen minutes, he was out on the harbor, sailing toward the Great Point lighthouse. He passed several of his friends who were out on their scallop boats who shouted to him as he sailed past. "Playboy! Must be nice to not have to work for a living!" They laughed as he returned their ribbing with a cheeky salute.

Once past Pocomo, there were no more scallop boats, and Matt had the inner harbor to himself. The wind stayed steady, and he was glad that he had gone back to the house for his warm clothes; it was much colder on the water than on land. Like Abby, he was struck by the allure of the island; he thought Nantucket was a beautifully wrapped present, just waiting for him to open it. His thoughts drifted to the prior night's conversation, and he wondered if he had damaged his relationship with her. He hoped not, but it was too late to unring that bell. He thought about what he would do with his now-free day and decided he'd still like to see Santa Claus arrive on Straight Wharf. He realized that he had seen Santa Claus arrive by Coast Guard cutter every year since he could remember, beginning when he was a small boy. It was one of his earliest and most favorite memories. He turned *The Lizzie* around and sailed for town, looking forward to rescuing his day with the reassuring tradition of his youth.

7

Abigail and Matthew

August 1846, Nantucket

After Abigail's premonition in July 1844, she came to understand two important things about Matthew. First, she realized that her husband's happiness was inextricably tied to the sea; and second, that she would not lose him to it as she had feared for most of her adult life. With this new insight, she knew that he needed to go back to sea to be happy. Over the summer and into the fall of 1844, the offers to captain a ship kept coming in, and Matthew had continued to say no, honoring his promise to her. Finally, when Jebidiah Macy, owner of the *President,* knocked on their door one afternoon in late October 1844, Abigail urged Matthew to take the commission, and he did. By August 1846, he had been at sea just short of two years and was due home within the month. Abigail had gotten the good news of his imminent return from Captain Austin of the *Young Eagle,* who had returned to Nantucket just the previous week. Captain Austin had gammed with Matthew off the coast of Chile in February 1846 and had brought a letter back for her. She learned that he was having a very successful voyage and that she could expect him no later than September.

ABIGAIL COULDN'T WAIT for Matthew to get home; she had never needed her husband more than she did now. Her world was falling apart and she was working around the clock to fix it. Since the Great Fire in July, which destroyed two-thirds of downtown Nantucket, she had been working eighteen hours a day, feeling as if every step forward were offset by three steps back. She and Alexander had lost everything—the only thing left of Gardner & Sons was the name—and she wasn't sure that would survive over the next few weeks. Luckily, her mother had her own money and didn't rely on Gardner & Sons to provide her with an income or Abigail would have had to add this to her list of worries. Alexander still had his farm, but he lost all the wool he had stored in their warehouse on the wharf. Luckily, the Starbucks' house on Union Street was untouched by the fire, as was Michael and Elizabeth's, but several of their close neighbors were not as lucky. She was very grateful that no one was hurt in the fire, but her heart broke that the business that had been in her family for three generations was in ruins.

Gardner & Sons lost everything: all of the agent's guidelines that had been carefully crafted over the years, all of the records, and, unfortunately, a large sum of cash, which they were just about to pay to the owner of the *Elizabeth Starbuck*. The fire, because it was fueled by casks of whale oil, was so hot that it melted their safe. They couldn't meet their financial obligations, and this gave her many sleepless nights. She was not consoled by the fact that nearly half of the businesses on Nantucket were in the same situation; both she and her brother held Gardner & Sons to a higher level of performance, due in great part to their father's philosophy of doing business with the highest ethical standards. They started out every day talking about what they should do to get their business restored to its former health. All of their sea captains were at sea, and they were reluctant to finance captains that they didn't know very well, especially without their guidelines. Whaling was a risky business, physically and financially, and they didn't have any working capital left; it was all tied up in the ships currently at sea. Their assets were greatly diminished and neither of them wanted to take on debt to expand the business when the outcome was so uncertain.

THE REST OF Nantucket was suffering as well. 'Ailani and Anuenue's dry goods business was doing very poorly—nearly all of their customers had no money to pay for anything. They were worried about losing their business and their little house, which they had grown to love. In the three years since they arrived on island, 'Ailani and Anuenue had made Nantucket their home. Yes, the weather was a challenge; they missed the tropical climate of the Sandwich Islands—but all other aspects were pleasing to the couple. They had made many good friends in New Guinea. Matthew's fears that they would be unhappy and would want to return to the Sandwich Islands never materialized. They attended services at the First Congregational Church every Sunday. Eunice Starbuck Hadwen's sponsorship had helped the couple tremendously. Because of her, Anuenue had more dress customers than she could keep up with. Many ladies waited several months for an original design by Anuenue, but never Eunice to whom Anuenue was fiercely loyal.

ANUENUE KNOCKED ON the door of 100 Main Street. Thaddeus opened the door and, seeing her, smiled. During her service to Eunice, Thaddeus developed a soft spot for the young woman. She reminded him of his granddaughter, Berta, who lived in New Bedford. After exchanging greetings, Thaddeus directed her to Eunice's private sitting room off of her bedroom on the second floor.

"Good morning, Mrs. Hadwen." Anuenue walked into the sitting room, carefully laying the garment she was carrying across the chair next to Eunice.

"Good morning, Anuenue. Lovely day, isn't it?" Eunice noticed that Anuenue looked very tired but didn't remark on it.

"Yes, I love warm weather. It reminds me of home. I have a new dress for you. Would you like to try it on?" She held up a lovely dove-gray dress with a pale blue collar instead of the more traditional white lace collar. The cut and the finishing touches were perfect for Eunice. She had stayed up late several nights to finish it quickly as they desperately needed the money.

"Anuenue, your dresses always fit me perfectly. It's lovely, dear. There's no need to try it on. Please sit down and have a cup of tea. I'd like to talk to you." Eunice poured her a cup of tea and motioned toward the chair opposite her. She sat, wondering what Eunice wanted. For a brief second, she was afraid that she had done something wrong. She worried that Eunice didn't want the dress.

"How are you and 'Ailani doing since the fire, dear? I heard from Abigail that you were both a big help on the night of the fire, taking care of the children while she and Alexander were trying to save their business."

The night of the Great Fire was terrifying. Flames were everywhere! They shot up into the night sky creating a scene that could have only been orchestrated by the devil himself. The smell and black smoke from the burning whale oil made being outside even more treacherous. On top of it all, townspeople started explosions hoping to contain the fire and the booms were deafening. It was very brave of 'Ailani and Anuenue to rush into the heart of the fire to help their friends.

"It's very sad, Mrs. Hadwen. It's sad to see the state of downtown, though I see many buildings are already being rebuilt." Anuenue was very modest—she didn't feel that she could take credit for doing something that she knew anyone with a good Christian heart would do.

"Please excuse my directness, Anuenue, but do you need some assistance?"

Anuenue was confused. What assistance was Eunice referring to? As she didn't immediately answer, Eunice continued. "My dear, do you need money? I would be happy to advance you some money to cover your expenses until your business is back on its feet."

Anuenue blushed and looked down at her hands, avoiding Eunice's direct gaze. She didn't know what to say. She was raised to be self-sufficient, and while she and 'Ailani were always grateful for others' help, she would never ask for it.

She stuttered, "I . . ."

Eunice, realizing that she had embarrassed Anuenue with her direct approach, softened her offer. "I'm sorry, my dear. I didn't mean to be so blunt. I'm happy to help you and 'Ailani, and be assured, it's not a gift. Think of it as my prepaying for the next six dresses." Seeing the relief on Anuenue's face, she added, "This is what family does for each other, and I've come to think of you both as my family."

After chatting for a little while longer and saying good-bye to Thaddeus, Anuenue stepped out into the August sunshine, feeling tremendously relieved. Like many Nantucketers, she and 'Ailani were having sleepless nights worrying about what would happen to their business and their home. She was eager to get home to share her good news with him.

As she stepped onto Main Street, she saw Abigail walking toward her. "Abigail! How nice to see you!" Anuenue was all smiles. She and 'Ailani finally agreed to call Abigail and Matthew by their first names just a few months before.

"Good morning, Anuenue. I was just on my way to cousin Eunice's to give her some news. Sarah is betrothed to Samuel. They asked for my permission last night. He's sailing today, and they'll be married when he returns. I shudder to think of how Matthew will react when he gets home."

Anuenue was surprised by the news. Like Matthew, she still saw Sarah as a little girl, but at sixteen, she was definitely old enough to be betrothed. Many girls were already married at sixteen.

"We'll want you to make her wedding dress, but we have plenty of time. I expect Samuel will be gone at least two years, if not longer. That's my only consolation. I know I'm not losing my little girl tomorrow!"

They chatted for a few more minutes before parting, promising to catch up later in the week. Abigail knocked on Eunice's door, greeted Thaddeus, and was directed upstairs to her cousin. She was enlisting her help to manage Matthew's reaction when he got home. She knew that, with her blessing, Matthew would be much more amenable to the idea of his little girl getting married. Between the Great Fire and this, Matthew was going to have quite the homecoming.

THREE MONTHS LATER, a lot had happened in the Starbuck household. Matthew had arrived on Nantucket at the end of September, having had a very successful voyage. This was a big relief for Abigail as it took some of the pressure off her and Gardner & Sons. Luckily, his family business was relatively untouched by the Great Fire, and they were able to pay him his lay. As she predicted, Matthew was astonished that Sarah was engaged, protesting that she was much too young. After she reminded him that they had known and loved Samuel their entire lives, and that they wouldn't be getting married for at least two years, Matthew conceded and blessed the betrothal. Gardner & Sons was back on track, albeit slowly. Alexander was much more engaged in the business, and this was a tremendous help for Abigail. By November, things were starting to improve. The evenings were getting cold, and every morning there was frost on the ground. It looked as if winter would come early this year. One evening, after supper, Matthew and Abigail were sitting by the fire in the kitchen.

"Abigail, I'd like to ask you something."

She looked up from her embroidery, happy for the distraction. She still disliked needlework and didn't know why she kept doing it.

"I've been offered the *Joseph Starbuck*, which will sail in two weeks. Now that things are better, I'd like to take the commission."

She had been expecting this, but it made her feel sad. She loved having him at home, especially since the last four months had been so difficult. She was just getting back on an even keel, and now he was leaving again. But she knew his life was the sea, so she put on a brave face. "If that's what you want, then you should do it. I'll miss you, as always."

"I want you to come with me." He smiled as he watched her reaction.

"Come with you? You want me to come with you? Matthew, it's impossible!"

"Hear me out, Abigail. Your family business is doing better. I'm sure Alexander could handle it on his own. He could find a bookkeeper to take over your accounting work."

"Yes, that's true. If he's willing to do it, he's more than capable. But I don't know any Nantucket wife who has been to sea."

"You're right. None has sailed from Nantucket so far. You'd be the first. But other captains' wives from America have gone to sea and had a great experience. Remember the stories of Mary Hayden Russell from New Bedford? She was originally from Nantucket."

"I don't know, Matthew. I don't know how we can organize everything in just two weeks. What about the children?"

"We'll bring Thomas with us, and Sarah can stay here. She can either live with Eunice or stay with Elizabeth and Michael. Either would be happy to have her."

"But what about her wedding? We'll miss it if we're away."

"I'm sure we can ask them to wait to get married until we're home and, besides, who knows when Samuel will be back? My last voyage was only two years. We might even be back before him."

Abigail had a hundred more questions, but in her heart, she knew that sailing with him would be the right thing to do. "Yes! I'll go with you. I might regret it six months from now when I'm homesick for Nantucket, but I'll keep an open mind. It will definitely be an adventure!"

EIGHT MONTHS LATER, after a harrowing rounding of
Cape Horn, Abigail stepped onto the deck of the ship
and looked out at the endless ocean. There was nothing but
blue, blue, and blue in all directions. The sun was bright,
and she had to shield her eyes as she scanned the horizon.
She never knew that there could be so many shades of blue!
She sat in her chair on deck, feeling better than she had
for weeks. She knew from Matthew's stories that rounding
Cape Horn would be difficult, but it was much worse than
she had imagined; at times, the waves were taller than their
ship, and it was freezing cold, for weeks. The difficulty was
compounded by the fact that she was six months pregnant
and was nauseous most of the way. She didn't know if she
was seasick or experiencing morning sickness, but it didn't
matter; the end effect was the same. She was both thrilled
and worried about being pregnant. She had wanted nothing
more than to have another baby and now she was getting
her wish, but she hadn't expected to have it aboard ship!
Matthew promised her that they would go to Talcahuano,
Chile, for the birth, so this reassured her a little. As they
sailed toward the Tropic of Capricorn and the west coast of
South America, the weather and sailing conditions improved
immensely. When it was like this, she could completely
understand his enduring love for the sea.

Because of her sickness, Abigail had moments of highs
and lows while on the *Joseph Starbuck*, but Thomas was
thriving. There was no task too onerous for him, and he
tackled all of his chores with the enthusiasm of a puppy
wanting to please its master. Matthew, as well as the rest
of the crew, was very patient with him, especially in his first
months on board. While he was a very capable boy on land,

many of his tasks were quite a challenge on the rolling deck of a whaling ship and he made a lot of mistakes in the early days. He was growing up fast aboard ship—a little too fast for his mother—though she was consoled by the thought of the new baby.

ABIGAIL REMEMBERED THE first whale they killed on this trip, just off the Falkland Islands in the South Atlantic. She was happy that Matthew didn't capitulate when Thomas begged to go out in one of the whaleboats when the lookout, perched on the mast high above the ship's deck, spotted the first whale. She knew how dangerous it was to capture and kill a whale. A male sperm whale could be sixty feet long and weigh up to fifty tons. Often, once the whale had been harpooned and before it was killed, it panicked at being restrained, smashing the whaleboat with its powerful tail flukes or jaws. The crew would hang on to the wreckage until the ship reached them or, worse, would drown or be killed in the attack. It took a very experienced sailor to hunt these giants of the sea, and Abigail didn't want Thomas to be in harm's way. He might be big for his age, but he was still her twelve-year-old son. She knew he'd have to get in a whaleboat eventually, but she hoped it would not be for at least two years.

Once the whale was killed, the whaleboat towed it back to the ship where the crew started processing it. It was a stinky, messy business that usually took two to three days with the crew working around the clock to process the blubber, baleen, and ivory. Abigail avoided going on deck during this time though Thomas reveled at being in the thick of things. He would help the crew by carrying chunks of blubber from the cutting room to the tryworks where it was boiled down into oil. Matthew let Thomas climb into the case, a cavity in the head of the second whale they caught, to scoop out the spermaceti with buckets. Spermaceti was high-quality oil used to make clean-burning candles. This task usually fell to the smallest crewmember, and Thomas was the perfect fit. He was so excited to be doing a man's job and offered to do this for every whale they caught. Abigail shuddered at the idea of her son in the whale's skull, but she knew that he was perfectly safe, so she didn't say anything. She did, however, hold her nose when he came below deck to tell her about his adventure—the smell, combined with her nausea, proved a powerful experience, and not one she wanted to repeat.

WITH THE EXCEPTION of some of the smells, Abigail grew to like life aboard ship, once her nausea had passed. At first, she had trouble sleeping as there were so many unusual noises as compared to the ones at home. Every time she heard a large creak or crack, she would jerk awake, momentarily worried that the ship had hit something! The crew was very kind to her, and she found ways to make herself useful, helping with the laundry and the baking, both of which she enjoyed as they were familiar tasks and reminded her of home. She was enthralled with each port of call, no matter how basic—they were all exotic to her. She loved the sights and smells of each new place and tried to find some small souvenir that she could take home for Sarah. She wasn't as homesick as she thought she would be though she did miss Sarah and her mother very much. Like all other Nantucketers on the high seas, she loved the gams when they were lucky enough to encounter another Nantucket whaling ship, even though they might be exchanging news that was several months old. As soon as she saw a whaling ship on the horizon, she wrote letters for Sarah and Phebe with the hope that the ship was on its way back to Nantucket.

She also enjoyed observing Matthew in his element. She had had a general understanding of what a sea captain on a whaling ship did, but seeing him in action gave her a much deeper insight into his day-to-day life aboard ship. He was much more serious than he was at home—rightfully so—as he was responsible for the lives of the crew and the ship itself. After rounding Cape Horn, she knew that the ship and all aboard could easily be lost if the captain made a wrong decision. She felt that they had grown much closer in the last months and this, along with the baby, made her as happy as she had ever been in her life.

SEVERAL WEEKS LATER, Matthew and Abigail were sitting on deck one evening after sunset; they were about a two-day sail away from Talcahuano, Chile. It was a beautiful evening with a warm breeze from the southwest, and the ship was making good progress toward port. It was pleasant on deck as the tryworks were shut down; they had processed the last whale ten days ago. When they were boiling blubber, no one could be on deck except for the crew. The stench alone, never mind the fact that the deck was awash in blubber and blood, kept Abigail belowdecks, no matter how nauseous she was.

The night sky was dazzling, and Abigail was enthralled with all of the constellations in the Southern Hemisphere. Matthew was very knowledgeable about the night sky and would spend hours explaining it to her, along with rudimentary navigation. She was particularly interested in the astrolabe, which came from London and had been in Matthew's family for three generations. With her affinity for mathematics, she picked up navigational principles quite quickly and could understand why Sarah enjoyed it.

"I'll write a letter to Maria." She tilted her head back to

take in the expansive night sky. "She would absolutely love to be where I am right now. I know she's seen drawings of the constellations, but they don't begin to describe the beauty of the sky. It's breathtaking."

"It's the darkness. When you're so far out at sea, there's no other light, and this magnifies the light from the stars. It's like being wrapped in a blanket of diamonds."

"I didn't realize you were a poet!" She laughed and reached for her husband's hand in the dark. They normally didn't show any physical affection in front of the crew, but except for the man on watch and the second mate at the helm, the crew was belowdecks for the evening. She decided she could be a little daring.

Matthew squeezed her hand, giving her a little thrill in the pit of her stomach. Even after fifteen years, his touch could still make her heart skip a beat, corny as that sounded.

"Are you feeling better?"

"Yes, much better ever since we rounded the Cape. I was worried about the baby because I was so sick, but now I feel well, and she's kicking all the time, so I know that she's fine."

"Oh, you know it's a girl?" Matthew was amused at his wife's certainty about the sex of their child.

"Yes, I'm quite certain. When I was pregnant with Sarah, it was exactly the same: months of nausea followed by months of kicking in the womb. It was completely different with Thomas. You don't remember because you were away for most of both of my pregnancies."

Inadvertently, her matter-of-fact pronouncement made Matthew feel sad. He always regretted missing the birth of both of his children though she never held it against him. Most sea captain fathers on Nantucket were away for their children's births. One, Captain Owen Chase of the infamous *Essex*, was even away for his child's conception, which was quite the scandal at the time. It was probably the only divorce on Nantucket that had the full blessing of the entire community, religious beliefs be damned.

But Matthew knew that Abigail's comment was not intended unkindly, so he took it in stride. "I look forward to meeting our daughter. She will have quite the story to tell her friends when she gets older, being born in Chile!"

"Oh, Matthew, will she still be a native Nantucketer?"

He laughed. "Yes, Abigail, she will. But I guess she can always claim to be Chilean in the future if she is so inclined."

TWO WEEKS LATER, the *Joseph Starbuck* was anchored in the harbor of Talcahuano, and Abigail moved in with the American consul's family, the William Crosbys. Matthew split his time between the town and the ship, using the time in port to make repairs and to restock provisions. Abigail enjoyed the company of Mary Crosby, the consul's wife. While she loved being on the ship, she missed female companionship. She also felt comforted that when it came time to deliver, she wouldn't have only the ship's doctor to rely on. She didn't, however, like Talcahuano very much. The port and its surroundings were very dirty, and there was a lot of activity day and night—for her, it was a little overwhelming after the serenity of the months at sea. Still, she tried to make the best of it, knowing that they were staying only until the baby was born.

A WEEK LATER, after twenty-four hours of labor, Abigail's prediction came true: she gave birth to a beautiful, healthy baby girl. They named her Emily. Abigail and Matthew were over-the-moon happy. Thomas was not as impressed as his parents. For a twelve-year-old boy, girls— even his own sister—were not too interesting. With the exception of missing her mother, as many women do during childbirth, Abigail was certain this was the happiest time of her life. And it was, until she came down with a mysterious fever that took all of them by surprise as they thought the dangerous time of childbirth had passed.

For four days and nights, she was in and out of consciousness. When she was conscious, she was delirious, making absolutely no sense. Matthew was beside himself with worry as they didn't know if she would survive. He never left her side for one minute, willing himself to stay awake every moment he could. After four days, the lack of sleep was catching up with him. On the fourth night, he laid his head down on her bed for just a minute and immediately fell asleep. Several hours later, toward the early hours of dawn, he woke, startled by the hand softly stroking the back of his head. He jerked his head up and looked at Abigail, who was awake and looking at him.

"Abigail!" He was shocked to see her awake and embarrassed to be caught sleeping.

"Hush, Matthew, it's fine. I'm fine. Rather, I will be, once I get my strength back. Where's Emily? Is she well? Did she get sick?" Her voice came out in a whisper, but there was no disguising her concern for her newborn child.

"She's good. She's with Mary. They brought in a wet nurse from the village, and she's thriving! I think she's grown two inches already." He smiled at the thought of his tiny daughter.

"I want to see her."

"And you will, my darling, as soon as the doctor gives you the all clear. We don't know where your fever came from, and we don't want to risk Emily catching it."

Reassured, Abigail closed her eyes and drifted off to sleep. The dream she had been having for the last four days came back as soon as she fell asleep. In it, Abigail could see two people, a man and a woman. They looked like her and Matthew, but similar to her premonition from two years ago, they looked wrong to her. Their clothes, their hair, and their surroundings were all wrong. She didn't know where they were; she didn't recognize any of the surroundings. She could see a room that looked a lot like one in Matthew's cousin, George Starbuck's house, the East Brick on Main Street—but one side of it was all glass, and from the view, it appeared to be several hundred feet in the air. How was this possible? It was all very confusing.

In her dream, dream-Abigail and dream-Matthew were talking, but Abigail couldn't make out any words. They were sitting side by side and had a funny object in front of them, which had a glass window that seemed to light up and change colors. They would point to the window during their conversation. While she couldn't understand what they were saying, she could tell that they got along very well and seemed happy together. As she watched them, she felt as if she was being wrapped in a warm, soft blanket. She could feel her whole being sink into the comforting embrace of this magical blanket, which made her feel restored and alive. Her body, which had been ravaged by the after-birth pains and the fever, felt strong as she watched dream-Abigail and dream-Matthew. She tried to talk to them; she wanted to ask them so many questions! But in her dream state, they couldn't hear her. Each dream ended the same way: that, even though she couldn't hear their words, she could hear with her heart—dream-Matthew and dream-Abigail loved each other very much.

Several hours later, Abigail awoke to the sun streaming in her window and Mary sitting in the chair by her bed, reading.

"You're awake!" Mary smiled, clearly happy to see her patient conscious.

"Where's Matthew?" Abigail's voice was weak from days of not speaking.

"He's on his ship. Once we knew you were out of danger, we sent out him out of the house for a few hours. He's been out of his mind with worry! We thought going to the ship would be a good distraction for him. He'll be back by supper."

"Where's Emily? Can I see her?"

"Yes, the doctor said your fever is not contagious. I'll go get her. Do you want any tea? Are you hungry?"

"Yes, I'm starving!"

"I'll tell cook to bring you weak sweet tea and dry toast. Let's see if you can keep it down. We were so worried that you were getting very dehydrated because you couldn't even keep down water. I'll be right back."

Abigail lay back against the pillows, exhausted from even that small exchange. She thought about her dream and seeing dream-Matthew and dream-Abigail happy together and wondered if that helped her recovery. As she was very practical by nature, she didn't believe that dream people could save her life, but she was not completely skeptical—too much of it seemed too realistic to dismiss out of hand. She decided, this time, to keep her dream to herself for now even though she was certain it was another premonition. If the right time presented itself later, she would tell Matthew. For now, it was her happy secret. Besides, she had a new baby to take care of. And considering her weakened state, she was afraid that her recovery would take longer than a couple of days.

SIX MONTHS LATER, Abigail stood on the dock, Emily in her arms. Mary Crosby was by her side, tears in her eyes at the thought of their departure. She had grown to love them both. Once Matthew was one hundred percent certain that Abigail was out of danger, he and the crew went whale hunting while she recovered. Her worries were correct; it took her nearly five months to recover from her mysterious fever. She and Emily couldn't sail with Matthew, as a whaling ship was no place to get over a near-death experience. She was looking forward to getting back to the *Joseph Starbuck* and to Matthew and Thomas.

Matthew's six months of hunting whales without Abigail were very productive. By the time he sailed back into Talcahuano, he had 1,800 barrels of whale oil, 90 percent of his quota, and they had been away only seventeen months. With luck, they could get the remainder from the Pacific and be home within the next eighteen months. After collecting Abigail and Emily, they would set sail for the Sandwich Islands, and if needed, they would sail farther to Tahiti. Abigail was very curious to see Maui and the Sandwich Islands after hearing so much about them from 'Ailani and Anuenue. She had two trunks of gifts and letters for their families, whom she was looking forward to meeting.

Emily adapted to life on the ship as if she were a natural-born sailor. By the time she was a year old, she was trying to tie simple knots, which her brother patiently showed her. The crew doted on the blue-eyed blonde-haired little girl. One of them carved her a little wagon out of ivory, which she rode up and down the deck as if she were the Queen of England. Despite all of the attention, she remained an unspoiled, charming child. But she was definitely Daddy's girl. She would perch on his shoulder like a parrot, to Abigail's amusement. She would watch father and daughter do their daily inspections and wasn't one bit surprised when one of Emily's first words was "shipshape!" The fact that this came out as "thipthape!" charmed the crew even more. Abigail made her a little captain's cap, which she never took off, even at night. She never felt jealous that Emily preferred her father to her; she remembered how she adored her father as a little girl and understood. She knew that Emily loved her, as she did Phebe, but there was a very special bond between fathers and daughters, and she was glad for it. She always felt that Sarah had missed sharing this closeness with Matthew because he was gone most of her childhood.

IN DECEMBER 1848, they sailed into the harbor on Maui and, despite all the stories from 'Ailani and Anuenue, Abigail was not prepared for the spectacular beauty of the island. The flowers alone were enough to take her breath away! The next five days were a blur; everyone on the island seemed to be a relation of 'Ailani and Anuenue, and each family expected the Starbucks to have a celebration at their home. They were the guests of honor at banquets every night, and the foods were glorious, especially after the simple fare aboard the *Joseph Starbuck*. Each relative seemed determined to outdo the others. They feasted on exotic fruits, such as papayas and mangoes, and each night a pig was spit-roasted. By their sixth day in port, Abigail and fourteen-month-old Emily needed a break from the endless festivities.

"Matthew, I'd like to stay on the ship today with Emily."

Abigail and Matthew were eating breakfast. "We need a little break. Emily needs her rest."

"Of course, my darling. I'll explain that you and Emily need your rest for a few days. I know the chief and his family will understand. We'll sail in three days, so maybe just one more day of celebrating? Would that work?"

"Yes, Matthew, that would be perfect."

"Where's Emily?"

"She's still sleeping. She was very tired last night, so I thought I'd let her sleep a little longer this morning. Are you going on shore?"

"Yes, I'm leaving now. I should be back before sunset, but no need to wait supper for me."

Abigail said good-bye to Matthew and looked in on Emily. The girl was sound asleep, her favorite stuffed bunny clutched firmly in her left hand. Her blonde curls framed her face, and her cheeks were lightly flushed, which Abigail attributed to the heat in the stateroom. She cracked a window open a little wider to get more air circulating. She crept out of the stateroom and went up on deck. She knew she would hear Emily as soon as she woke as she always let out a screech like the first mate's return-to-ship whistle. She opened her book and was immediately lost in *King Lear*. After an hour, her mother's intuition told her something was very, very wrong. She jumped up and raced to the stateroom. Emily hadn't moved since the last time she checked her, and Abigail realized that she was unconscious, not just sleeping.

"Mr. Jones!" she shouted for the second mate. "Mr. Jones, hurry!"

Mr. Jones ran into the stateroom and saw Abigail's wild-eyed stare and the unconscious little girl in her arms. He bolted from the room and shouted instructions to an oarsman. "Get a starboard whaleboat ready to be lowered! We have to take Mrs. Starbuck and the child to shore right now!" The ship's doctor had gone ashore with Matthew to get supplies.

In minutes, the whaleboat was ready to launch. Mr. Jones placed Abigail and Emily in the boat as gently as if they were the finest pieces of china and lowered it, as quickly as he could, to the ocean thirty feet below. With three of the crew, he grabbed an oar, and they all rowed as if they were being chased by the devil himself. Fifteen minutes later, they were on shore. Mr. Jones leapt out of the boat and raced to the first person he saw, shouting for help. Within seconds, everyone was rushing to assist Abigail and Emily, who was still unconscious. They brought her to the chief's house and sent for the medicine man and the ship's doctor. Abigail was frantic. Where was Matthew? What should she do? She didn't even know what was wrong with Emily!

The chief's wife, Kale'a, took Emily from Abigail and laid her on the bed in the sleeping chamber and covered her with a light sheet. A servant brought a cool bowl of water, scented with ginger and hibiscus. Kale'a dipped a clean white cloth in the bowl and placed it on Emily's forehead. She was burning up, and the flush in her cheeks had blossomed to angry red blotches that covered her face, neck, and chest. Still unconscious, she started thrashing around, and Kale'a gently restrained her, afraid that she would hurt herself. Abigail let out a sob—she needed Matthew—where was he? Normally stoic, all of her composure was gone as she watched her daughter's condition deteriorate.

Seconds later, Matthew burst through the door of the chief's house. "Where's Emily?" he shouted; he was in full sea captain's mode. "I want to see my daughter!"

Mr. Jones had found him and told him what had happened

as they ran to the chief's house. Seeing the panic in Matthew's eyes, Abigail took a deep breath and regained some of her composure. Emily needed one parent to stay strong, and after seeing her husband, Abigail knew she would have to be that parent.

OVER THE NEXT eight hours, Emily's condition didn't change. The medicine man and the ship's doctor agreed on a course of treatment, which was to keep her as comfortable as they could, try to get her temperature down, and, if possible, keep fluids in her. She didn't get better, but they were glad to see she didn't get any worse. She didn't wake up, no matter how many times Matthew beseeched her to please wake up for Daddy. At midnight, Matthew told Abigail to get some rest; he would stay up with Emily during the night, and she could take over in the morning. She didn't want to leave her side, but he was insistent. Against her better instincts, she did as he asked; this was no time to argue with him, especially not in front of Kale'a. She didn't go far; Kale'a made a bed for her just outside the door of the sleeping chamber. Once she was alone, she broke down, crying silently into her pillow. She started negotiating with God, *Spare Emily and take me!* She desperately missed Phebe, knowing that her mother would understand her anguish and helplessness at this moment. She cried herself to sleep—the sheer exhaustion from the stress of the day was the only reason she could sleep at all at a time like this.

SHE WOKE JUST before dawn and saw Matthew standing in front of her, ghostly silent, his eyes clouded and unfocused. She jumped to her feet. "Is she better? Did she wake up? It's my turn to sit with her." He didn't respond; he just stood there as still and silent as a marble statue.

She moved to go around him and into the sleeping chamber, but he blocked her path. "Matthew, please move!" she shouted, so frustrated that he was blocking the path to her child!

He broke out of his stupor and grabbed her by the upper arms, holding onto her tightly. "She's gone."

She looked at him, unable to take in what he just said. He repeated it. "She's gone, Abigail. She died thirty minutes ago."

If he hadn't been holding her, she would have collapsed to the ground. Instead, she balled her hands into fists and starting striking his chest. "Get out of my way! I have to go to her! She needs her mother!" Abigail's cries were like daggers to Matthew's heart. He released her and stepped aside.

She staggered into the sleeping chamber and saw Emily, lying peacefully on the bed. Someone had combed her hair and washed her face and placed a spray of purple orchids in her hands, which were laid on her little chest as if in prayer. The angry red splotches on her cheeks had subsided, and she looked as if she were sleeping. She looked so beautiful. Abigail fell to her knees, sobbing, and took one of her daughter's tiny hands in her own, noticing that it was already getting cold. Until this moment, she had always thought that the pain of childbirth was the worst that she had ever experienced, but now she knew the truth; it wasn't even one one-thousandth of the pain of losing your child. She felt her chest tightening and the room beginning to spin. She could hear her breath coming in short bursts, but it was as if it were from far away. Mercifully, she fainted.

SIX MONTHS LATER, Abigail stood at the railing of the *Joseph Starbuck* as they approached Nantucket. The horror that was Emily's death was as fresh in her mind as if it were yesterday. She thought back to the last six months and wondered how she had even survived. If she was inconsolable, Matthew was lost; he was a shell of his former self. Despite the tragedy, duty called, and they had continued their voyage. They were able to get their whale oil quota quite quickly after leaving Maui and could sail straight home. She didn't think she could have stood it if they had to stay at sea for another year; the six months seemed interminable.

They packed the child in salt and placed her in a lead-lined coffin for the long journey home. Abigail had insisted that Emily was to be buried on Nantucket. She couldn't bear to leave her little girl on Maui even though 'Ailani and Anuenue's relatives had promised to look after her. For the remainder of the voyage, Matthew and Abigail hardly spoke to one another, and when they did, it was to keep up appearances with the crew. Thomas started spending more and more time with the crew as he found it too difficult to be around his parents. Everyone was painfully aware that Emily's coffin was part of the ship's cargo. The crew was also subdued; they missed Emily nearly as much as her parents did and they, too, were happy to be sailing straight home.

As THE *JOSEPH Starbuck* approached Old North Wharf, Abigail could see the townspeople standing there, silently, which was very unusual for an arriving ship. Normally, the wharf was bustling with noise and activity. She looked closer and saw that each one was wearing black, and many were carrying Bibles. She saw Phebe and Sarah whose faces was streaming with tears as were 'Ailani's and Anuenue's, who were by their side. Matthew finished giving docking instructions and came over to where Abigail was standing. He stood by her side, but he didn't touch her. She wished with her whole heart that she could hold his hand, but when she went to reach for it, something prevented her. Would she ever be able to forgive him for letting her sleep while her precious child died?

Quietly, every man on the crew disembarked, except for the first and second mates. They looked to Matthew, who nodded his head. They descended into the hold and came back on deck, carrying the tiny coffin between them. They proceeded down the gangplank where Phebe was waiting. She laid her hand on the coffin and whispered a silent prayer. Matthew, Abigail, and Thomas followed the coffin, and at the bottom of the gangplank Abigail collapsed into her mother's arms, unable to retain her composure one minute more. Phebe's eyes met Matthew's over Abigail's head, and she reached out a hand to touch her son-in-law's sleeve. He looked at her gratefully, thankful for the small gesture of consolation.

"I'll go with Emily to the church and meet with Pastor Williams," said Matthew to Phebe.

"He's expecting you, Matthew. I'll take Abigail home."

"Thank you, Phebe. I'll be there as soon as I can."

With this, Matthew and Thomas walked to the wagon where the mates had loaded Emily's coffin. As they proceeded up the wharf to Main Street, their neighbors and friends parted to clear a path, murmuring words of condolence and prayers. Matthew tried to acknowledge each one but found it was too hard. He took Thomas's hand, who for once didn't protest the public display of affection, and together they walked with Emily to the church.

THE NEXT TWO days went by in a blur. Phebe had organized as much of the funeral as she could, but Abigail and Matthew still had to make some decisions about the service, which they did. They were polite to each other, but Phebe could see that they were not relying on each other for comfort. This put a tremendous burden on Sarah and Thomas as they didn't know how to deal with their parents who were ghosts of their former selves. Phebe kept her thoughts to herself; she decided to get through the funeral before discussing it with Abigail. Like it or not, Abigail needed Matthew, and he needed her. Sadly, tragically, children died. But they had two beautiful children, and Sarah and Thomas needed their parents. They were sad too but felt unable to express their feelings to their parents who were so obviously suffering—what was the loss of a sister compared to the loss of a daughter? They told Phebe their feelings, and it broke her heart. It made her even more determined to speak to Abigail, and Matthew, if she had to, after the funeral.

THE WEATHER THE day of the funeral reflected their mood. It had rained all night, and the day dawned cold and raw. After the service, only the immediate family went to the cemetery. Their friends respected their privacy and let them have their last minutes with Emily alone.

Abigail looked at Matthew across the open gravesite as the tiny coffin was lowered into the ground. The pain in her eyes was magnified by the pain in his. They couldn't watch their darling Emily being committed to the earth. With Phebe by her side, clutching her arm to hold her upright, Abigail choked back a sob. She longed to reach out to Matthew, but she held back, hating her need for him and at the same time, wishing she could ease his pain and be comforted by him. The deep connection that they had achieved during the two years before Emily's death was a gossamer thread holding their marriage together. But like the threads of a spider's web, she knew a strong storm could easily break them. She wondered if Emily's death would be that storm. In that moment, watching the agony on the face of the man she loved, she resolved it would not be. She straightened her back and stood tall. She told herself that when they got home, she and Matthew would take a first step to putting Emily's death behind them, and be the parents that their living children deserved. It wouldn't be easy, and it would take a long time, but Abigail knew in her heart that they could survive this tragedy; the time of grieving in isolation was over. Phebe could sense the change in her daughter, whom she knew better than she knew herself. For the first time since getting the letter telling her about Emily's death, she smiled, a small sad smile, but a smile nonetheless.

OVER THE NEXT few months, Abigail and Matthew allowed themselves to have some happy moments in spite of feeling devastated about losing Emily. They still grieved, but they did so in private, together. This alone made the loss more bearable. They threw themselves into planning Sarah and Samuel's wedding, which was going to be on August 22. Samuel had arrived back on Nantucket two months after the Starbucks returned. As Abigail expected, Sarah was going to move into Elizabeth and Michael's house after the wedding. The house was definitely big enough, especially as Michael and Samuel were away for years at a time. Abigail was thrilled with this arrangement as was Matthew. Anuenue made Sarah's wedding dress, which was absolutely lovely and complimented her best features. On her wedding day, Sarah was radiant.

"Are you nervous, my darling?" Abigail secured the wreath of flowers to Sarah's hair. They were in Abigail and Matthew's bedroom, putting the finishing touches on Sarah's wedding outfit.

"No, Mother, I'm not."

"We love Samuel as one of our own. Both your father and I are very happy that you're marrying him."

"Thank you, Mother. This means a lot to both of us."

Impulsively, Abigail threw her arms around Sarah, nearly squeezing the breath out of her.

Startled, Sarah laughed. "What was that for?"

"I was just remembering the day I married your father. I couldn't wait for us to start our lives together. He was so handsome! He wore his first mate's uniform for the ceremony. He took my breath away!" She grew serious. "And even though we've had some hard times, I would marry him again. He is the love of my life."

Sarah blushed; she had never had such a conversation with her mother before. Her mother was normally pretty reticent about her feelings, especially about her father.

Abigail, seeing Sarah's blush, turned away from her and pretended to look for something to give her time to compose herself. The moment passed, and mother and daughter descended the stairs, each eagerly anticipating the day ahead and their lives to come.

8

Abby and Matt

*T*he wind was howling and rain pounded the windows of Abby's office. The sound was so loud, she wondered if it was hailing instead of just raining. *It just doesn't matter*, she thought, *my mood is way worse than anything the weather could throw at me.*

As she predicted, the situation between her and Peter Coffin significantly deteriorated after their run-in in July. He moved from veiled challenges to being an outright adversary, and she didn't have much leverage to change the situation. Advisory board members either voluntarily retired—which he was not about to do—or they died. On her dark days, she didn't think the latter was such a bad option.

She spent more time with the remaining advisory board members, assuming that this could help, and to a point, it did. But meeting after meeting, Peter threw his weight around, and two of the board members were fairly weak; they didn't agree with him, but they didn't oppose him either. She couldn't consistently count on the remaining four board members to vote her way. She was frustrated with the extra work she had to do to prove his challenges were wrong.

She had received some very good news this week: Star-Taker 2.0 was in the hunt for a multiyear multimillion dollar navy contract. She and Matt had traveled to the Pentagon in the first week of January to meet with the head of procurement for the navy. She was notified this week that they would be invited to bid on the contract to outfit the entire US fleet with StarTaker 2.0s. If they won it, both of their firms would be set for at least the next twenty years. Not only would they be supplying the hardware and software, they would also get a multiyear service and training contract. It looked very promising. The only roadblock was her advisory board. They had to approve her investment in a factory to build enough StarTaker 2.0 units as their existing manufacturing capacity was insufficient to meet the navy's demands. It was a catch-22 situation. To win the contract, they had to prove they had the capacity to deliver the StarTaker 2.0s; but if they didn't get the contract, they couldn't afford the new factory. She knew that they had to take the risk, but she wasn't sure she could convince the advisory board. Unfortunately, she had already used her CEO override for this financial year, so she had no choice but to get their approval.

"Hi, Matt. It's me," Abby called Matt on his cell. "Where are you? I thought you were coming to Boston today."

Matt looked out his office window at the fog blanketing the island. He had planned to fly to Boston that morning, but nothing was flying.

"Hi, Abby. I was coming this morning, but we're fogged in. The airport's closed."

"My advisory board meeting is in two days. I really need your help with the proposal for expanding our manufacturing footprint. As usual, I'm expecting a battle."

Matt could hear the frustration in her voice. He knew that she hated the situation with the advisory board, but as she was only thirty-three, she would have to put up with it for another seven years. He wasn't too thrilled with it either. It also affected Starbuck Enterprises, but he would never complain. Abby helped him a lot after the crash of Lehman Brothers. If she hadn't reached out to her customers and suppliers, he would have had to lay off nearly half of his workforce. Her introductions gave him new contracts that replaced the ones that were canceled on short notice and kept Starbuck Enterprises afloat. They were mostly short-term contracts, so he wasn't out of the woods yet, but it was something.

They chatted for a few more minutes and arranged the logistics for the next day. Matt would get to Boston as soon as he could. Until then, they would use the online collaboration tools they had to share and change documents so they could hit the ground running when he got to her office.

Abby was relieved that their relationship hadn't changed after their awkward dinner discussion during Christmas Stroll. She had worried that it would. Their first conversation afterward was a bit odd, but she attributed it to both of them being nervous. She needed Matt to stay on top of his game to bring StarTaker 2.0 to market by October, and it appeared that everything was going as well as could be expected if she could just get her advisory board in line.

PETER COFFIN HUNG up the phone. He had just received a call from the commercial real estate agent who was finding potential manufacturing properties for Gardner

& Sons. He had thought that Abby was going to propose expanding manufacturing capacity, but until this call, he wasn't certain. In the last few months, she was playing her cards close to her vest. As he hung up the phone, he smiled, thrilled to finally have the lever that would bring Gardner & Sons—and more importantly Abby—to their knees. How dare she go behind his back! He would teach her a lesson. He was the rightful heir to Gardner & Sons—Bill's premature death had scuttled his plans. Before Bill's death, his secret plan was to marry Abby; after all, Bill had treated him like a son, and Peter believed that he would have approved of their union. When the time was right, he intended to make her fall madly in love with him, and once they were married, he could take over as CEO of Gardner & Sons. She could stay home and raise his children as all women should do. A woman as a CEO of a multimillion dollar firm? It went against the natural order of things! He always thought Bill was misguided to name her as his heir-apparent. Couldn't he see that Peter was much more capable?

HE WASN'T SURE when, exactly, his brilliant plan had gone wrong. He had expected Abby to lean on him more after Bill's death, but she didn't. In fact, she started to avoid him and their big brother–little sister relationship evaporated. Around this time, she became much more involved with Edward Fanning, so maybe this had something to do with it. Peter never liked Edward. He thought Edward was typical old New England money, walking around as if he were entitled to everything he got. Nothing could be further from the truth, but Peter's view was so distorted that he saw only what he wanted to see.

In the year after Bill's death, he and Abby grew further apart. Instead of playing it smart, Peter took out his frustrations on her by challenging her decisions as CEO. He abandoned his plan to marry her and decided to destroy her instead. He knew how much her family's firm meant to her; he thought nearly destroying the business and forcing her to resign would be the best way to ruin her personally. He was aware that he was walking a tightrope. In destroying Abby, he had to be careful not to destroy Gardner & Sons, or there would be no business left for him to rescue. On one hand, he wasn't happy that it had deteriorated to this; he was attracted to Abby and spent many a happy moment fantasizing about getting her into bed, but destroying her was also a kick. He could live with this option too. He assumed that, with no other Gardner heir and with him as chairman of the advisory board, he was the logical candidate to inherit the CEO role once she failed.

LUCKILY, ABBY SUSPECTED nothing about Peter's dark plans. If she had, she might have found a way to follow through with her instinct in July to throw him out of the nineteenth-floor windows.

She was cautiously optimistic about the navy contract. They still had a long way to go—bidding for government work was not a speedy process—but she felt good about their chances. StarTaker had always been the market leader before, and StarTaker 2.0 was getting a lot of good buzz in the sailing community. They were on schedule and would have their first prototype ready by the end of April when they would begin six months of tests before it was launched in October.

Her most pressing issue was to find manufacturing capacity. They had a factory in Walpole, Massachusetts, but they needed double their current capacity, and their site couldn't be expanded. It was surrounded by residential properties, and it would take too long and cost too much to acquire the needed land even if the residents would sell their homes, which she doubted. Many of their employees lived in Walpole and some of their homes bordered Gardner & Sons' factory. She was hoping they could find something else within twenty-five miles of Walpole as she wanted to have her experienced manufacturing employees oversee the new construction. She heard from her realtor that there were several promising properties to view, which she and Matt would go see as soon as he could get to Boston for a few days.

AT NOON, MATT looked out his office window at the fog, which looked as if it had settled in for the day, like a piece of cotton batting wrapped around fine china. He kept his cell phone within easy reach; the Gardner & Sons' flight dispatcher was going to call him as soon as the plane left Logan. He was looking forward to getting to Boston. He was very excited about the navy contract, and it felt good to be jazzed about something. The last few months hadn't been too easy. He and Abby were able to put the Christmas Stroll conversation behind them, but his dreams hadn't stopped. He no longer had the same dream, however. Last night, he dreamt that they were on a whaling ship in the South Pacific. He could see her sitting on deck, intently reading a book. She looked glorious in the tropical climate! She wore her hair loosely tied at her neck, and it softly curled to her waist. Her dress was made out of lightweight linen, and it flowed around her, softly hugging her body when it was caught in the tropical breeze. If he wasn't mistaken, he thought she looked like she was pregnant. As he watched the fog swirl against his window, he knew that he definitely wouldn't be telling Abby about this dream. He smiled to himself. If this dream was true, then they had had an exciting life. His dreams no longer disturbed him. It was as if his telling Abby had given his psyche permission to just enjoy the show instead of being tortured by it. *Enough woolgathering for one morning*, he thought, *time to get back to work.* He opened the spreadsheet with the StarTaker 2.0 sales projections and went back to work.

TWO DAYS LATER, Abby and Matt walked into the boardroom at Gardner & Sons. Abby had asked for and gotten permission for Matt to attend the advisory board meeting, which was highly unusual. He understood that he didn't have a speaking role for the upcoming presentation and discussion, but he wanted to be in the room to support Abby. She was nervous. She knew she had three votes in her favor, but she wasn't sure she'd get the fourth.

Peter called the meeting to order and, dispensing with pleasantries, asked Abby to start her presentation immediately. Normally, the advisory board reviewed old business for the first thirty minutes, but Peter wanted to put Abby off her stride by changing the normal operating procedure. She had expected that he would have some trick up his sleeve, so this little stunt had no effect on her. Two hours later, she completed her presentation with its recommendation that Gardner & Sons invest in a new manufacturing site in order to win the navy contract. She proposed taking out a ten-year fifteen-million-dollar loan to finance the project and already had the commitment from Bank of America.

"Let me get this straight," said Peter as Abby finished speaking. "You went ahead and got the financing commitment without having our approval for the project?"

"Yes," said Abby, matter-of-factly, without elaborating further.

"In the future, I would appreciate it if you would follow the proper protocol, Abby. You should have gotten our approval for the project first before securing financing." Peter's tone was dismissive; he spoke to Abby as if he were speaking to a five-year-old child.

Matt sat up straighter in his seat, dying to jump in. Abby saw him move, met his eyes with hers, and nearly imperceptibly shook her head "no." She didn't need him to make the situation worse. At this point, she had gotten used to Peter's condescending behavior toward her.

"Let's vote." Peter surprised everyone with the abrupt change in the discussion. "All in favor of expanding Gardner & Sons's manufacturing capacity and taking on fifteen million in debt, raise your hand."

The vote was three in favor and three against. The board members who opposed the proposal were concerned about incurring such a large debt. Up until now, Gardner & Sons only had short-term financing to bridge cash flow shortfalls; it hadn't had multimillion dollar debt since her grandfather's days as CEO. Peter had not yet voted. Abby was struggling to keep her composure. She knew that Peter would vote no, and she wouldn't be able to override the vote until July when the new financial year started. By then, they would lose the navy contract. The bids were due on April 2.

"I vote yes, on one condition," Peter said, to shocked silence in the room. No one thought he would vote yes. "I will vote yes if, and only if, Gardner & Sons goes public and issues common stock to raise the fifteen million needed."

The three board members who had previously opposed the proposal changed their votes to yes with the amendment Peter proposed.

"No. Absolutely not." Abby struggled to control the fury

in her voice. "Gardner & Sons is my family business, and I will not take it public. Neither my father, nor my grandfather, ever wanted the company to go public, and I won't do it. I will not relinquish control of my family business to shareholders."

"In which case, my vote is no." Peter was happy to be forcing Abby into a corner; his Machiavellian plan was coming together nicely!

Mark Mullen, the longest-serving board member and the one Abby was closest to, jumped in. "Abby, don't dismiss the idea out of hand. Your family would retain the largest block of voting stock, and while there are a lot of disadvantages to being a public company, there are advantages as well. Issuing stock is a great way to raise capital, and if you ever wanted to significantly expand Gardner & Sons in the future, you'd most likely be forced to go down this path."

Abby was seething and, at the same time, unsure of how to proceed. If she refused to consider it, she wouldn't get the approval to go forward with her manufacturing proposal. But she was very, very concerned. She felt that Peter had an ulterior motive for taking Gardner & Sons public, but on the spot, she couldn't think clearly enough to make a decision. She looked at Matt. Now it was his turn to shake his head "no." She looked at the board members, trying to gauge where their loyalties lay. Unfortunately, except for Mark, she knew where they lay: in their pockets—if Gardner & Sons were to go public, each one of them would make a lot of money. She believed that only Mark had the company's best interests at heart.

"Ladies and gentlemen, I propose the following: considering the magnitude of your amendment to my proposal, I need a week to review the facts. I request that we meet again in one week, and I will either resubmit my proposal with your amendment or withdraw it."

Before anyone else could answer, Mark spoke for the group. "That sounds fair, Abby. Let's meet again a week from today, same time."

Peter scowled, unhappy that she had wiggled out of making an immediate decision. But he realized that pushing too hard for an answer right now would alienate the other board members, so he smiled like the Grinch and pretended to be pleased with the suggestion. He adjourned the meeting and, with the other board members, left the building. He got into his waiting Mercedes S500 and headed for his office. While he didn't get exactly what he wanted, he was pretty satisfied with the turn of events. Once Gardner & Sons went public, he would be in a much better position to control the company. He had already set up several offshore companies who would buy the stock on the first day of trading, each one buying a small percentage of the shares which, when combined, would be larger than the Gardner family holdings. It was never about money—his family was very wealthy—it was about status. His family's business was in convenience stores, waste management, and a chain of low-cost motels. They were hardly the businesses that befitted someone of his superior stature.

As soon as the advisory board members left, Caroline stuck her head into the boardroom. She saw Abby sitting at the head of the table, not saying anything. Matt had stood up and was collecting his papers. She guessed that it hadn't gone well.

"Would either of you like a coffee?" Caroline knew that Abby would tell her what had happened when she was ready.

"Do you have any of that great Starbucks coffee, Caroline?" Matt attempted to lighten the moment.

"I'll check, Matt. I don't think we got the shipment from your family's warehouse this week."

He laughed. He always enjoyed how Caroline could match his comments one-for-one. In fact, he was pretty sure that if they were keeping score, she'd be well ahead. Caroline stepped out to get the coffee.

Abby didn't say anything during this exchange, but she did smile. "Well, it's not a 'no.'" She was trying to look on the positive side.

"Abby, I know you said that you'd consider it, but I hope you only said that to buy us some more time. You can't possibly be serious about taking Gardner & Sons public!"

"Do you have fifteen million dollars in your back pocket, Matt? I sure don't."

"No, I don't have it today. But you heard the dissenting board members; their objection was to the debt, not to the proposal. If we eliminate the debt, you'll have your majority," Matt said, as if he might find fifteen million dollars on the sidewalk when he left the building.

Caroline came back to the boardroom with three mugs of coffee, half-and-half, a bottle of Maker's Mark bourbon, and three glasses.

"Now that's what I'm talking about!" said Matt, eyeing the Maker's Mark. "*This* is what I call Starbucks coffee!"

The three of them laughed. Abby told Caroline what had happened, and she immediately agreed with Matt—in no circumstances should they consider taking Gardner & Sons public. She told Abby that Bill had been approached several times to do exactly that, and he refused each time. He felt that the company was his family's legacy, not just in name, but also to give back to society by making things that could benefit mankind. Every time a lost sailor found his way because of StarTaker, Bill took it as a sign that the Gardners, in a small way, were contributing to the positive energy of the universe. Abby never knew that her father felt this way.

"Your father was more of a romantic than you realized. When he was young, he had such dreams about saving the world! Then, one thing led to another and before we knew it, life kind of caught up with us. Your grandfather retired and your father was committed to the business full time. He never regretted it, but he always had a soft spot in his heart for doing good."

"I guess that explains why he never wanted to expand Gardner & Sons' products beyond navigational aids. He always reinvested in StarTaker, which I think some people would have viewed as a risk—having all of your eggs in one basket," said Abby.

"He would love StarTaker 2.0," added Caroline. "You and Matt have to fight to protect it! If the company were to go public, I don't know what would happen to it."

"We will, Caroline," promised Matt fervently, getting caught up in the emotion of the moment. Whoever thought that business was only facts and figures never worked for something, and someone, they believed in.

"How about I take you two lovely ladies to dinner? I think we've earned a night out and tomorrow, well . . . I'm guessing it's 'noses to grindstones' for the next week."

Abby and Caroline agreed and promised to meet him at one of their favorite restaurants in the Back Bay, Post 390, at 7:00 p.m. He left the office to go check in at the Four Seasons, and Abby and Caroline followed closely behind, intending to go home before dinner. As they stepped onto Rowes Wharf, Abby ran full tilt into Edward, whom she hadn't seen since Thanksgiving.

"Edward!" Abby was startled to see him.

"Abby, Caroline, how nice to see you both. How are you?"

"We're well, Edward, lovely to see you too," said Caroline. "Abby, I have some errands to run. I'll meet you at the restaurant."

After Caroline left, it was a little awkward between Abby and Edward. They both started to talk at once, and then paused at the same time, only to both start talking again at the same time.

Laughing, Edward asked Abby, "Do you have time for a quick drink?"

"Sure, I'd like that."

They walked around the corner to the Alley Bar and found a table in the corner. They had often met there after work when they were dating and the bartender recognized them. For a moment, it made her a bit nostalgic, and sad, because she had had many wonderful times with him. They ordered their usual drinks.

"You look great, Edward." He did; he looked wonderful.

"I'm seeing someone," he blurted and blushed because this was the first thing out of his mouth.

"I'm really happy for you!"

"Her name is Lynda, and we met in December. She's a lawyer as well. She's an assistant district attorney here in Boston. She's my crime-fighting caped crusader." The warmth and affection in his voice came through clearly.

"Well, then, you'd better keep her. It's not easy to find a caped crusader." Abby smiled at him; seeing him happy made her feel happy, too.

"What about you, Abby? What's new with you? Are you dating anyone?"

"No, I'm not. To be honest, StarTaker 2.0 has been occupying my days and a lot of my weekends. It's been going very well, at least until today."

"What happened today?"

"We had an advisory board meeting, and it was awful. I think I got maneuvered into a corner by Peter."

"Tell me."

Abby was relieved to tell the story to Edward. He knew her so well, and he had lived through many of her earlier run-ins with Peter; he completely understood what she was facing with the latest challenge. It was a relief to be open and candid about the problems she was facing. Of course, she had the unwavering support of her mother and Matt, but she sometimes hesitated to show them how worried she was—she felt that, as the CEO, she should stay strong. Right or wrong, this was how she felt, and she wasn't going to change her personality anytime soon. Edward listened as Abby talked about the day and about the opportunity with the navy.

"Thank you, Edward. It was good of you to let me rabbit on about my worries. If Lynda ever decides to freelance as a caped crusader, let me know. I'm sure I could use the help." She felt a little embarrassed that she had been monopolizing the conversation and tried to steer it back to him.

"So let me see if I understood you correctly. If you had fifteen million dollars, you would get the approval you need from your advisory board, and you wouldn't have to take Gardner & Sons public?"

"Yes, I'm sure I would. But I don't have angel investors in my pocket, so—"

"Let me help you," Edward interrupted her.

She looked at him, confused. They never spoke about money when they were dating, but she was pretty sure he didn't have millions of dollars. "I don't understand."

"I have the money you need, and I would be happy to give it to you as a personal loan. You wouldn't have to declare it to your board. It would stay private between you and me."

"You have fifteen million dollars?" Abby was incredulous.

"To be honest, I have a lot more. My maternal grand-father left me considerable commercial and residential real estate holdings in downtown Boston, which I developed, and I have a sizeable income from them every year. I typically reinvest the money, but in the last three years, I've had no time to find suitable investments, so the money's just sitting in the bank."

"I couldn't take your money, even as a loan."

"Abby, I believe in you. I've always believed in you. I know StarTaker 2.0 will be a huge success. I can charge you an exorbitant interest rate if that eases your conscience." He was smiling as he offered to overcharge her on interest.

"Edward, I don't know what to say. It's incredibly generous, and I must admit, it's appealing."

"Just promise me that you'll videotape Peter's face when you tell him that the financing issue is off the table. You know that I like being a little vindictive on your behalf."

They finished their drinks and promised to speak again in the next couple of days. She insisted that he sleep on his offer; she wanted to be sure that he had no regrets in offering her such a large sum of money. She had never imagined that one day he would be her knight in shining armor, but remembering his kindness to her all the years that they had dated, she realized that she was lucky to have had him in her life. It seems that they would be staying connected after all.

ABBY WALKED INTO Post 390 and saw her mother and Matt sitting at a corner table, clearly engaged in a heated debate about something. He started speaking before she even sat down.

"Abby, tell your mother that she is *not* going to sell her

house to finance our project. Would you believe it? She's already called a realtor and set up an appointment for tomorrow!"

"Mother! Are you crazy?"

"No, I'm not. It's my house. I can do what I want with it. Besides, you know I've been talking about selling it for years."

"Yes, I know. Every winter when you get the oil bill, you swear you're selling. But come on, you've never been serious before."

"I'm serious now. The agent from Sotheby's is coming over tomorrow at 10:00 a.m."

"Thank you for making such a generous offer, but there's no need. I think I've found the money."

Caroline and Matt looked at Abby, astonished. Matt blurted, "What are you talking about? We've been apart for two hours. Where did you find fifteen million dollars in two hours?"

Caroline realized where the money was coming from and looked at Abby with a question in her eyes.

"Yes, Edward offered me a private loan. Who knew that he had so much money? I never did." While they were dating, Edward had a lovely two-bedroom apartment in the Carlton House and drove a nice car, an Audi Q7, but you'd never know he was a multimillionaire.

Matt jumped in. "Edward? When did you see him? Did you call him?"

"No. Mother and I bumped into him as we were leaving the office. We grabbed a quick drink." She turned to Caroline and added, "Oh, and he's dating an assistant district attorney named Lynda. He seems very happy."

For a moment, no one said anything. Caroline wanted

to ask Abby more about her drink with Edward but didn't want to do it in front of Matt. She would ask her when they got home later that evening. Matt, too, was a little confused and a little jealous—he wanted to be the person Abby could count on! It seemed odd to him that Edward would appear out of thin air and solve their most pressing problem in a matter of minutes.

Breaking the awkward silence, Caroline said, "In that case, now that we're not saving every penny, I'm upgrading my burger to a lobster roll!"

ONE WEEK LATER, the board reconvened. Abby opened the meeting by asking the formerly opposing board members that, if taking on fifteen million dollars in debt was off the table, would they vote yes to her original proposal? They agreed that they would. Peter sat through Abby's opening comments, feeling very smug. He didn't know why she was beating a dead horse and revisiting the question; but if it made it easier for her to accept that Gardner & Sons would have to go public to raise the funding, he'd let her carry on.

"In which case, ladies and gentlemen, thank you for your vote of confidence. The original proposal is approved. Any other business before we adjourn?"

"Wait just a minute!" said Peter. "Aren't you forgetting something?"

"No, I don't think I am. Oh, wait—are you talking about the fifteen million dollars that we'll use to finance the new manufacturing capacity?"

"Yes, you know that's exactly what I'm talking about. You don't have approval to proceed."

"But, Peter, I do. I have fifteen million dollars. I don't need financing." Abby enjoyed watching Peter's face turn bright red and was very sorry she couldn't videotape this moment for Edward.

"You borrowed the money without getting board approval? This is a very serious infraction, young lady!" Peter was nearly shouting. *Why*, thought Abby, *does he always refer to me as "young lady" when he is irritated?*

"Gardner & Sons didn't borrow the money, Peter. You can check with our chief financial officer. We have no new debt. And as long as the money is legally obtained, it's none of your business where it came from. Feel free to speak to Michael O'Malley. He'll confirm what I just told you."

Peter stood up and stormed out, clearly unhappy to be outmaneuvered by Abby. Mark Mullen broke the tension by congratulating her and was joined quickly by the rest of the advisory board members.

After the board members left, Abby told Caroline the good news and called Matt. He was on Nantucket working with the development team. While he would have loved to be there to see Peter's face when Abby gave him the news, they both agreed this would be a waste of time. As promised, she called Edward to tell him about Peter's reaction. They agreed to meet later in the week to sign the promissory note for the personal loan. For the first time in weeks, Abby felt a sense of optimism. Now, she could focus her efforts on preparing their bid for the navy; it was nice to get back to work and put the board politics behind her, at least for now.

PETER SPOKE TO Michael O'Malley and learned that the money was legitimately obtained. He stormed out of the building and waved off his driver, deciding to walk back to his office instead. He could not believe that Abby had outfoxed him! He was going to find out where she got the money; it was just too suspicious for him to accept that it was all on the up-and-up. Peter assumed that everyone, especially Abby, had it out for him. He didn't start out as a bad person, at least not when Bill was alive, but years of feeling "less than" with no strong person to guide him had made him very bitter and distorted his view of the world. He viewed everything through dark-colored glasses—especially where Abby was concerned. He also assumed, incorrectly, that her triumphing over him was jealous payback for his relationship with her father. There was one point, though, that he and Abby could agree upon: they couldn't continue in this manner. One of them had to go!

9

Abigail and Matthew

May 1850, Nantucket and the Pacific

Abigail waddled down Union Street on her way to the Atheneum. There was no other way to describe it; she was huge with this baby, and there were still two months to go. It was just starting to get warm, and the trees were budding. She loved the spring. It brought such happy anticipation, especially this year with the baby on its way. She was looking forward to seeing Maria and getting a new book. She had finished reading *Othello*, but it wasn't one of her favorites of Shakespeare's. She was in the mood for a comedy. It had been seventeen months since Emily had died, and Abigail was just starting to feel like her old self. After Emily's funeral, she told herself that she had to go on for Sarah's and Thomas's sakes, but it wasn't easy. She had many, many dark days. She had good friends on the island that had experienced the same terrible loss of a child, and they were a comfort to her. Matthew also struggled, but as a man, he had less opportunity to show his feelings. This is why, when he asked, she was happy for him to go to sea again. She knew this would help him heal as the baby would help her. She realized that the baby wasn't a replacement for Emily. Luckily, she wasn't as nauseous this time around; she was convinced it was a boy, which she told Matthew before he sailed—to his great amusement at his wife's unwavering certainty in predicting the sex of their child.

MATTHEW HAD BEEN gone for five months. He was the captain of the *President* again, one of his favorite whaling ships. At first, he didn't want to leave her because of her pregnancy, but she assured him that she would be fine. She had her mother and her friends, and Elizabeth and Sarah were right next door. As his last two voyages had been very successful commercially, they were optimistic that their luck had turned and that this voyage could be as short as two years. Thomas sailed with him, as did 'Ailani. With Sarah married and Thomas gone, Abigail was lonely at night in the big house by herself. Phebe offered that she could move home, but Abigail wanted to stay in her own house. In the end, they came up with an excellent solution: Anuenue and her firstborn child, a two-year-old boy named Matthew, moved into the house with Abigail to keep her company. They affectionately called him "Little Matthew" so as not to confuse the two. They were quite touched that 'Ailani and Anuenue had named their first child after Matthew. She loved having them; it was wonderful to have a baby in the house again, and she was very happy for her friends. She thought of Little Matthew as her "practice" grandchild; something she would never dare say to Sarah!

WHILE ABIGAIL WAS waddling to the Atheneum, Matthew stood on the deck of the *President*, 'Ailani by his side. They were just north of the Falkland Islands, and they had already killed three sperm whales; hunting had been good in the South Atlantic. It was a very auspicious start to the voyage. There was no way for them to know that it was going to turn horribly, horribly wrong.

"Are you excited to go home?" asked Matthew.

"Yes, Captain, I am. I can't believe that we've been away for seven years. But to be honest, Nantucket is home now." 'Ailani took in the vastness of the South Atlantic and remembered their voyage to Nantucket seven years before. To him, it seemed like a lifetime ago. He and Anuenue were so happy on Nantucket and with the birth of Little Matthew two years before; their lives were full. 'Ailani hoped to take his son to the Sandwich Islands one day; maybe Anuenue could also be convinced to sail with him, but if not, he knew that they would teach their son about his heritage in the best way that they could.

"When will we reach the Sandwich Islands?"

"With luck, about four months from now. It all depends on the Cape Horn rounding. I know of ships that had to turn back and reach the South Pacific by sailing east and rounding the Cape of Good Hope. Pray to God that doesn't happen to us, or it will add nearly a year to our journey."

"I will pray to God, Captain. Thank you for asking me."

Matthew winced. He had forgotten how deep 'Ailani's faith was and yet again, had inadvertently mentioned God casually. Since the death of Emily, Matthew's relationship with God was not very good. No matter how many times Pastor Williams tried to explain "God's will" to him, he couldn't accept it. He couldn't accept a God who could be so cruel to his beautiful Emily.

TWO MONTHS LATER, as she predicted, Abigail delivered a strong beautiful baby boy who looked just like Matthew. He had a lot of dark brown curly hair and his eyes

were a deep, deep blue. She hoped that they wouldn't change
as he got older as was sometimes the case. They had agreed
to name him Jonah. From birth, he was a very good-natured
baby. Little Matthew was mesmerized by his new little
"brother," and life was good again in the Starbuck household.
With Sarah, Anuenue, and Phebe as built-in babysitters,
it was easy for Abigail to continue working at Gardner &
Sons, which she loved. During her last months of pregnancy,
Alexander brought the accounting books to her house—her
climbing the stairs to the office made both Alexander and
Phebe very nervous—though Abigail assured them that she
was fine. They were worried that she would fall as her center
of gravity was so off! While she was at sea with Matthew
in 1846, Alexander had borrowed some money from his
brother-in-law's family and rebuilt the warehouse and office.
All of Gardner & Sons' captains had had very successful
voyages during this time, and he was able to repay the loan
within two years. She was happy, unaware that the second-
most-trying time of her life was about to begin.

MATTHEW WATCHED AS the crew dropped anchor in
the harbor of Maui as the sun set on the horizon.
It still amazed him how quickly the sun set in the tropics;
it went from light to dark in a matter of minutes. They
would wait until tomorrow to go ashore. It was four months
after his conversation with 'Ailani, and he conceded that his
prayers might have helped; it was the easiest Cape Horn
rounding that he had ever had. They had gotten eight more
whales and, as of today, were at 70 percent of their quota.
As he looked toward the lights of the buildings surrounding the harbor, he remembered, with sadness, the last time
he was here. He forced himself to think of happy memories
of Emily and not their traumatic last days. He thought of

Abigail and hoped that she and little Jonah were doing well. Even though he knew it was logistically impossible, he was hoping for some news of his family. He smiled, wondering if Jonah was actually a girl. Abigail refused to consider any girls' names before he left as she was completely certain that the baby was a boy.

THE NEXT DAY, 'Ailani was standing by the *President's* railing beginning at 6:00 a.m., ready to jump into the first boat going ashore. For all of his certainty that Nantucket was his home, now that he was within swimming distance of his family he nearly dove off the side of the ship and swam to shore. Instead, he decided to maintain some semblance of dignity and waited for Matthew. Matthew, knowing that 'Ailani would be anxious to get ashore, was ready to go by 6:30 a.m. The quay would normally be relatively quiet at this time of the morning. But news had gotten out that it was Captain Starbuck, so the quay was buzzing with activity. Since the tragedy with Emily, the islanders had embraced the Starbucks as their own, and they were excited to see Matthew. They had no idea that 'Ailani was with him.

In fifteen minutes, they were pulling alongside of the quay. The local people had seen 'Ailani in the boat as it approached, and a young boy raced to get the chief, Ewelani, and his wife, Kale'a, 'Ailani's parents. There were jubilant shouts all around as strong hands reached in and lifted 'Ailani off the boat before he even got a chance to stand up. The homecoming was everything 'Ailani hoped it would be and more. He had tears in his eyes as he embraced his parents. Yes, Nantucket might be home, but Maui would always be part of his heart.

The next few days were spent restocking the *President* and making repairs. Matthew relieved 'Ailani of his duties so he could spend all of his time with his family. On their last evening in port, Matthew dined with Ewelani and his family.

"Where will you sail from here?" asked Ewelani. 'Ailani and Kale'a were sitting off to the side, deep in conversation.

"Toward St. Mary's Island and the western coast of South America. I heard from Captain Veeder of the *Emotre* that the whaling is good there right now. I hope to get our quota and then sail directly back to Nantucket."

Ewelani lowered his voice; he didn't want 'Ailani and Kale'a to hear what he was about to say. "Be careful, Matthew. There are Spanish pirates in the area. They captured and killed the *New London's* captain and held the crew hostage for days."

"That's terrible! What happened?"

"After the captain was killed, the first mate led the escape and, together with the rest of the crew, overpowered the attackers who were aboard the ship. The wind was favorable, and they were able to outrace the attacking ship, the *Santa Theresa*. We haven't seen the *Santa Theresa* here, and she's not welcome, but I believe she's still out there."

"I will be very careful, Ewelani. Thank you for the warning. Do you know if they have cannons on board?"

"I believe that they do. Please don't say anything in front of Kale'a. I don't want her to worry."

Early the next morning, the *President* set sail. It was a glorious day; the wind was favorable, and there wasn't a cloud in the sky. 'Ailani stood on deck and watched his beloved island until it disappeared below the horizon. He promised God that he would come back with Anuenue and Little Matthew. It was important to him that his parents meet their grandson. After five days in port, having been relieved of his duties, he was anxious to get back to work. He felt a little guilty that his fellow crewmembers had to cover for him though none of them minded.

Heeding Ewelani's warning, Matthew had a quiet word with his first and second mates, Mr. Morse and Mr. Brock. They prepared as well as they could, moving the guns and ammunition from the strongbox in the hold into Matthew's cabin. He was very worried about the cannons. He thought he could outrace the *Santa Theresa*, but if she attacked with cannons, there was a good chance they'd sink the *President*. He told Mr. Morse and Mr. Brock to prepare the whaleboats as if they had to abandon ship, placing stores of water, salted cod, and hardtack into the after cuddy. He told them: if anyone asked what they were doing, they were to say that he was trying something new. He had heard that other captains were stocking the whaleboats for longer times at sea, separated from the ship. He knew that the more seasoned crew would not believe this, but they would respect his authority and not ask any questions. If he could, he wanted to keep the news of the pirate ship from Thomas as long as possible. There was little likelihood that they would cross paths with the *Santa Theresa*. He didn't want Thomas telling Abigail about pirates when they got home—or the both of them would be sheep farming for the rest of their days.

JUST BEFORE THEY left Maui, Matthew had heard that the whale hunting was excellent just north of the barrier reef surrounding the Sandwich Islands, so he decided to take a short detour before sailing southeast to St. Mary's.

Five days later, they reached the barrier reef northwest of the Sandwich Islands. The next morning dawned clear and bright with a strong wind from the southeast. He was hoping that they could get their remaining quota of whale oil and sail for home. They had been gone eight months and little Jonah would be two months old by now; he couldn't wait to see him.

"Captain!" shouted Mr. Brock. "Storm clouds on the western horizon!"

Matthew looked to the west and saw that, indeed, there were threatening black storm clouds on the distant horizon. While tropical storms were common at this latitude, these were not those types of clouds. It looked like a large storm was heading straight for them.

"Prepare for rough weather, Mr. Brock. Shorten the sails and prepare to turn away from the wind. I want to cover more distance today." He knew that the *President* could handle herself in rough weather; she had many times before under his command. She was small for a whaling ship, 293 tons, which made her fast and very easy to maneuver. Still, it was better to be prepared. Who knew how long the storm could last?

The crew efficiently battened down the ship and secured the whaleboats. Luckily, the tryworks were cold—dealing with hot coals on a rolling ship in high seas was not very easy. There was nothing left to do but wait. Most of the crew was on deck, except for the cook, who thought he'd better prepare a meal while he still could. The storm was approaching fast, and the dance of the clouds across the growing waves mesmerized the crew, which is why they didn't see the *Santa Theresa* until she was nearly upon them, cannons blazing!

"Captain!" shouted Mr. Morse, "Pirate gun boat off port side! They're firing at us!"

Matthew spun around and saw the *Santa Theresa* bearing down on them. He shouted to Mr. Morse, who had already taken the wheel from the second mate and was taking evasive maneuvers. "Sail her northeast! We have to outrun her! Mr. Brock, get the arms for the crew!" He knew that muskets couldn't beat cannons, but he also knew that the crew would feel less vulnerable with guns in their hands.

Luckily, the increasing winds were in their favor, and they were quickly able to put enough distance between them and the *Santa Theresa* to be out of cannon range, for now. Matthew was not sure how long he could keep her at bay. His heart was pounding; he was a very experienced captain and had sailed under all kinds of conditions since he was twelve years old, but he had never been under cannon attack before.

"Thomas," he shouted over the winds, "come here!"

Thomas ran to his father's side. Matthew could see that the boy was afraid although he was trying to show a brave face.

"Don't worry, son. We're much lighter than her, and we can outrun her. I want you to stay by my side."

"Aye, aye, Captain!" said Thomas in his bravest voice.

The winds had reached gale force. The storm, which had appeared to be a long way off only a few minutes before, descended on them in all its fury. Matthew searched the horizon in all directions, but he couldn't see the *Santa Theresa* anywhere. He felt a small flicker of hope, which was short-lived as a forty-foot wave crashed over the deck, knocking half the crew off their feet; if they hadn't been experienced sailors, some of them would have gone overboard. The next wave hit the *President* broadside! She heeled over on her starboard side, the masts with their yards dipping toward the rolling ocean, dangerously close to broaching. Luckily, she recovered just in time. The crew raced to take down the sails. For the next thirty minutes, it was all hands on deck to secure the ship as she rolled and pitched like a rubber ball between two big cats. Matthew knew that even if the *Santa Theresa* was right behind them, she wasn't a danger. They were both fighting for survival in the worst storm he had ever seen. The waves seemed to come from several directions at once, making it impossible for Mr. Morse to hold her so that she faced directly into the wave. They bounced to and fro, losing all sense of direction. The sky was as dark as night, and the crew was afraid—no man on the *President* had ever experienced a storm like this one. The noise from the wind and waves was deafening; Matthew had to shout directly into Mr. Morse's ear to be heard, which is why they didn't hear the collision between the *President* and the barrier reef. As she struck the reef, propelled by the full force of the storm, the ship shuddered as if it had been blasted by twenty cannons. Matthew grabbed for Thomas as he was thrown against the aft companionway. He looked around, expecting to see the *Santa Theresa* even though he knew it was impossible—no captain could hit a target with cannons in these seas. Then, it struck him—they must have hit the barrier reef north of the Sandwich Islands! Amazingly, the *President* came to nearly a complete stop—she was stuck hard and fast on the reef. Matthew got to his feet and ran two decks below where his worst fears came true; the ship had a gaping hole in her starboard side the size of a sperm whale, and she was taking on water. It was already up to his knees!

He raced back up to the main deck and shouted, "Prepare to abandon ship!" The crew looked at him incredulously—in this storm? He wanted them to abandon ship in the worst

storm they had ever seen? Just as they collectively hesitated—about to object—the *President* shuddered and rolled
jerkily to her starboard side. They were taking on water
faster than Matthew had expected.

"All men to the whaleboats! Now!"

He ran back down to his cabin and grabbed the astrolabe,
his captain's log, his maps, and his pistol. When he came back
on deck, the men were launching two of the three starboard
whaleboats. The three port whaleboats were going to be a
problem; they were swinging over the deck and not over the
rolling ocean. Mr. Brock solved the problem. Together with
the harpooner and six of the crew, they cut the ropes to the
port whaleboats and were able to lower them to the deck.
From there, they lifted them over the railing and dropped
them into the violent sea below. There was no time to waste;
the men had to jump in and swim to them, as impossible as
that sounded. It was a terrible solution, but the *President's*
crew wouldn't all fit in three whaleboats. They had to risk
the jump; they needed all six whaleboats if they were all to
survive.

Matthew, Thomas, 'Ailani, and Mr. Morse left in the last
starboard whaleboat, together with four other crewmembers, including the cook. Matthew had wanted Thomas to go
in the first one, but he wouldn't obey him. If they survived
this, he was going to give him a good talking-to!

Amazingly, all six whaleboats stayed afloat, and everyone
made it to one of them; they were all safe. They rowed sev-
enty-five yards away from the ship. Matthew was afraid that,
when she finally sunk, she might take them down with her.
They watched, silently, as the violent sea pounded the ship.
She was now completely submerged along her starboard
side—only the railing of the port side was visible through
the sea spray. Five minutes later, she was gone. Everyone sat

in stunned silence. They were in the middle of the Pacific Ocean, hundreds of miles from the nearest land, and their ship was gone.

As soon as she sunk, the crew of the shipwrecked *President* got a small mercy; the storm also abated. The six whaleboats rowed to within shouting distance of one another. Matthew did a roll call, relieved that everyone was alive and uninjured. They used a one-hundred-foot length of rope to tie the whaleboats together.

"Get some sleep, men!" Matthew shouted. "We'll chart our course in the morning." Matthew saw 'Ailani and Thomas huddled together in the stern of the whaleboat, and he carefully made his way over to them, murmuring encouragement to each crewmember as he passed.

"What happens now, Father?"

"It'll be fine, Thomas. We're not the first ship to shipwreck. Many of our Nantucket brethren have survived worst trials than this one. I have my astrolabe and my maps. We'll find the nearest land and head for there. Now, get some sleep. You'll need your strength for rowing."

Matthew met 'Ailani's worried eyes over Thomas's head. He gave him a reassuring nod and lay down, pretending to sleep. He thanked God for sparing Thomas; he didn't know what he would have done if he had lost him and, surprising even himself, fell asleep.

THE NEXT DAY dawned clear and bright with no evidence of the violent storm of the day before, except for the six whaleboats loosely tethered together in the middle of the Pacific. Matthew's forethought was more than fortuitous; they had enough hardtack, salted cod, and water to last at least one month. He was sure that they would reach land before their supplies ran out. After all, they were only a five days' sail from the Sandwich Islands when the storm struck. While it was hardly desirable, whaleboat crews could row seven to eight miles a day, even in rough seas. According to his calculations, they were about twenty-one days away from the nearest land. He wasn't as worried about food as he was about water; it would be hard to row long distances on rationed amounts of water.

Matthew, together with Mr. Morse and Mr. Brock, plotted their course and set up a schedule for which boat should take the lead, setting the pace, and which ones should follow. They couldn't stay tied together—it was impossible to row like this—but they didn't want to get separated. His other worry, besides the potential shortage of water, was that the *Santa Theresa* would find them. He didn't want them to go from being shipwrecked to being prisoners! He decided to ignore this problem for now; there was nothing he could do about it. With the sun blazing overhead, the six boats set out with Matthew's taking the first lead. The crew was in good spirits—his plan made sense to them, and they were happy to be underway. Every stroke of the oar brought them closer to land.

By THE THIRD week, things had deteriorated alarmingly. They had had two weeks of overcast night skies, which made it impossible for Matthew to take their position using the astrolabe. He had to calculate their location using dead reckoning, which was always a last resort for sailors, especially ones trying to find an island in the vast Pacific Ocean. There were occasional squalls, during which it was very difficult for the six whaleboats to stay together. The squalls at least brought fresh water, and as he feared, water was the problem. To row at full strength all day long, the men needed at least two gallons of water a day; this was impossible. They were surviving on two cups of water a day, which made their progress much slower. Four of the crew were very weak; the blazing sun and the salt water were torturing everyone's skin, covering it in boils and open sores. Only Thomas seemed immune. Yes, he was sunburned, but with the resiliency of youth, he didn't suffer as badly as most of the others. He also was in surprisingly good spirits. Perhaps it was because he had so little sea experience; he had no idea of how bad things could get, but Matthew attributed it to his nature. Thomas had been a happy-go-lucky person since birth.

THE NEXT NIGHT, three of the crew died during the night. This was a turning point for the crew of the *President* as they each knew this could happen to them. They had no choice but to keep rowing, and they did, but the deaths of their shipmates broke the spirit in many of them. There was an air of hopelessness that hadn't existed before. That night, two of the boats disappeared. Matthew never knew if it was an accident or deliberate. The remaining four boats stayed in the area for a day where they last saw their shipmates, but they couldn't stay longer; they were dangerously close to running out of all supplies, not just water. It hadn't rained for a week, and try as they might, they had no luck catching fish. They were in an area of the Pacific that is notoriously devoid of all living things. He watched his remaining crew get weaker with each passing day, but there was nothing to do but keep rowing. He was most concerned about 'Ailani whose condition had worsened in the last two days. Matthew suspected that he was giving his water and hardtack to Thomas, but he didn't ask him. He couldn't dishonor his friend's selfless gesture; he knew that if he wasn't the captain, and responsible for everyone, he would do exactly the same.

TWO WEEKS LATER, five weeks after the shipwreck, Matthew looked up at the crystal-clear night sky. There was still no land in sight—somewhere in the first two weeks he must have made a miscalculation, and now they might be way off course. He would try to take a reading tonight, but he was so tired, and it was so hard to concentrate to do the three hours of calculations it took to get a position with the astrolabe.

It was hardest to keep his spirits up at night. He remembered the nights aboard the *Joseph Starbuck* when Abigail was with him, and the thought of never seeing her again brought him to tears. At least, under the cover of darkness, the others wouldn't see him cry. He didn't know how much longer they could survive. 'Ailani was in terrible shape; he was very weak and no longer able to stand. Of all them, Thomas was the fittest, and if Matthew was honest with himself, the better leader. He kept everyone's spirits high during the day, looking on this disaster as if it were a normal rite of passage for a seagoing lad. But it wasn't a rite of passage; it was Matthew's worst nightmare. His only consolation was that neither Thomas nor 'Ailani knew what might lie ahead. If they didn't catch some fish or get some rain in the next two days, they would be forced to draw lots to determine which one of them they would have to kill and eat so that the others could survive. Matthew regretted burying his three crewmembers at sea, but three weeks ago, they expected to reach land within the week.

Cannibalism and drawing lots was an accepted practice when lost at sea. In 1820, Captain Pollard of the *Essex* had no choice but to draw lots after his ship was sunk by a rogue whale. What made it even more tragic was that the boy who drew the short straw was his cousin, Owen Coffin. Captain Pollard and his crew were adrift at sea for more than three months before some of them were rescued; of the original twenty-three crew, only eight survived. Eating Owen saved their lives. Although Captain Pollard was exonerated when he returned to Nantucket—except by his aunt, Owen's mother—he suffered knowing that he had committed incest cannibalism.

The other crewmembers knew that they might have to resort to cannibalism, and they avoided Matthew's eyes during the day; they couldn't imagine what would happen if either Thomas or 'Ailani drew the short straw. In the darkness, Matthew's breath caught in his chest. *Please God,* he thought, *if it has to be someone, let it be me!* He made a deal with the God that he hardly believed in—that if they all survived this, he would never go to sea again. He fell into a troubled sleep, dreading the coming dawn.

BY MAY 1851, Matthew had been away for seventeen months. One morning, Abigail was sitting in the kitchen, playing with ten-month-old baby Jonah when there was a knock on her back door. She looked up and saw her brother, Alexander.

"Come in!" She wondered why he knocked; he never knocked.

"Abigail, I have some news. The *Rose* sailed into port today."

"Oh, yes? Great! Did they have a successful voyage? Do you have a letter for me from Matthew? I know not to expect one from Thomas. He dislikes writing letters nearly as much as studying the Bible. I wonder—" As she often did, Abigail asked many questions at once, not giving her conversation partner a chance to jump in.

"Abigail!" Alexander raised his voice, interrupting her before she could go on.

She finally saw the look in his eyes and cold, dark terror clutched at her heart.

"What's wrong?" She tried to keep the panic out of her voice so she wouldn't scare the baby.

She instinctively pulled Jonah to her chest, who squealed with joy, thinking they were playing a game.

"Alexander?" Her tone was pleading.

At that moment, Phebe appeared at the back door and hurried into the house.

"It's Matthew. I have bad news. He's lost at sea." Alexander stood in front of his sister, taking both of her hands in his as his mother took Jonah from her arms.

"How do you know this? He could be anywhere! Maybe he went to the Kamchatka Peninsula!" Abigail was frantic.

"Two whaleboats from the *President* were rescued by Captain Smith of the *Omega* about two hundred miles from the Sandwich Islands. Captain Smith returned immediately to Maui as the men were in bad shape. The *President* sank in a terrible storm four weeks before. The six whaleboats stayed together as long as they could, but they got separated. The rescued men were in no shape to sail, so Captain Smith sent a letter back with Captain Coleman on the *Rose*. That's how we know what happened."

Phebe started to cry, scaring Jonah, who joined in, wailing at the top of his lungs. Abigail took her little boy back from her mother, hugging him so tightly that his wails got even louder.

"What about Thomas and 'Ailani?" Abigail asked with a sob in her voice.

"They're both lost too. I think they're probably with Matthew. I can't imagine that they'd be in separate boats."

At that moment, Anuenue walked into the kitchen and saw the dramatic scene unfolding before her.

"Please, Mr. Gardner, tell me what's happened!" Anuenue stood there, her back ramrod straight as if she were bracing for a physical blow.

"I'm sorry, Anuenue. The *President* has shipwrecked, and all we know is that Matthew, 'Ailani, Thomas, and twenty-four crewmembers are still missing. They rescued twenty-one of them, so there's still hope."

Phebe asked, "What happens now? What do we do? We must be able to do something!"

"We wait, Mother. Unfortunately, that's all we can do." Alexander would have given his right arm to have a better answer for his sister and mother.

Abigail leapt up. "I'm going to the wharf! Where's the *Rose* docked? I need to see Captain Coleman right away! Mother, can you watch Jonah?"

"Wait, Abigail, stop!" Alexander grabbed her upper right arm as she tried to go by him. "He can't tell you any more. I've told you everything! You need to tell Sarah. She needs to hear this from you."

Abigail collapsed into Matthew's chair by the fire and covered her face with her hands. Sarah! She had completely forgotten about Sarah. How could she tell her darling daughter that her father and brother were missing? And poor Jonah! He might never meet his father. She felt the room start to spin and, using all of her strength, grabbed a hold of the arms of the chair to stay conscious. Not this time! She was not going to faint this time! She was weak when Emily died, but now—now she was going to be strong. Matthew and Thomas were coming back to her; she knew it

in her heart. She'd know if Matthew was dead, and since she
didn't know that he *was* dead, by deduction, he had to still
be alive. He was alive and coming back to her; she was not
losing him to the sea. She sat up, squared her shoulders, and
decided to be the wife and mother her family deserved: brave,
strong, and optimistic—it wouldn't be easy, but she consoled
herself with the fact that whatever Matthew and Thomas
were facing was much harder. For her husband and her son,
she could be brave. She stood up, took Jonah in her arms, said
good-bye to Phebe and Alexander, and left the house. She
went across the backyard to tell Sarah.

10

Abby and Matt

April 2009, Boston and Nantucket

att stood on Straight Wharf at 7:00 a.m. and watched the yachts and sailboats coming and going in the harbor. It had been an unusually warm April. Boat owners took advantage of the good weather to put their boats in the water earlier this year. He had bought a forty-seven-foot sailboat four years ago, the *Patience*, and she was docked at Straight Wharf. He loved the *Patience*, but he was afraid she'd spend more time at dock than she would on the open water this summer.

They had completed the StarTaker 2.0 prototype three weeks ahead of schedule, which was a big milestone for the team. Everyone was very proud of this accomplishment. It was also a great sign of confidence for the navy; they were overdelivering on their promises—surely, that had to count in their favor? He had one of the prototypes in his hand; he was taking it to the *Patience*. StarTaker 2.0 would be tested by the team as part of its development cycle, but he also wanted to test it on his own. It was a sophisticated piece of equipment; you needed to be an experienced sailor with an expert understanding of navigational principles to use it. No sailors should be out in the open ocean, in the conditions StarTaker 2.0 was designed for, unless they were very experienced sailors and strong navigators.

He boarded the *Patience* and went below. As always, everything was shipshape. He was fastidious in keeping his sailboat ready to sail at a moment's notice. He puttered around inside for about fifteen minutes and then went up on deck, StarTaker 2.0 in hand. The device was elegant; there was no better single word to describe it. He liked the physical design of it; it felt good in his hands. If he could find the time, he hoped to try it out in the next couple of weeks. He put it in the cabin, locked the cabin door, and headed back to his office.

IN BOSTON, ABBY wasn't having such an easy start to her day. As she did most days lately, she reached the office by 7:00 a.m. The weather was beautiful, unusually warm for April, but she hardly noticed. She was worried about an email that she had received late last night from the deputy assistant secretary of the navy, Mr. Royer, who was the head of procurement. It appeared that the navy wanted to solicit a second round of bids. One of the three bidders had dropped out, leaving only Gardner & Sons and one other firm, and this didn't comply with the navy's procurement policy.

Abby and Matt had thought that they would have an answer by May 15. She still believed that they had the best chance of winning the bid, but now they wouldn't have an answer from the navy until August at the earliest. They had started construction on the new manufacturing site in Danvers, Massachusetts; it was an old Sylvania lightbulb factory and perfect for their needs, but they were quickly burning through the fifteen million dollars she had borrowed from Edward. She knew it was a risk to start construction before the navy contract was won, but she had no choice. She had had the timing carefully planned; the navy contract would have been awarded on May 15, and the next phase of construction that required a large amount of capital would begin on June 1. They could spend the money knowing they had the navy contract in the bag. But now, she would be in much riskier position.

Her original plan was that if they lost the contract, she would halt construction on the new manufacturing site on May 18 until StarTaker 2.0 launched in the market in October. She would resume fitting out the new factory based on demand from the general public, which she anticipated would be much lower than if they had the navy contract. If she had to do this, she would incur some penalties, but it would be much worse if she continued to spend money without a matching income stream. Her father had always taught her to take calculated risks, and her plan B was a sound one. She knew that Edward would not push her to repay the money, but she didn't want to take advantage of their relationship. She felt guilty enough as it was. But now that the bid was delayed, she was taking a much larger risk. For the umpteenth time since her father died, she wished that she could speak to him. Her cell phone rang; it was Matt.

"Yes, Matt. What do you need?" She was abrupt and unusually curt with him and regretted it immediately.

"Yikes! No coffee yet, I guess."

"Sorry. I'm in a foul mood. We got bad news last night. I was just about to call you."

"Didn't we get the navy contract?" Matt asked, immediately concerned.

"No, that's not it. They're asking for more bids, so we won't have an answer until August 14. I got an email late last night from Mr. Royer."

"Isn't he happy with our bid?"

"For a contract of this size, they are mandated by law to have at least three bidders. There were only two when the bid closed last night."

"So what happens now?" Abby's firm had the lead on the bid process.

"Actually, nothing happens now. That's the problem. We have to decide if we should continue our construction project or if we should put it immediately on hold."

"We can't put it on hold until after the navy decides, can we? Don't we have to demonstrate that we have the capacity ready to go?"

"Yes, we do. But I also have to consider what's best for Gardner & Sons in the long term. If we don't get the navy contract, by August I will have spent twelve of Edward's fifteen million dollars with no income in sight."

"Don't you think StarTaker 2.0 will be a success?"

Abby had one nerve left, and Matt was jumping all over it. She took a deep breath, not wanting to bite his head off twice in ten minutes. "Yes, I'm sure it will be a success. The only question is when. I don't need double today's production capacity by October if we only grow 5 to 10 percent a year, which is the likely scenario for the private sector market."

He understood her point, and he didn't want to push her, but he felt that she was being overly negative. "Is there something else going on?"

"I have an advisory board meeting today."

"That explains your good mood." He was hoping to get a laugh out of her. "You're always happy on the days you see Peter. It's a wonder you don't invite him to drop by more often."

"Meh," said Abby, conceding a small smile. She wasn't ready to be cajoled out of her crabby mood just yet. "Look, I've got to go. If you don't need anything right now, I'll talk to you tomorrow."

They hung up. Matt had called her to tell her that he was going to take StarTaker 2.0 on a test drive, but in light of their discussion, he decided it could wait.

OVER THE NEXT four weeks, it was business as usual. The advisory board meeting went as well it could with Peter openly gloating at the setback though he couldn't take any action because of it. Abby knew it was just another piece of ammunition that he was storing up, like a squirrel with its nuts. Matt was able to get in a couple of night sails in the harbor with StarTaker 2.0 and he found that it worked exactly as they had planned. Now, it was just a question of waiting for the navy's response. After a long discussion with Caroline and Matt, Abby decided to continue the construction project—yes, she was nervous—but as Matt rightly pointed out, she was confident about StarTaker 2.0's potential.

SHE FLEW TO Nantucket early one May morning. April's warm weather continued into May; it felt like a July day when she stepped off the plane. Matt picked her up, and they went straight to the office where they spent the day in project reviews with the team and Dr. Eva. They finished at 5:00 p.m., and Matt asked Abby if she'd like to grab a drink at the Rope Walk before flying back to Boston. She agreed and they headed into town.

"Do you want to see my sailboat?" he asked as they were walking to the restaurant.

"Where is it?"

"I keep her on Straight Wharf. It's one of the few luxuries I allow myself. We've had the slip in our family for three generations, and I don't want to give it up."

"Sure." Abby was enjoying the sea breeze coming off the harbor.

Removing their shoes, they stepped onto the deck of the *Patience*. The beautiful forty-seven-foot sailboat had been lovingly restored, with teak decks and dazzling brass and mahogany trim.

"I can see why you love her. She's gorgeous. Why did you name her the *Patience*?"

Matt laughed. "So I could tell everyone that I finally had some patience."

She snorted a most unladylike snort, which he graciously ignored and changed the subject.

"We can have a drink here, if you like. I'm sure I have a bottle of wine in the fridge."

"That would be nice. C'mon, I'll help you." They went below, and Matt took a bottle of Sancerre out of the refrigerator. She saw the StarTaker 2.0 sitting on the table and picked it up. She, too, thought it felt nice in her hands. While she was an expert in math and navigational principles, she had only limited sailing experience. She could imagine that a true sailor would like using StarTaker 2.0.

They sat on the deck and watched the activity on the other boats docked near the *Patience*. "Have you tried StarTaker 2.0?"

"Twice. It works great. I could compare the calculation in real time with GPS, and it was 100 percent accurate. In fact, I'm sure it was more precise than GPS."

"What were the conditions?"

"Light winds and a cloudless sky. I had a full view of the night sky so I was able to take an accurate reading."

"That's great. Have you told the team?"

"Yes. They make me fill out detailed testing sheets each time I use it."

Abby laughed. She could see from the look on his face that he was not a fan of being a test rat.

"I'm actually thinking of testing it on a much longer sail."

"Oh?"

"There's an unofficial race next week from Nantucket to Bermuda." He tried to appear nonchalant. "I was thinking of going. I'd be gone for eight to ten days."

Abby looked surprised; even with the delay from the navy, there was still a lot going on. She wasn't sure they could afford for him to be away for ten days. She was scheduling customer meetings with yacht brokers and navigational supply companies to preview StarTaker 2.0; she needed him at these meetings.

"Is that OK?" he asked, seeing the look on her face. "I won't go if it's a problem."

She saw his look of pure longing and decided that she could postpone the customer meetings for a couple of weeks. The last seven months hadn't been easy for him with the near collapse of his business in October and November.

"Absolutely. No problem from my side. By the way, what's an 'unofficial' race?"

"It's with six of my friends whom I've known since kindergarten. It's single-man sailing. We each have a sailboat. It's a combination of 'boy's night out' and extended camping trip."

They finished their drink, and Abby insisted that Matt put her into a taxi. Twenty minutes later, she was flying back to Logan.

THE FOLLOWING TUESDAY, Matt was at the wharf by 5:30 a.m. He and Abby had spoken the previous evening, and he agreed to check in when he got to Bermuda in four to five days. The sky was overcast with a light wind from the southwest. He saw his friends who were all docked nearby. After good-natured kidding about who was going to beat whom, they agreed to a 6:00 a.m. start time—no cheating! Unlike the others, Matt had been ready to go since the night before, so he sat on his deck with his coffee and surveyed the harbor. The gulls were swooping and squawking, hoping for a better breakfast than a cup of coffee. He smiled at their antics. He was struck, as he often was, by how much he loved Nantucket. Taking in a deep breath of the salty sea air, he could feel his emotional attachment to the island tug at his heart. Just then, the sun broke through the early morning clouds. He thought this was a good omen—the heavens opening up to illuminate the island he loved—one last time. One last time? He wondered where *that* thought came from. He shrugged it off as just another manifestation of all of his crazy dreams about Abby. Looking at his watch, he saw that he had fifteen minutes before they were to set sail; time to cast off.

THIS IS JUST what the doctor ordered, thought Matt as he stared at the night sky two nights later. He was approximately four hundred nautical miles northwest of Bermuda, and as far as he could determine, he was in the lead. It was hard to be certain because everyone else gave a slightly false position during their daily 8:00 a.m. check-ins, trying to convince the others that they were in the lead. Boys will be boys. It didn't matter to him if he won or not; he felt as if he had already won just by getting this time on the sea. He noticed the wind was starting to pick up as he turned on StarTaker 2.0. *Funny,* he thought, *the weather forecast didn't predict strong winds.* He got distracted by StarTaker 2.0 and didn't give the changing weather another thought until fifteen minutes later when he realized that he could be sailing into trouble. Because it was night, he had difficulty seeing in the distance, but from what he could see, the waves were increasing to ten to twelve feet with whitecaps. They were coming at him from the southeast and were breaking quickly. This wasn't good. He hurried below deck, took a reading from the weather fax, put on his foul-weather gear—a bright yellow jacket with navy blue pants—and stored StarTaker 2.0. *It must be a local squall,* he thought as he quickly scanned the report. There was no indication a storm was heading his way. Just to be safe, he secured everything in the cabin before going back up on deck.

When he got back up on deck, it was as if he had landed on a different planet. The waves were now thirty feet high, and they seemed to be coming at him from all directions! According to his wind speed indicator, the wind was blowing at fifty-five knots, just short of gale-force wind, and it had started to rain heavily. In his thirty years of sailing, he had never seen a storm come up so quickly. He was in for one heck of a ride. Even with the dramatic change in the weather, it never occurred to him that anything could go seriously wrong. He quickly lowered all the sails except for his storm jib. He started his engine and tried as well as he could to steer at a forty-five degree angle into the waves. The engine on the *Patience* was powerful, but not powerful enough to cope with a raging sea. The first fingers of doubt started to tickle his brain—he might be in serious trouble.

He wondered if his friends were also in the middle of this storm; he doubted it as they would have radioed him. He had to warn them! He tried to hail them on the VHF radio, but all he got was static. He hesitated; should he call the Coast Guard and at least report his position, while he still could? Yes, he decided, this was the prudent thing to do. He looked at his GPS and was shocked; there was no reading. How could there be no location coordinates? The screen was blank. He toggled the on/off switch. Nothing. No radio, no GPS—was he in the middle of an electrical storm? Just as that thought popped into his head, lightning flashed and he heard a loud crack, like a gunshot. His main mast had split like a toothpick five feet from the deck and was hanging off the side of the boat! He felt the compression from the change in atmosphere deep in his chest, which caused a moment of panic to course through his body. He was definitely in trouble now. With the rain pounding him from all sides, he assessed the damage. In the violently rolling seas, there was nothing he could do. The trailing mast was acting like a pivot point, and the *Patience* was circling around it. His biggest worry was that she would capsize. He deployed the sea anchor and went below, trying both the GPS and the radio again—they were still dead. He reached for his Emergency Position Indicating Radio Beacon. It, too, was dead. He remembered StarTaker 2.0! It was functioning beautifully, and he had a signal. *It's worth a try*, he thought as he pressed an SOS and send, which was the last thing he remembered until he came to the next day.

MATT SLOWLY CAME back to consciousness and looked around, completely disoriented. He was lying on his back in his life raft, but he had no idea how he got there. He remembered the storm, the mast breaking, and sending a signal via StarTaker 2.0; but those were the last things he remembered. He looked around him. He had on his foul-weather gear, but somehow, he had lost a sneaker. He felt as if he had been run over by a truck, but as far as he could tell, he didn't have any serious injuries. He was so thirsty! He jerked up to sitting, only to be rewarded by a pounding in his head from the sudden movement. He put his hand to his forehead and felt a lump the size of an egg. From his sitting position, he scanned the horizon—ocean as far as he could see in all directions. Where was the *Patience*? His best guess was that she had sunk. *This is not going to be one of my better days*, he thought ruefully. His naturally optimistic nature still couldn't register the seriousness of his situation.

His first task: get water. He looked in the stowage pocket and found a single two-gallon container of drinking water, which unfortunately appeared to be two-thirds empty. The bottle was leaking. Matt took a small sip, forcing himself not to gulp down the rest of the water in the bottle. He leaned against the side of the life raft and did a quick assessment: the *Patience* was gone, he didn't know his location, he had limited water, and he had no radio. He searched the life raft for what he did have and found some useful things: fishing hooks and lines, a small knife, a medicine kit, a small folding oar, a large sheet of plastic, and three flares. He also found the antique astrolabe that had been in his family for nine gen-erations. He had it aboard the *Patience*; he must have grabbed it when he abandoned ship though he couldn't remember doing it. He wished that he had grabbed the prototype Star-Taker 2.0 instead.

"OK, buddy," he said out loud, his voice croaking from not having spoken for twenty-four hours. "Time to focus!" He felt better just saying this out loud.

He had three significant problems: no way of contacting

anyone (the rescue teams would have to find him), limited water (if it didn't rain, he had four days of water at best), and no shelter (he was going to fry in the cloudless sky). He wasn't worried about food; he could last a couple of weeks without eating if he had to, but the lack of water and shelter worried him. He had read stories of shipwrecked sailors who had survived for many days lost at sea, but all of them had had water. He knew that when he missed today's 8:00 a.m. daily check-in, his buddies would raise an alarm, so he felt confident that search and rescue should already be underway.

And it would have been had his friends taken his absence seriously. When Matt missed his first check-in, his friends thought it was gamesmanship—he was trying to outfox them to win the race. In hindsight, this was a stupid assumption, but they had all been friends for over thirty years and were known for playing some pretty idiotic jokes on each other. It wasn't until the second day when Matt wasn't on the call that they realized something was terribly wrong. By then, Matt had been drifting on the open sea for two days.

By his fourth day on the Atlantic, Matt's optimistic nature was taking a pounding, like his body. He had forced himself to stay clothed even though the temperatures were in the upper nineties during the day and the sun was relentless. Every part of him that was exposed to the sun had a second-degree sunburn. He tried covering himself with the plastic sheet, but it made him sweat too much; he couldn't afford to lose any more water. Waves regularly broke over the side of the raft, and he had no choice but to bail to keep it afloat. The salt water on his sunburned skin was torturous, but there was nothing he could do about it. He had been able to catch a couple of small fish, and it had rained twice—briefly—but at least enough to extend his supply of drinking water. In four days, he hadn't seen another boat or a plane. He was worried that he was being carried northeast, along the Gulfstream, farther out into the Atlantic. The hardest part of his situation was the feeling of helplessness; all he could do was wait for someone to rescue him, which went against his nature. He was normally the person who did the rescuing!

His thoughts drifted to Abby. She must know by now that he was lost, and he could imagine that she was very worried. Without him, StarTaker 2.0 was at risk; but he knew, in his heart, this wasn't the main reason she'd be worried. Somehow, over the last months, they had grown closer than just business associates though neither of them would ever admit it. Maybe it was his telling her about his dreams—which he still thought were visions—or maybe it was just that, in building StarTaker 2.0, they were creating something amazing together, and this feeling couldn't help but spill over to their personal relationship. He could feel himself getting weaker every day, but he was made out of strong stock; he had to see Abby again. Their last meeting on the deck of the *Patience* would not be their final chapter.

TWO DAYS BEFORE, Abby looked at the screen on her cell phone as it rang: caller ID UNKNOWN. She was right in the middle of her weekly review of the construction budget and hated to be interrupted. But as very few people had this number, she took the call.

"Yes, this is Abby." She was distracted by the spreadsheet on her screen.

"Am I speaking to Abby Gardner?" It was a woman's voice on the phone.

"Yes, this is she. Who is this?"

"I'm Senior Chief Petty Officer Beverly Gibson. I'm the

officer-in-charge of the Coast Guard Brant Point Station on Nantucket."

Abby gripped the phone tightly in her hand and tried to keep her voice even. "How can I help you, ma'am?"

"I'm calling to inform you that the *Patience* has been reported missing. The captain, Matt Starbuck, listed you as one of his emergency contacts."

If Abby hadn't been sitting down, she would have fallen down. It felt as if the breath had been knocked out of her.

"I don't understand. How can it be missing?"

"That's what we're trying to determine, Ms. Gardner. It appears to have gotten caught in a violent squall and possibly sunk. We just don't know. Cruise ships in the area reported severe weather three days ago."

"How long has it been missing?" Abby was trying to make sense of what the chief was saying.

"As best as we can tell, two days. We're coordinating all search and rescue efforts from Brant Point Station in cooperation with Air Station Cape Cod and the Bermudian authorities."

She had to take a deep breath before she asked, "Any sign of Matt?"

"No, I'm afraid there isn't. His last contact was on Monday when he joined the daily 8:00 a.m. check-in call. Since then, there were no further transmissions."

"What can I do?" She was desperate to have something to do.

"Unfortunately, nothing. He's in good hands, Ms. Gardner. If he's out there, we'll find him. I'll call you as soon as I know anything. I'll give you my number. Call anytime."

"If he's out there . . ." She shuddered at the chief's remark. She took the chief's number, thanked her, and hung up the phone. She sat back in her chair, dazed. She got up, asked her mother to come into her office, and quickly told her what had happened. Caroline was shocked and looked like she was going to cry.

"Mother! There's no time for tears! Call our pilot and tell him I will be at Logan in thirty minutes. I'm going to Nantucket. Cancel my meetings indefinitely. Also, please book me a room at the Union Street Inn."

"For how long? Would you like me to come with you?"

"No, I need you to stay here and hold down the fort. I'm not coming back until Matt is found, safe and sound."

Five minutes later, she was in a cab on her way to Logan.

11

Abigail and Matthew

October 1850, the Pacific and Nantucket

"Father! Father! Wake up!" Thomas shouted at the sleeping Matthew. "It's a ship!" All pretense of Thomas calling Matthew "Captain" had disappeared in the last few weeks, like Matthew's waning hope for rescue.

He sat up and looked east—on the horizon was a whaling ship—flying American colors—and she was headed straight for them! Everyone on the whaleboat got a burst of energy with the sight of her and cheered. Except for 'Ailani who lay eerily motionless in the bow.

No, thought Matthew, *not when we're about to be rescued. He can't be dead!* He went to 'Ailani's side and gently put his fingers on his neck, searching for a pulse. It was weak, but it was there. He sank to his knees alongside of his friend, thanking God.

"Father, will they see us?" Thomas asked anxiously. The ocean was vast, and they were just a speck compared to their surroundings.

"Take an oar, wrap your shirt around it, and set it on fire! Quick!"

Thomas did as he was asked and was joined by three others. In minutes, they got an answering signal from the fast-approaching whaling ship; they saw them and were sailing to their rescue! Matthew felt the tears streaming down his face and, as he looked around, so did all of the others, except for Thomas, who was whooping and hollering. He was going to be the hero of all of his friends when he got home!

Hang on my friend, Matthew thought as he looked at 'Ailani. *Just hang on; help is on the way.*

ONE MONTH LATER, they were back on Maui. Matthew, Thomas, and 'Ailani were at Ewelani and Kale'a's house, and the rest of the crew were scattered among their relatives. Everyone, except for 'Ailani, was recovering quickly. They were reunited with their former crewmates who were still on Maui—sadly, they had had a harder time than Matthew and his whaleboats, and four more men were lost. They were a close-knit crew, and this was very difficult for some of the younger crewmembers.

Matthew, too, was struggling with the loss of the *President.* He had never lost a ship before nor been on one that had been lost. As the captain, he took full responsibility for the loss of the ship, its cargo, and most importantly, his seven crewmembers who died. He spent a lot of time alone during his first weeks of recovery, coming to terms with what had happened. He thanked God that 'Ailani and Thomas were safe. Thomas, especially, seemed to come through it all unscathed and spent his days on shore recounting the run-in with the pirate ship and the storm to anyone who would listen.

Matthew learned that a letter about his shipwreck had

been sent to Nantucket and that Abigail would know that they were lost at sea. This broke his heart as there was no way for him to let her know that they were safe. The earliest that they would be home, once they found a ship returning to Nantucket, would be in eight months. By then, she would have been facing an uncertain future for several months. He couldn't do anything about it, and his only comfort was that she was the strongest person he knew.

TWO MONTHS LATER, after their evening meal, Matthew sat with Ewelani under the stars.

"Matthew, I hear that Captain Cathcart and the *James Loper* will sail for Nantucket in two days. Will you sail with her?" The *James Loper* had arrived in port three days before.

"Yes. They have room for as many as want to go. I think some of the crew will stay here and look for another ship. Not all of them have deep ties to Nantucket, and they're whalers, after all, who need to make a living."

"That's not your fault," Ewelani replied gently, knowing that Matthew was suffering.

"It is, Ewelani." Matthew took full responsibility for the situation. "I accept that it is, and I also know that I can't change it now. I just wish I had sailed straight for St. Mary's as I had planned."

Ewelani looked at Matthew, whom he had grown to love like a son, and searched for the words that would ease his conscience. He knew his faith was shaken after Emily's death, and he wasn't sure if he still believed in God.

"Son, I've known you now for many years. You are a good man. You would never take unnecessary risks, and from what I understand, your actions saved many of your men. I can't tell you to put it behind you. I am sure the seven souls you lost will stay with you the rest of your life, but this burden is one you can bear. As a chief, I've made many difficult decisions and regretted a few. From this regret, I learned to accept that I am only a man, trying his best. I know this will be true for you."

Matthew looked at his friend and felt a loosening in his chest. He didn't realize, until that moment, how much anxiety he was keeping bottled inside.

"Will you take 'Ailani with you?"

"Do you think he's strong enough to make the trip?"

"Yes, I do. He's still weak—he won't be much help—but he's strong enough to sail. Besides, as it is true for you, his best medicine is waiting for him on Nantucket."

Matthew smiled and took the chief's hand, clasping it with both of his. "I will remember your kindness and friendship the rest of my days."

IT WAS AUGUST 1851, and Abigail was in the office at Gardner & Sons, doing the accounting from the *Elizabeth Starbuck*, which had sailed into port two days before. It was another successful journey and her captain, Captain Alexander Chase, was stopping by later that day to get his orders for his next trip; he wanted to turn around as quickly as he could. Work had been a salvation for Abigail in the last three months.

When she first heard about the *President's* shipwreck, she wanted to go to bed and sleep and never wake up. After losing Emily, and now, maybe Matthew and Thomas, she didn't think she could survive so much loss. It was Jonah who saved her. He had no idea that his father and brother, whom he had never met, were missing. As a toddler, his view of the world was focused solely on Abigail, Anuenue, and Little Matthew. His tunnel vision was what helped Abigail get through the first days after learning of Matthew's shipwreck when she thought she would drown in waves of worry. She woodenly walked through those days—Sarah and Phebe were with her nearly around the clock—and slowly, she started to come back to life. She drew on the same fortitude that helped her and Matthew rebuild their lives after Emily's funeral. She truly believed that if he were dead, she'd know it her heart, and this comforted her. She just wished that she had some news!

She also had the full support of the Nantucket community, who understood the dangers of a life at sea. She was not the only sea captain's wife who had faced an uncertain future, and the community rallied around her. In the first months, there was a constant stream of women stopping by her house, bringing food and small toys for Jonah and Little Matthew. In the early days, she would have much rather had time alone and said as much, but the women knew that this would not be good for her. They brushed her objections aside and kept coming by every day. Abigail tried to keep a brave face for Anuenue who was facing the same tragic loss. Anuenue felt the same for her friend, so they both put on brave faces in support of each other.

All of these things, together with her work, helped her tremendously. In the three months since she learned that their men were missing, she had come to accept that, no matter what the outcome was, she would be OK. If they were gone, her heart would break, but she would survive, and over time learn to be at peace with it. Like Matthew, she was not a proponent of "God's will," but she was pragmatic and accepted that what would be, would be.

HEARING A KNOCK on the office door, she called out, "Come in!"

Captain Chase walked in, hat in hand. "Good morning, Mrs. Starbuck."

"Good morning, Captain. I was just completing your accounting. Congratulations on a successful voyage. Please, have a seat."

"Thank you. We're quite anxious to go back out. The *Elizabeth Starbuck* needed very few repairs, so we can turn around quite quickly."

"I have an appointment with the owner, Mr. Rotch, at 9:00 a.m. tomorrow. Once we get his sign-off, you're good to go, Captain." Abigail was all business.

Chase thanked her, stood up, and turned to leave. He paused. "Mrs. Starbuck . . . Abigail, may I say something of a personal nature to you?"

"Of course, Captain."

"My cousin, Owen Chase, survived the shipwreck of the *Essex*. I won't insult your intelligence by saying that it was easy or that he came through it unscathed. He had terrible nightmares for many years after he got back. But I will say this: he survived! And over time, he was well again."

"Thank you, Captain. I truly believe that Matthew's still alive and is coming back to me."

"As you should! I've known Matthew my whole life, and he is one of the best captains I know. He will survive this."

She stood up and impulsively gave Captain Chase a quick hug and a kiss on his whiskered cheek. Startled, he awkwardly hugged her back—women! So unpredictable! No wonder, like most men, he preferred the routine of life at sea.

After Captain Chase left, she looked out the office window

at the activity on the wharf. Two more ships had come in that morning, and there were hundreds of people scurrying to and fro. She smiled to herself, comforted by Captain Chase's words and amused by the look on his face when she hugged him. She grabbed her cloak and hat; it was time to go home.

A MONTH LATER, she was spending the morning at home with Jonah. He was now fourteen months old and just starting to walk. He was very stubborn—every time she tried to help him by holding his little hands he'd shake her off, take two wobbly steps, and fall over like a sack of corn. He'd laugh and laugh, terribly amused by the whole activity, and get up to try again. She was sitting with her back to the door, and Jonah was laughing so loudly that she didn't realize for several minutes that there was someone standing behind her. She felt the hairs go up on the back of her neck, and she exclaimed, softly, "Matthew!"

She turned to face the door, and there he was, smiling at her with tears streaming down his face. She leapt to her feet and threw herself in his arms, sobbing and laughing at the same time. Jonah looked at the scene, quite perplexed. Why was Mama jumping up and down?

"Matthew! When did you arrive? Why didn't anyone tell me? Where's Thomas and 'Ailani? Are they well? Are you well? You look tired. Do you need to sit down?"

Matthew laughed. "Oh, my darling Abigail. It's good to know that some things never change. One question at a time, please!"

She covered his face in kisses and couldn't stop touching him. Yes, this was her Matthew, but she could see in his eyes that the last months had taken a terrible toll on him. He had lost so much weight, and his hair was nearly all gray; but to her, he had never looked handsomer.

"Thomas will be along shortly. He ran into his friends as we disembarked the *James Loper*, and 'Ailani is waiting outside. He wanted to give us a few minutes alone."

"Jonah!" She had completely forgotten the baby in her excitement at seeing Matthew. "Darling, here's your son."

She scooped Jonah up off the floor and handed him to Matthew. Jonah immediately grabbed one of the gold buttons on his jacket and tried to eat it, not at all intimidated by the strange man who was now holding him.

"Hello, my son," said Matthew softly. At hearing his father's voice, Jonah raised his deep blue eyes to meet his father's, which were the same shade of cerulean blue. Matthew knew, without any doubt, that this was the only sea blue he would ever need, for the rest of his life.

12

Abby and Matt

May 2009, Nantucket and Boston

Abby reached Nantucket a little over an hour after she left her office in Boston. She grabbed a taxi and went straight to the Brant Point Coast Guard Station and asked to see Chief Gibson.

"Hello, Ms. Gardner."

"Please, it's Abby."

"And I'm Beverly. I'm sorry. I don't have any more news for you."

"Can you tell me more about the search? Are they looking with a single plane or many planes?"

For the next twenty minutes, Beverly described the search and rescue protocol to Abby who took copious notes. She wanted to review them later, looking for any clues that might be helpful. At the end of their conversation, she gave Beverly all of her contact details.

AN HOUR LATER, after checking in at the Union Street Inn, she was walking west on Main Street. She had left Boston in such a hurry; she needed a few essentials until her pilot came back with the bag Caroline was packing for her. Town was bustling, the official opening to the summer season, Memorial Day, was only a few weeks away. All the activity was a blur to Abby; she could think only of Matt. She stopped at Congdon's Pharmacy for toiletries and Murray's for a nightgown and underwear. She looked at her cell phone every few minutes, but there were no missed calls. She didn't know what to do with herself; she was never very good at waiting. She decided to walk around town and turned onto Fair Street. On her right was the Nantucket Historical Association, known by its abbreviation as the NHA. On impulse, she went in.

"Good afternoon," said the gray-haired woman at the desk. "Can I help you?"

Abby looked around. She was standing in the middle of a large library with several big library tables where people were looking at old documents and making notes.

"Yes, please. How would I find information on the Gardner family?" She had used the NHA's online resource many times when she was a teenager, but she had never visited it before today.

The librarian gave her several options and pointed her to the collections that she felt were closest to Abby's interest. Abby pulled the files and found an empty place at one of the library tables. She put her cell phone on the table and turned it to vibrate only, ready to leap up and run outside if Beverly called. One of the collections contained rare books, so she donned white cotton gloves to handle them.

FOR THE NEXT two hours, Abby was lost in the world of the Gardners. She didn't know exactly which ones were her ancestors—she'd have to ask her mother—but she guessed that she was related in some way to many of them. She was just about to leave when she noticed a small black leather-bound book. She opened it gently, as it was clearly very old, and read the inscription: "The personal journal of Abigail Gardner Starbuck, December 26, 1876." Abby's breath caught in her chest as she turned the first page and read:

Dear Journal,

I have never written in a journal before, but there's always a first! Matthew gave me this lovely book for Christmas, so I feel compelled to put it to good use. I'm not quite sure what I should write about. I don't think my life is so interesting or so unusual that it warrants writing about it, but Matthew assured me that the words would come to me. As Sarah, Thomas, and Jonah are grown and long gone, I definitely have more time to write. Maybe I should write something for our fifteen grandchildren? I could tell them how it was to live on Nantucket during the golden years of whaling! With the precipitous decline in the industry, I'm afraid that Samuel and Thomas may be the last sea captains in our combined families. Let's see . . .

The journal went on to describe Abigail's daily life, but Abby couldn't read any more. She needed fresh air. She collected the material she had and returned it to the librarian.

"Are you OK, dear?" the librarian asked with concern in her voice. "You're very pale. You look like you've just seen a ghost!"

"I'm fine. Thank you for your help." She walked out into the warm May air and took several deep, gulping breaths.

JUST AS SHE stepped out of the library, Abby's phone vibrated. "Abby, it's Eva. The testing team has found something odd." Eva didn't ask if there was any news of Matt because she knew that Abby would call her immediately if she had heard something.

"What did they find?"

"They got a coordinate signal that doesn't make sense; it indicates that the device is 240 nautical miles southeast of Nantucket. We're testing ten devices at different places on the island, but none offshore yet. It doesn't make sense."

Abby started running toward the Brant Point Station, eliciting odd looks from the people on Main Street. "Call Chief Gibson at the Brant Point Station! It has to be from Matt. He took a prototype StarTaker 2.0 with him! What's the time stamp on it?"

"Forty-eight hours ago. Abby, with the information from this signal, we have the software to calculate where Matt might be. I just need to get the weather and ocean current data from the last two days. I could have an answer within the hour."

"I'm on my way to Brant Point Station." She kept running toward the station. "I'll give Chief Gibson the background on StarTaker 2.0. Maybe they can refine the search area right away!"

By evening, Eva and her team had provided the Coast Guard with three likely locations where Matt could be based on StarTaker 2.0's last known position. It significantly changed the search area, both in size and in location. Abby prayed it was correct; otherwise, they could be sending him to his death.

EVEN WITH THE new data, the search area was still hundreds of square miles. Her excitement about Star-Taker 2.0's transmission quickly turned to frustration as the search entered its second day. Eva's team provided updates to the Coast Guard every four hours around the clock. No one at Starbuck Enterprises could sleep while Matt was lost.

The entire island seemed to be looking for Matt. There were vigils at all of the churches, and everywhere Abby went she saw green ribbons tied around everything. When she asked why a green ribbon, she was told that it was Matt's favorite color. *What must it be like,* she wondered, *to live in a community that knows your favorite color?*

Each day, she spent most of the day either walking around town or sitting on the dock where Matt had his slip for the *Patience.* She knew that it looked odd—a woman sitting cross-legged on the dock not near anyone or anything—but no one remarked on it. On the contrary, many of Matt's friends stopped by to see if she needed anything. She appreciated their kindness, but she didn't need anything. She was waiting.

While she waited, she thought about Abigail Gardner Starbuck's journal. It had shaken her. Because it was so closely aligned with Matt's dreams, it made her feel very uneasy. She still didn't think he was seeing the past in his dreams, but she wasn't as sure as she was before. When Matt was found safe and sound—because he *had* to be found—she'd check with her mother to find out more about her ancestors. It would definitely be odd if Abigail Gardner Starbuck was her ancestor.

THE NEXT DAY Abby's phone rang, and she saw on the screen that it was Mark Mullen. She groaned. Hadn't her mother told everyone to leave her alone? She didn't want to think about Gardner & Sons right now!

"Hi, Mark. It's Abby." She decided to accept his call; other than worrying, she really wasn't doing anything.

"Abby, I'm so sorry to disturb you, but Caroline told me it would be OK if I called. First, any news of Matt?" Mark's kindness came pouring through the phone.

"No, not yet. Thanks for asking."

"I'll make this quick, but there's something I thought you should know about right away. Last night, Peter called an emergency meeting of the advisory board."

Abby waited for Mark to finish speaking as she didn't trust herself to say anything.

"In summary, he tried to oust you as CEO of Gardner & Sons for 'dereliction of duties.' He said that your abrupt departure to Nantucket, and the lack of any contact for four days, proved that you were incapable of running Gardner & Sons."

"Are you *kidding* me?" Abby burst out, saying the first thing that came to mind.

"There's more. He said that if you were no longer CEO, he would be the best candidate to replace you and would step in as acting CEO, immediately, pending formal approval."

"Mark, I can't come back to Boston right now!" Abby said, nearly in tears, her voice cracking.

"There's no need, Abby. This was the last straw for me and the rest of the advisory board members. We unanimously voted him off the board."

"What?" Abby was completely confused. This wasn't possible!

"Yes, there was a fourth amendment to the bylaws that your father had put through when he made the other changes. He deliberately never told you about it. I'll explain more when Matt is found, and you're back, but both myself and Michael O'Malley were aware of it."

"Are you telling me that he's really gone? Peter Coffin no longer is the chairman?" For the first time in four days, Abby heard some good news.

"Yes, he was escorted out of the building last night. Michael called security and had him escorted out."

"Who's the new chairperson?"

"I am. I hope that's OK for you."

"Mark, it's wonderful!"

They talked for a few more minutes about the next steps with the change in leadership and what to do about Peter's equity in Gardner & Sons. As Abby hung up the phone, she was grateful that her mother had encouraged him to call her. While nothing short of Matt being found would make her happy right now, the call from Mark eliminated one of her big worries, and that was good.

ON HER FIFTH day on the island, Abby woke at 6:00 a.m. She decided to start the day's vigil at the Brant Point lighthouse. This way, she'd also be near the Coast Guard station if there were any news. Somehow, she felt that physical proximity mattered in some way, though she couldn't say why. She grabbed her folding beach chair that she had bought at the Grand Union, stopped by the Bean for a cup of coffee, and walked fifteen minutes to Brant Point. There were two men fishing near the lighthouse; they nodded "good morning" to her as she set up her chair to face the opening to the harbor.

Two hours later, her cell phone rang; it was Beverly.

Beverly dispensed with pleasantries and launched right in. "Abby, there's news."

"I'm at the lighthouse. I can be to you in three minutes."

"I'm in my office."

They both hung up without saying good-bye. Abby sprinted to the Coast Guard station, leaving her chair behind—some lucky tourist could have it.

Breathless, she burst into Beverly's office, knocking as she pushed open the door.

"Abby, it's not good news. They've spotted a life raft that they think could be Matt's."

"But that's great news!" Abby didn't understand how this could be bad news.

"There's a man on it, but he's not moving. They're fighting twenty-foot seas and forty-five knot winds; the rescue divers will go in for a closer look as soon as it's safe, but if the wind picks up, the helicopter will have to return to base."

"They can't leave him out there!" Abby was frantic. Here was the first piece of good news in a nearly a week, and it might turn out to be even worse than no news.

"Abby, the rescue team will do everything they can. The pilot grew up with Matt. Do you think he wants to leave his friend behind?"

"Can I wait here?"

"Sure. I'll have Seaman Miller take you to the lounge. I'll come to you as soon as I hear anything else."

AFTER TWO AGONIZING hours, Beverly appeared in the door of the lounge. Abby tried to stand up but couldn't and collapsed back onto the couch. Beverly walked over to her and took her hands in hers. Seeing the sympathetic look in Beverly's eyes, Abby started crying.

"Abby, you need to be strong. They have Matt. He's alive, but he's in very bad shape. The rescue divers were able to reach him, and he's on the helicopter, but he's unconscious and not responding."

"Where will they take him?" Abby was trying not to cry in front of this woman who had been so kind to her over the last five days.

"To Massachusetts General Hospital in Boston. It's the closest trauma center, and it's excellent. I've informed his family. They're heading to Boston now. Matt should arrive in the next two hours."

Abby stood up. There was no reason to stay at the station any longer. On impulse, she pulled Beverly into a hug. Beverly hugged her back; sometimes being an officer meant giving someone a big hug.

"Will you go to Mass General?"

"Yes, I just need to grab my things at the Union Street Inn and head to the airport." Abby had kept her pilot and plane on standby, ready to go on short notice.

"Seaman Miller is at your disposal. He'll drive you to the inn and wait for you."

"Thank you." Abby was genuinely touched at the kind offer.

When she got to the inn, she asked Seaman Miller if he could wait for twenty minutes. It was only forty-five minutes to Boston; she had a little time before Matt would arrive at the hospital. She called her mother and told her what had happened. Caroline promised to go to the hospital immediately and would meet Abby there.

She left the inn and walked south on Union Street,

coming quickly to number fifteen, Matt's house. She went to the back door, lifted the mat, and sure enough, there was a key. She let herself in and looked around. She was in the kitchen; the fireplace that Matt had described to her was on her right. In front of it were two chairs that looked as if they had been there since the house was first built. She sat down and closed her eyes.

Her mind was immediately flooded by images of her and Matt in the 1800s. She could see, in her mind's eye, what Matt had described to her over Stroll weekend six months before. More unnerving, she could see it was exactly as Abigail Gardner Starbuck had described in her journal. Although her thoughts were fully occupied with worrying about Matt, Abby sensed an idea forming in the back of her mind. Could it be true? Could she and Matt have been married in a prior life?

She opened her eyes; the visions were breaking her heart. She whispered to the empty room, "Matt, come back to me. I know now what you've known all along. I'm so sorry I doubted you. You *have* to come back to me." She sat there for a further fifteen minutes, praying to God and the universe that she would get a chance to tell him what she should have recognized months ago—that she loved him, not only now, but for eternity.

NINETY MINUTES LATER, she raced into the Trauma Center at Mass General. Her mother jumped up as she came in. Thirty people, whom Abby realized were Matt's family, surrounded Caroline. She looked at all of them and, if the situation had been less serious, would have found it very funny that thirty Starbucks were each holding Starbucks coffees.

"Abby, this is Phoebe, Matt's mom. And this is Rick, his dad," said Caroline.

Rick immediately pulled Abby into a hug that squeezed the air out of her lungs; this was no time for conventional niceties. Phoebe gently released Abby from Rick's bear hug and gave her a quick hug of her own.

"Abby, dear, it's so nice to finally meet you. Matt talks about you all the time." Phoebe and Caroline exchanged quick, knowing glances over Abby's right shoulder.

"How is he? Any change?"

She had talked to her mother as soon as she had landed. Caroline told her that Matt had just arrived and was going into intensive care.

"No, he's still unconscious. The doctors are with him now and will give us an update in a few minutes. Wait with us," said Phoebe.

Phoebe introduced Abby to the other twenty-eight Starbucks, but she knew the names didn't register. The glazed look in Abby's eyes reflected how everyone felt. For such a large group, it was remarkably quiet.

The trauma surgeon, Dr. Morris, appeared and gave everyone a quick update. No major injuries, external or internal, which was good. But she didn't know why he was unconscious. He was severely dehydrated, so she thought that he could have been unconscious for the last three days or so. They were pumping fluids into him, and they should know more in the next twenty-four hours.

Lilly, never being the shy sister, asked the question that was hanging in the air. "He's going to make it, Doctor, isn't he?"

"His vital signs are strong, and his preliminary tests show no significant injury. As I said, I'm not sure why he hasn't regained consciousness. We'll be doing a brain scan shortly, and after that, I should have more news."

"Can we see him?" Phoebe asked.

Dr. Morris looked at the big crowd. "Just two of you and only for a few minutes. Until I know more, I want to keep him as quiet as possible."

It was decided that the visitors should be Phoebe and Rick, who donned gowns, gloves, and masks—with Matt's weakened state, they were taking no chance of infection. They came out ten minutes later, and Phoebe couldn't hold back her tears. All the family gathered around her to reassure her—Matt's strong! He's a fighter!

SIX DAYS LATER, it was just Phoebe and Abby in the ICU waiting room. Everyone had to get back to work though they promised to come immediately if his condition changed. They took turns during the day spending time at Matt's bedside as he was allowed only one visitor at a time. His condition was stable, and all the tests showed that there was nothing physically wrong with him; he just wouldn't wake up. Phoebe was staying with Caroline; the two mothers had grown very close in the last few days. She had intended to stay in a hotel, but Caroline wouldn't hear of it, using the argument that Phoebe would do the same for her if the situation were reversed.

Abby hadn't been to the office since Matt disappeared. She delegated her duties to her chief financial officer, Christopher Folger, and got daily updates from Caroline who had also gone back to work. Everything appeared to be in order, but right now, for the first time she could ever remember, work was not important to her. Yes, it would be easy to run into the office for a few hours or to work remotely on her laptop, but she couldn't concentrate on work; she could think only about Matt and what she had to tell him. He had to wake up!

MATT WAS DREAMING. In his dreams, he could see himself and Abby, not Abigail and Matthew. There were many new, modern things that he didn't recognize so he guessed that it must be the future. His dream state was very advanced—from believing that he never dreamt; he now could dream and try to make sense of his dreams while dreaming. He and Abby were very, very happy, and it appeared that they had two children, a girl and a boy. He saw them in Nantucket, and Boston, as well as in other locations, such as Paris, London, and Mexico City. The activities and locations varied, but the common thread was their love for each other. As he watched them, he felt as if he were being wrapped in a soft, warm blanket—not only to keep him warm—but also to keep him safe. He could feel his whole being sink into the comforting embrace of this magical blanket, which made him feel restored and alive. His body, which had been ravaged by the brutal days at sea, felt strong as he watched dream-Abby and dream-Matt.

ABBY WAS EXHAUSTED. She was sitting by Matt's bed, holding his hand, careful not to disturb the IV. She had convinced Phoebe to take a long break, and Caroline had come by to pick her up. They were going out to lunch, then a little shopping on Boylston Street, and then home. Phoebe would come back in the evening. Abby couldn't remember the last time she had slept well. She knew that she dozed off from time to time. The days were starting to blur together; she had been in the hospital for seven straight days. At some point, she'd have to leave, but she couldn't, not just yet. She decided to lay her head on his bed, for just a moment—she was so tired! As she drifted off to sleep, she murmured, "Come back to me, Matt! I need you. I've needed you all of my life, and in all my lives before. I believe you. I love you." She fell into a deep sleep.

She woke slowly, feeling a hand caressing the back of her head. She imagined it was her mother, stroking her head to comfort her as she did so often when she was a little girl. She smiled, keeping her eyes closed, and attempted to drift back to sleep. She was so tired.

"Abby?" a male voice whispered.

Her eyes flew open! This voice wasn't Caroline's!

She sat up, turned, and saw Matt looking at her.

"You're awake! I'll the call the nurse!" Abby frantically looked for the nurse's call button and, not finding it, leapt up.

"Abby, sit. We can get the nurse in a minute." Matt smiled weakly at her.

She sat down, unsure of what to do or say. For days, she had been begging God and the universe to bring Matt back to her; but now that he was here, she felt shy and uncertain. She was flooded with insecurities. He had told her about his dreams, but he had never said that he wanted them to be together in this life; she didn't know what to say, so she decided to start with the facts about his rescue.

"Eva and StarTaker 2.0 saved you, Matt. Somehow, you must have sent a signal before you passed out, and the team used that signal to narrow the search for the Coast Guard."

"Hitting 'send' on StarTaker 2.0 is the last thing I remember. Looking around now, I'm guessing I didn't have the relaxing trip I hoped to have." He added impishly, "Did I lose the race?"

Abby choked back a laugh and a sob at the same time; she couldn't just chitchat any longer.

She took a deep breath and began. "Matt, I have to tell you something. I believe you. I was in Nantucket when you were lost. I went to your house and sat in your kitchen. I had the same visions as you. There's more. I found a journal from Abigail Gardner Starbuck, but it can wait until you're stronger."

Matt looked at Abby with love in his eyes. He had known for months that he loved her, deeply. He never doubted that they were married in a previous life. When he was lost at sea, his dreams were full of her. He was 100 percent certain it was what kept him alive. But before he could tell her, he needed her to reach out to him. Up until now, he had been the one taking the emotional risk; if they were to start a relationship as equals, he needed her to be brave on his behalf. He didn't have to wait long.

"Matt, there's something else. I'm just going to say it. I love you! There, it's said," Abby said it fiercely as if she were challenging him to say: "No, you don't." Tears were streaming down her face.

Matt smiled, gently raised her hand to his lips, and kissed it. "I love you too." And then, there was nothing else that needed to be said.

TWO MONTHS LATER, Matt stood by the altar at the front of the First Congregational Church on Center Street in Nantucket, looking back toward the entrance. The late afternoon July sun streamed through the stained-glass windows and flooded the church with a kaleidoscope of colors. He saw his family and Caroline sitting in the front three rows. The Fannings were all there, including Edward and Lynda, who had just gotten engaged. The first notes of Pachelbel's *Canon in D* floated in the air, and then she was there. Abby was standing in the entrance of the church, backlit, as she was the very first time he saw her. If she had taken his breath away then, it was nothing compared to how he felt now. Tears of joy filled his eyes as she slowly walked toward him—toward their new life, together.

Epilogue

Abigail and Matthew

December 1876, Nantucket

Abigail laid down her writing quill, satisfied with the first entry in her journal. What a funny Christmas present from Matthew! She was quite sure that she didn't have anything interesting to write about, but he insisted that she did, so she was going to give it a try.

THE STARBUCKS' LIVES were much happier after their tragedies in the mid-1800s: the death of Emily, the Great Fire, and the shipwreck of the *President*. Matthew honored his promise to God and never sailed again as a captain of a whaling ship. He did, however, help to launch the first steamship service between Nantucket and Hyannis on the mainland, in 1854, and was known to occasionally captain one of the steamships—just to keep his skills up—or so he told Abigail.

They had fifteen grandchildren! Sarah, Thomas, and Jonah were all happily married; and they stayed on Nantucket unlike many of their friends' children who left the

island as the golden days of whaling came to an end. Abigail
was happy that her sons weren't enticed by the Gold Rush
in California, which created a mass exodus from Nantucket
in 1849.

Phebe died at the age of ninety-six. While Abigail still
missed her every day, she knew that her mother had a rich,
full life. She could only hope that Sarah would say the same
about her when her time came.

'Ailani and Anuenue stayed on Nantucket as well, though
they did go back to the Sandwich Islands for five years
several years before. Sadly, Ewelani had died in the interim
and didn't get to meet his grandson, Little Matthew. They
never had any more children, but they found a welcome
home for their abundant love with the Starbuck grandchildren. Little Matthew went on to be a master basket maker
like his father, and his baskets were in collections as far away
as Washington, DC, and London.

January 1, 1877

Dear Journal,

*This is my second entry, and I'm finding that I quite
enjoy writing in you! I have no idea who will ever read
my musings, but that doesn't matter. I shall keep at it and
maybe one day my namesake, Little Abigail, will be able to
read what her grandmother was all about.*

*It's the start of the New Year, and we had a glorious
day today! The entire family attended service at the First
Congregational Church. The new pastor is an excellent
orator. He gave us all much food for thought. We went to
Sarah and Samuel's for our midday meal. The weather
was very pleasant for a January day, so we took advantage of the sunshine and mild temperature: we went for a*

walk to the new Brant Point Lighthouse, which replaced the one that burned down three years ago. After living through the Great Fire, any fire makes me nervous!

I am looking forward to this evening at home when it will be just Matthew and me. I want to share with him my thoughts about the theme of Pastor Francis's homily: "stop judging." As I write in you, dear journal, I know that there were never two better words of advice! If I have had a happy life, and I absolutely know deep in my heart that I have, it's because I haven't wasted one precious minute judging others or the people I love or even myself.

I would be thrilled if we could all live our lives as the stars are in heaven—timeless in their beauty, brilliant in their light, and clear in their purpose. No one would ever feel diminished or less-than. We all would shine brightly. What a gift this would be!

As I reread my scribbling, I can see that I am getting very philosophical, which was never my strong suit. I'll revert back to my practical nature and save some space for more to come . . .

At the start of this New Year, with gratitude for my life, love for my family, and devotion to the love of my life, Matthew, I remain,

Your Abigail

Acknowledgments

I have so many people to thank! Writing this book has been a wonderful experience and many people contributed to its creation.

Anne Cooney and Debora Goudemond were the first two people to read *The World Is Decorated with Stars* when its working title was still the very imaginatively named *Novel*. They gave me wonderful feedback, which helped me tremendously. Their early encouragement and coaching motivated me to write faster. As soon as I had given them new material, they couldn't wait for more . . .

Lori Drumm and Leo Schultz were also early readers whose insights helped me to form Abigail's and Matthew's characters and personalities. Their comments guided me to my characters' authentic voices, and I am immensely grateful.

I also want to thank Pat Drumm. She read the final drafts with eagle eyes, catching many mistakes that I never would have caught. Unasked, she gave me pages of review notes that I treasured—each one improved the story and made many of the scenes more authentic. I am so grateful for her generous help.

Grael Norton, from Wheatmark, was instrumental in bringing *The World Is Decorated with Stars* to publication. When I had finished the first three chapters and an outline, I asked Grael if I should keep writing it. It was very different from anything I had written before, and I wasn't sure if it was any good. He didn't hesitate for one second to help me even though I was a long way away from a finished book. His professional advice, encouragement, and kindness spurred me to keep going!

I want to thank Lori Leavitt, my account manager at Wheatmark, whose professional advice, guidance, and direction helped turn my final draft into the book you're holding in your hands. This is my second project with Lori, and I am thrilled that we got to work together again. Thanks, too, to the copyeditor and proofreader for contributing to the final result—I would not have such a professional-looking book without your expertise!

Many thanks to Yvonne Parks from Pear Creative who designed the cover, which brought tears to my eyes the first time I saw it. Her talent gave my efforts a "face." It was a joy to work with her.

I used four books as reference for this novel, and any mistakes in historical facts are truly my own. They were *Sometimes Think of Me, Notable Nantucket Women Through the Centuries*, embroidered narratives by Susan Boardman, biographies by Betsy Tyler; *Away Off Shore, Nantucket Island and Its People, 1602–1890,* by Nathaniel Philbrick; *Revenge of the Whale, The True Story of the Essex,* by Nathaniel Philbrick; and *Leviathan, The History of Whaling in America,* by Eric Jay Dolin. Each of these books made the history of Nantucket and whaling come alive. I hope that I have also been able to contribute the same even in a small way.

As so many people do, I write about what I know. The family scenes are based on my own family. I am extremely lucky and thankful to have a wonderful family, starting with my parents, Larry and Dee Kronau, who not only live the values modeled by the characters in this book, but also have always believed in me—whether I was a janitor or a computer programmer or an author.

Last and never least, I thank my husband, Michael Reitermann, for his love, support, and belief in me. If I can write authentically about enduring love, it's because of him.

Book Club Reader's Guide

Abigail and Matthew, 1800s

1. Abigail lived in the 1800s but in many ways she faced challenges similar to ones today. What are three challenges that she faced that would resonate with you today?

2. For all of her independence and self-sufficiency, Abigail's life could also be seen as very lonely. Do you think this was true? Why or why not?

3. Imagine yourself in Abigail's shoes when Matthew would leave for another voyage. Whaling was a dangerous profession and many men were lost at sea. How did Abigail cope with the years of uncertainty about Matthew's fate?

4. When Matthew first returned from a voyage, he had trouble adjusting to life on land. Why? Do you think this was true each time he returned?

5. Abigail took a big leap of faith when she went to sea with Matthew in 1846. What would she find the most rewarding about joining him on the voyage? What would be the most challenging element?

6. Abigail's and Matthew's careers were an integral part

of the story. The ups and downs about their livelihoods mirror the experience of many working couples
today. Do you agree? Why or why not?

7. You could say that Nantucket itself was also a character in this book. What are three things about the
island that made this story unique?

Abby and Matt, 2008-9

1. Abby is an only child and Matt comes from a large
family. How do you think this influences their relationship?

2. Abby is very uncomfortable with Matt's references
to their having been married in a prior life. In what
might seem to be an unusual twist, Matt is much more
accepting of his visions. Discuss their different points
of view.

3. Abby's interactions with Peter Coffin evolve during
the course of the book. In the beginning, she defers to
his challenges. By the end, she's no longer willing to
put up with his antics. What do you think causes this
change?

4. Why do you think Matt never left Nantucket?

5. If someone told you that you were married to him or
her in previous life, would you believe it? Why or why
not?

6. If Abigail, Matthew, Abby and Matt had been real
people, could you imagine being their friend? Why or
why not?

CPSIA information can be obtained at www.ICGtesting.com
Printed in the USA
LVOW11s0559171014

409214LV00005B/431/P